PRICHARD FAMILY SERIES
Volume One

Paper Dreams

*Blessings!
To Mary, My new friend!*

Joyce Richards Case

Joyce Case

Romans 15:13

Inspiring Voices®
A Service of **Guideposts**

Copyright © 2014 Joyce Richards Case.

All rights reserved. No part of this book may be used or reproduced by any means, graphic, electronic, or mechanical, including photocopying, recording, taping or by any information storage retrieval system without the written permission of the publisher except in the case of brief quotations embodied in critical articles and reviews.

Inspiring Voices books may be ordered through booksellers or by contacting:

Inspiring Voices
1663 Liberty Drive
Bloomington, IN 47403
www.inspiringvoices.com
1 (866) 697-5313

Because of the dynamic nature of the Internet, any web addresses or links contained in this book may have changed since publication and may no longer be valid. The views expressed in this work are solely those of the author and do not necessarily reflect the views of the publisher, and the publisher hereby disclaims any responsibility for them.

Any people depicted in stock imagery provided by Thinkstock are models, and such images are being used for illustrative purposes only. Certain stock imagery © Thinkstock.

ISBN: 978-1-4624-0974-7 (sc)
ISBN: 978-1-4624-0975-4 (e)

Library of Congress Control Number: 2014908930

Printed in the United States of America.

Inspiring Voices rev. date: 06/11/2014

ACKNOWLEDGEMENTS

A special note from Joyce:

I have to admit, when there's a book to read my excitement takes me directly to chapter one. Thinking the author is just thanking a group of people who are strangers to me, the acknowledgements page is usually overlooked. However, after the last chapter is absorbed, I sometimes turn the book in my hands cherishing the thoughts within. Opening the book again, my appreciation leads me to read about those who made the publishing possible. For a brief time they too touched my life bringing the author's words and purpose to me. I wish it were possible for those "strangers" to realize how much I appreciate the part they contributed to my insight, enjoyment, and encouragement.

It is my prayer that God will use these pages to speak to you of His eternal love and forgiveness. I give thanks to the Lord, who placed in my heart this series about a couple who met staggering challenges, yet came through and was used by God in untold ways. As the family in this series is able to do, my hope is that you also may be given the privilege of seeing God's intervention when your personal hardships are overcome.

For my husband, Jerold, without whom this book would not have been possible, gratitude seems a small word. I appreciate beyond measure the encouragement given by my daughters, Valarie and Valinda, and I know if she were here Dorinda would also support my efforts. A special acknowledgement goes to the Life Writing Group of New Iberia, Louisiana, and Kim Graham for inspiring me to keep on keeping on. Judy Dauterive steered me through the murky waters of grammatical fiascoes, and I extend utmost thanks to my dear, cheerleader friend, Betty Leblanc.

As you read the fictional portrayal of *The Prichard Family Series*, I humbly thank you for holding this story in your hands, and I hope in your heart.

Interspersed throughout *The Prichard Family Series* are newspaper columns written by the character, Winston Prichard. They are printed some forty years after the timeline of events in the story.

THE RICHLAND RECORD

More Than a Newspaper—a Community Service
A Weekly Publication Serving the Greater Richland Area
Richland, Texas   Thursday, March 23, 1967
Winston Randolph Prichard, Editor and Publisher

News and Views of a Tactless Texan

The future has a way of showing up suddenly as an unannounced, unwelcome, present. If asked by a youth the way to welcome the future without regret, I would reply, "Start building toward tomorrow today, find a godly, praying spouse, and benefit from your mistakes and errors of others." Better yet, go to the Good Book, it's filled with sage advice, especially in Proverbs. One of my favorites is chapter 19:20 "Listen to counsel and accept discipline, that you may be wise the rest of your days." By no means do I claim to be a wise scholar, but I'm of the opinion that my longevity, in both age and decades in the printing industry, merit a measure of worthy insights. We all make mistakes, but if they are selfishly executed and impulsively repeated, the consequences delay the purpose of our being.

When a person reaches a certain age of maturity, his extended past encompasses a myriad of reflections. The past has worked together to bring him to this moment. And within the divine gift of this moment it is possible to make recompense and change where needed. Recalling hard times congers realization of how far he's come. It enforces the knowledge of how God, in His infinite wisdom guided and taught life's lessons along the way. It takes some of us (of which I am one), longer to grasp those lessons and live accordingly.

My lifelong dream of owning a publishing business came to fruition years ago with no thanks to my mistakes, erroneous personal decisions, and misuse of funds. In fact, it's a miracle. I wouldn't care to relive painful events which were thankfully mingled with pleasant experiences. Those of you who, like me, are nearing their allotted three score and ten have lived through two World Wars, the Korean Conflict, the Great Depression, and suffered losses of loved ones. But through the years, my personal obstacles, which are too numerous to recount, were the major setbacks to overcome. In each circumstance, at various times, the good Lord surrounded me with His angels of mercy who brought me to fulfillment of my boyhood ambition of becoming an editor.

Enduring the brunt of our hardships, my wife, Hope, has been the constant angel through the struggles. Without her by my side, this publication would not exist. I'm eternally grateful for her faith in me and most of all, the Almighty. The story of our amazing journey to this pinnacle is one I hope to write one day when I can figure out how to bare my soul without destroying my reputation. Perhaps the importance of confirming that miracles do happen would be more important than the opinion of naysayers and my blotted reputation.

As subscribers to the *Record* can attest, I freely express personal views and welcome rebuttals in Letters to the Editor. It has been gratifying that the majority of readers have indulged my declarations with favorable comments. The opposition either chooses not to submit disapproval or simply dismisses my editorializing as the ramblings of an opinionated old gent. Some may agree that their assessment is correct.

I sign off each week's column with the printer's symbol -30-. I have been asked the meaning. It is traditionally used by journalists to indicate the end of a story. With the backward reading type tumbling out of the linotype one story after another, there had to be a noticeable indication of the end of each article. Also in a telegraphed message, it was the telegraphers' code meaning the completion of a message. With that bit of proofreaders' trivia, I sign off with -30- for this week.

1

Hempstead, Texas—March 1928—

The porch step gave way. The wind was knocked out of her as she landed with a plop on the hard-packed dirt.

Octavia Jane rushed to the edge of the porch. "Hope, are you all right?"

Gulping to catch her breath, Hope stood and wiped her hands across the freshly ironed dress. "I'm okay, Mama." She stooped to pick up the shim that had worked its way out from under the weathered step.

Octavia leaned over the railing as far as her rotund body allowed and realizing the problem, her frustration overshadowed concern. With a clouded face, she turned to her husband sitting in his cane chair. "I told you a hundred times to fix that step, Hollis." Her balled fists, were perched on ample hips. "Hope could've broken her neck."

Hollis glanced to see his Sugar in one piece and then directed his attention back to whittling. "Now, Tave, I said I'd get to it." His words were sorghum thick.

Stepping closer to Hollis, Octavia's eyes were set in anger. "Get to it?" Her voice was loud enough to shake the leaning timbers precariously supporting the tin roof. "When? When are you going to get to it? I swan, you've been saying that since Betsy fell off it and twisted her foot."

Hope's wish for starting a day without her parents bickering was splintered. She took out her agitation on the wooden shim and kicked it back in place. "It's all right, Mama. I should've remembered to step over it."

With a long stride, she returned to the porch and assumed her position as self-appointed referee. She placed a hand on her daddy's shoulder. "I'll help you fix it when I get home from work, Papa."

He glanced at his daughter and then focused downward busying himself with his project. "Aw no, Shug. I got some wood in back of the outhouse. I'll look through it directly."

Octavia stood to her full four foot, ten height and her eyebrows arched over dark, squinted eyes. "Humph. You'll likely find a good whittling stick and take to your chair. Then you'll sit there 'til time to get on to the funeral home."

Taller than her mother, Hope easily placed an arm around her shoulders. "I'm sure he'll see to it." She gave a meaningful gaze toward Hollis. "Won't you, Papa?"

He grunted and shifted in his chair.

Studying her papa's large hands, Hope marveled at his skill at forming a unique walking cane from a stick of cedar, yet he evaded fixing the steps and most other repairs. She resisted the urge to pat his wispy white hair into place and smooth his bushy mustache as she had as a child. At the same time, she was provoked enough to give it a yank, but knew it wouldn't make a difference in her daddy's lackadaisical ways.

Losing her temper would only stoke the smoldering embers between her parents. Hope forced an even tone. "If you could saw a brace to size before you go to work, I'll nail it together after supper. We wouldn't want anyone else to stumble and get hurt if it works its way out again."

Hollis chuckled. "That shim ain't likely to wiggle out too soon the way you kicked it in there, Sugar."

Mama pulled away and threw up her hands. "Oh, Lord, he's come up with another excuse."

Hope could see there was no changing Papa or Mama this day or any other. Resigned, she brushed a kiss across Hollis's cheek and met her mother's eyes with a plea for armistice. "I need to get going." She rushed off the porch, skipping over the offending step.

"Wait, Sister." A barefoot girl ran out of the house letting the screen door slam. "I wanna give you a kiss."

Hope's pink and rose flowered skirt twirled as she pivoted and ran back to lend puckered lips to her little sister. "How could I ever leave without a smooch from you, Betsy girl?"

The youngest sister, Pearl, watched from behind the rusted screen door. Hope motioned to her. "Hey there, Pearly Mae, come give me a hug."

"Na-uh."

"Okay for you then. But I better get a hug when I get home." At the hog-wire fence, Hope carefully removed the wire loop from the cedar post holding the lean-to gate. She stepped onto the dirt path and hooked the loop back on the post. "I'll see y'all at noon."

As she turned to wave, Hope heard her mother. "Hollis, when are you going to get to the broken hinge on that gate?"

Live in peace with one another.
—1Thessalonians 5:13b NASB

2

The same morning—

Hitchhiking, Winn looked hopefully at a roadster as it whizzed by on Texas State Highway 290. It slowed and pulled to a stop just beyond the Brenham city limit sign. A fair-haired girl stuck her head out the passenger side window and waved him on. Winn took off running, but when he reached the back of the auto, she yelled, "Now, Johnny, step on it now!" The car sped away in a cloud of dust. Shrill laughter burst in Winn's ears.

The March wind carried his hat across the highway. Cursing, he dropped his scuffed suitcases and chased it. The brown fedora was rescued just before ending its flight in the ditch. Brushing it off, he stood and looked across the gently rolling hill stretched out beyond the barbed wire fence. Grazing cattle made a tranquil setting in contrast to Winn's impatience. A breeze broomed dust in his face as another car sped by, then stopped and backed up. He waited. An attractive young woman peered out the window and gave him the once-over. She said, "Hey there, need a ride?"

Winn thought her voice implied an invitation of a more personal nature. His guard was in place. "Yes, ma'am, I do if you're headed east."

She pouted. "What a shame, I'm going to Austin. If you want a lift east you're on the wrong side of the road."

"I know, I was just . . ." She stepped on the gas, and his voice escalated. "Getting my hat." He held it up as proof and then let his arm fall to his side. *Just as well. I don't need any distractions.*

Trudging back to his worn valises, Winn plopped the hat on his head and wiped a hand over his face. It felt gritty. Picking up the bags, he continued to walk, looking over his shoulder periodically to see if an opportunity for a ride might be approaching.

A Model A came into view. As it went by, Winn could see there was no room for him and gave a nod when the driver waved. Troubling thoughts began to whirl through his mind. *I don't think I'll ever find what I'm looking for. How far can I get with seventeen dollars in my pocket?* He kept a steady pace with long strides. *When will the past stop gnawing at my gut?*

He breathed deeply of the country air and shook his head to rid rambling taunts of failure. *I've been down and out before. Somehow something always turns up. I've stared hard times in the face enough to know every wart and wrinkle.*

The pastoral countryside was reminiscent of the time he had lived in Georgia with his grandparents and walked to town from their grist mill. Thinking of them pulled the corners of his mouth into a smile. It was a reprieve from the downward spiral of his brooding. *Boy oh boy, things might've been different if I'd lived the way they taught me.*

A rock in his path caused him to stumble, and a pinched face replaced the smile. His stylish shoes scuffed as he shuffled across loose gravel to regain his balance. Again he cursed and spoke out loud. "Why should today be any different? I keep bouncing around from town to town, making a mess of things. Maybe if I had stayed in San Antonio, everything would've worked out." He kicked a tree branch aside. "No, I had to leave."

Winn heard a rumbling behind him and turned to see a dilapidated truck. It slowed, and an elderly man called to him through the open window. "You wanna hop in, or you just out for a stroll?" The driver wheezed a chuckle that ended in a cough.

"Yes, sir. I'd be much obliged for a lift." He threw the bags in the back and hopped in the cab. The smile returned—the one he sincerely presented simply because he liked people. "Winn Prichard's my name."

Pumping Winn's outstretched hand, the driver gruffly said, "McDonald's mine, and I don't wanna hear no cracks 'bout Old McDonald had a farm."

It was said so seriously, Winn wasn't sure it was meant jokingly until a grin crept across McDonald's whiskered face. He made that wheezing sound and coughed again.

"That's a promise." Winn laughed at the man's humor, but mostly at his chuckle.

The truck lumbered along at a snail's pace. Winn wondered if he would have been better off refusing the man's offer and waited for a ride with more promise. He wanted to make it the short distance to Hempstead by noon.

The old farmer spit out his window leaving a brown stream to mesh with the accumulated tobacco juice on his rusted door. "You a Fuller Brush man or a preacher?"

Winn straightened his bow tie. "Neither. I'm a newspaper man. Been working at the paper over in Giddings."

"Uh huh." He gave Winn a sideways glance. "So whatcha doing out here?"

"The printing plant hit on hard times and had to let some employees go. I got a ride as far as Brenham. The paper there couldn't use another linotype operator, so I'm heading to Hempstead to see if I can get on with the paper there."

"Nice place, Hempstead. Did you know it's called 'Six-Shooter Junction'?" Winn opened his mouth to say he was aware it had been known as a Wild West town, but the old gent went on. "Back in aught five, Judge Pinckney and three other men was shot dead right there in the courthouse, mind you. A fight broke out in a meeting with the Texas Rangers and all of a sudden shots were fired." He looked at his passenger more than the road, as the truck veered around a curve.

Grabbing the dashboard with both hands, Winn looked to see the tires graze the edge of the ditch. Unconcerned, McDonald slowly turned the wheel back on course while talking nonstop. "Yep, four folks lay dead and bullet holes was all over the courthouse walls."

Winn sat back and took a deep breath. He suspected McDonald was a lonesome soul who reveled in having someone to talk to and he was a good listener. It reminded him of years ago when he sat with Grandpa Prichard, listening to his lore. The truck stopped at a crossroads to allow a horse-drawn wagon to pass. McDonald stopped his story and stuck his head out the window to holler a greeting to the man in the wagon.

A spring in the lumpy seat poked Winn in the rear of his pants. He shifted. "I read about the skirmish in a western magazine. Sure is interesting to hear about it from someone who lived here at the time." Winn was relieved when the community came into view.

"Yep, that's the way it was. I can tell you anything else you wanna know 'bout happenings around here. Hempstead's known for its melons and its murders." McDonald guided his truck to Brazos Street and parked in front of Sophie's Café. "Here you are, 'Six Shooter Junction'." He picked up a wadded bandana from the seat and wiped it across his stained whiskers.

"Much obliged for the ride, Mr. McDonald, and thanks for filling me in on Hempstead history." Winn agilely stepped over the running board and retrieved his suitcases from the bed of the truck.

The door on the driver's side opened with a creak and McDonald slowly found his footing. Seeing the old gentleman appeared to be a bit wobbly, Winn sprinted around the truck and gave him a hand. With Winn's support, he stepped onto the sidewalk. "Thank you, Lad. Been sittin' too long, old man rheumatis got me all stove up."

When assured McDonald could make it on his own, Winn stepped back to push the truck door closed. "Which way is the newspaper office, Mr. McDonald?"

"Just up yonder on the corner, a block past the new courthouse." He pointed up the street. "Miss Adkins owns the *Hempstead News*; she's a right nice little lady. Good luck to you."

"Thanks." Winn waved and took quick inventory of his appearance. His brown suit and white shirt were clean but could have gained a little more prestige from an iron. *Glad I bought this suit before I got canned.*

Seeing road dust on his two-tone shoes, he stood on one foot and rubbed his right shoe on the back of the left pant leg. He buffed the other shoe the same way. *That'll have to do for now.* Crossing the street, he picked up his pace. A woman was walking ahead of him, he slowed to watch the energetic bounce in her step. He liked the way the wind tousled her light brown tresses. For a few steps he swayed in time with the soft swing of her flowered print skirt, but straightened when he realized how foolish he must appear.

Stopping for a moment, Winn set the grips down and adjusted his hat lower on his brow lest the unpredictable breeze carry it away again.

> *There is one thing which gives radiance to everything.*
> *It is the idea of something around the corner.*
> —G.K. Chesterton

3

Hope slipped her key in the lock and twisted the worn brass doorknob. Entering the print shop, she gave the dark green door shade a gentle tug and in a graceful motion pulled the string on a large hanging light. As it swayed back and forth, she paused to watch the funnel of illumination settle on the rough wood counter where current issues of newspapers were neatly stacked.

Hearing the door, she turned and saw a man holding two suitcases. Startled, her hand fluttered to the crocheted lace collar of her pink and rose dress. "Oh!" Focusing on his engaging smile, she quickly recovered. "Hello."

"Good afternoon." Winn set the bags on the floor and took off his hat. *Hmm, her front looks as good as her back.* "It wasn't my intention to startle you, ma'am. Guess you were closed for the noon hour."

Hope walked around to the back of the counter but couldn't take her eyes away from the stranger's. They were brown, a warm brown, like creamy milk chocolate she thought. He was tall and had very nice features indeed. "Yes, we close at noon and open at one." She waited an awkward moment and then said, "Is there something I can help you with, sir?"

While admiring the lady's fresh-scrubbed look, he took in the familiar aroma of ink and turpentine. Stepping closer to the counter, he flashed his beguiling smile. "My name is Winn Prichard, Miss Adkins, and I'm the fastest linotype operator this side of the Mississippi." His head cocked slightly as if giving his statement a second thought. "Maybe even the whole United States for that matter, and I'm looking for a newspaper that can use a 'Jim Dandy' typesetter."

Hope was taken aback. Flattered that he mistook her for Miss Adkins, she muted a giggle at his lofty introduction. "Um, Mr. Prichard did you say?"

The door slammed. A stooped man with downward eyes tramped toward the back shop mumbling. "Gotta get some baking soda. That lunch special Sophie calls beef stew oughta be called chili powder stew."

Hope said, "You have heartburn again, Orville?"

He shot a sour look over his shoulder and said, "Nope, I take baking soda 'cause it makes my hair grow."

The couple watched Orville's comical stride for a moment. Then facing each other, they both smiled. Captivated by the man's friendly face, Hope was about to speak, but he hurried on. "I've been working at the paper over in Giddings, but unfortunately the owner has hit on hard times and . . ."

Hope put a hand up to stop him, "Mr. Prichard, I'm . . ."

The door was pushed open again, this time with a gust of wind. The newspapers on the counter took flight. They both turned to see a woman haphazardly attempting to control a large handbag, her skirt, clipboard and a stack of loose papers. With her first step in the door the load tumbled and scattered across the floor. Winn and Hope rushed to help her.

The woman's hat was askew and hair windblown with loose strands wildly free from the bun at the nape of her neck. She said, "Whoever named March the windy month is right. I'm surprised I wasn't swept all the way to Houston."

She continued her diatribe as the three of them transferred the clutter from the floor to a desk behind the counter. A large pearl tipped hat pin was waging a losing battle as her hat flopped on the side of her head. Finally taking a breath, she removed the pin and the hat. Pushing back the rebellious hair, she looked at Winn and realized she had been groveling on the floor for her papers with a stranger. "Thank you ahh, Mr . . ."

Hope rushed to make introductions, "This is Mr. Prichard. And Mr. Prichard . . ." She held out her hand toward the woman. "This is Miss Adkins, the owner." Pinching her lower lip with her teeth, Hope took a step back.

Winn's embarrassment was preempted by disappointment that conversation with the attractive young lady seemed to be at an end. He felt heat rise to his cheeks and gave Hope an apologetic look. His gaze was forthright toward Miss Adkins as he shook her extended hand. "Pleased to meet you, Miss Adkins, I've heard some nice things about you and the *Hempstead News.*"

Seeing she was no longer needed, Hope turned to go. *He's charming as well as handsome.*

Winn turned toward Hope. "Uh, Miss . . . I apologize for my mistake. I suppose I didn't give you a chance to correct me."

"That's quite all right, Mr. Prichard." She walked to the back shop and donned her printer's apron. *I hope Miss Adkins needs another linotype operator.* Stepping on a wooden box to work across the job press, she picked up a roller from the ink tray. While saturating the black goo on type in the press bed, her thoughts were far from the task at hand.

Winn explained his mistake to the publisher. Miss Adkins laughed. "I don't know if you need to sit, Mr. Prichard, but I do." She sat at her desk and directed the man to do the same in the wooden straight-back chair across from her.

As he voiced his request for a job, Winn forced his mind to stay focused on Miss Adkins and did not allow his eyes to seek out her female employee.

Hope willed herself to concentrate on her job as she stepped down from the box and shoved it aside. She pumped the cast iron foot pedal causing the bed to open and close for manual insertion of each sheet of paper.

Miss Adkins explained to Winn that Orville had been with the plant for years. "Why, he practically lives here." She nodded toward the job press. "Hope started working here last fall. She began by sweeping the floor and cleaning up after press day, but was eager to learn the trade. Now she handles most of the job printing. I sell the advertising and write the news, Orville sets the type and we all pitch in on press day."

Hope glanced at the front desk and was disappointed to see Miss Adkins shake her head. *Guess she's not going to hire him, wish we could've talked longer.*

Miss Adkins rooted underneath the accumulated pile on her desk and located a scrap of paper and pencil. "Hempstead is just not big enough to support a paper any larger than four or six pages weekly, Mr. Prichard. A big issue for us is eight pages. I subscribe to United Press and Associated Press syndicated news services, so I can't use another typesetter or full time shop man."

She scribbled on the paper as she talked. "The Baldwin Paper salesman was by here a few days ago and said the paper in Liberty is growing. They might be looking for another printer. I'm acquainted with the editor at the *Vindicator*, Mr. Spencer, and he publishes a first-rate paper. I'm writing his name down if you're interested."

"Yes, I am. Much obliged, Miss Adkins."

When she handed the information to him, he glanced at the note, biding time to think of an excuse to talk to Hope. "I'll need to catch a bus, how far is the depot?"

"Just a few blocks down Brazos Street at Butch's filling station." She pointed to the right and said, "I'm sorry we can't use you, Mr. Prichard."

"I understand and appreciate your kindness, Miss Adkins." They both stood and shook hands. "I do have a favor to ask if I may."

"What's that, Mr. Prichard?"

"I may be in for quite a bit of walking before finding employment and a place to stay. I wonder if it would be in the way if I stow one of my suitcases here and send for it later? There's nothing of value in it."

"Well of course, you may leave it here. It won't be in the way." She looked over her shoulder. "Just put it back in the corner behind my desk, no one will bother it there."

Winn placed the valise where she indicated and nodded. "Thank you, Miss Adkins." He turned to walk away, but then looked back with an afterthought. "Oh yes, I'd like to bid Miss Hope good-bye if you don't mind my interrupting her work for a few minutes."

"I don't mind at all. She never leaves for the day until all her work is finished, so don't worry about that." She smiled and looked at Hope whose eyes were riveted on her work.

When Hope sensed his nearness, her heart quickened and she felt color redden her face. Concentrating, she didn't miss a beat in her rhythmic motions. She pumped the foot pedal, taking a printed circular out of the bed with her left hand and feeding a sheet of stock into it with her right.

Winn stood at the side of the press waiting until she made eye contact. He noticed her left hand was bare of a ring. Hope stopped pumping. She wasn't sure why he approached, but whatever was on his mind, she didn't want their conversation to be shouted over machine clatter. The only noise was Orville's steady clicking at the linotype.

She spoke first. "Miss Adkins doesn't need America's fastest linotype operator?"

He laughed and glanced down at his hat, brushing an imaginary piece of lint from the brim. Looking into her dark brown eyes, he took in the epitome of innocence. The freckles sprinkled across her nose betrayed youth in recent past, yet the sculpture under the printer's apron revealed Hope had crossed the threshold of womanhood. "No, I'll be moving on. Miss Adkins recommended the paper over in Liberty."

"How far away is Liberty?" *Oh no, it sounds as if I'm too interested.* She wanted to suck the question back into her mouth. *There I go, saying whatever pops into my head, just like Papa says I do.*

Winn's face broke into a grin. *Hmm, she's curious about the distance I might be from Hempstead.* "Northeast of Houston, a few hours bus ride is all." He looked at the printed handbills. "That's a nice looking circular. Miss Adkins says you do most of the job press work."

"Thank you, I like job printing. Orville and Miss Adkins have taught me a great deal about the business."

Winn was enthralled. *I could have a real conversation with this girl. I never met one who gave a flip about what interests me. Can't imagine Darlene even walking into a print shop—might get her manicured nails dirty.*

Hope couldn't seem to stop talking about what she loved. "Composing and printing jobs in different typefaces is so interesting." He was staring and she was a bit breathless. *Uh-oh, I'm making a fool of myself.* "I'm . . . I'm going to be a printer."

"Is that right?" He nodded approvingly. "It's a wonderful profession. Once printer's ink gets in your blood, you won't be happy doing anything else. I was editor of my own paper back in Georgia until I moved with my family a few years ago."

The expression on Hope's face clouded. "Oh, you have a family, Mr. Prichard?" *Dear Lord, I did it again and he's a married man.*

"Yes, Miss . . . Hope, I don't know your last name."

Her voice lacked the enthusiasm it held a moment ago. "Davidson."

"Yes, Miss Davidson. I moved with my parents and two younger brothers." He noticed the relief in Hope's demeanor and went on to tell her that his daddy was the circulation manager for the *San Antonio Light.* "He would like for me to work there, but I'm looking for a small town to start my own publication."

He could have conversed with her all afternoon, but stepped back and said, "I'm keeping you from your work, Miss Davidson. Is it all right if I call you Hope?" *What am I thinking, she's just a young girl and with my past, how can I consider any kind of relationship?*

Hope loved his soft southern drawl and easy manner. "Yes . . . that is, yes you can call me Hope—not yes you're keeping me from my work." She laughed and glanced toward Miss Adkins, who was engrossed in reorganizing the pile of papers on her desk.

He liked her laugh. "Still—I need to get on to the bus depot."

Hope stuck out her hand. "It's been a pleasure talking with you, Mr. Prichard." She noticed ink smudges on her fingers and quickly withdrew her hand.

"I'm used to printer's ink, Hope. Nothing's wrong with indications of hard work." Holding out his hand, he invited the handshake and she complied with a smile. He noticed her front teeth slightly overlapped, but the curve of her full lips framed them nicely.

He said, "By the way, Miss Adkins told me I could leave one of my suitcases here. It's over behind her desk." He waved in that direction. "Figured I can send for it later." He took a few backward steps. "It's been very nice meeting you, Hope, and good luck with your printing career."

Well, that sounds pretty final. "Thank you, Mr. Prichard."

"Winn. Actually it's Winston, that's what my family calls me, but to my friends I'm Winn."

"Okay, Winn. I'll say a prayer and ask God to lead you to a job and a good location for you to start a newspaper."

He searched her eyes and saw complete sincerity. "That's mighty kind of you, Hope. A man needs all the prayers he can get."

He turned to leave and stopped by Miss Adkins's desk to express his appreciation again. Hope watched him pick up the one suitcase and before leaving, he turned and caught her staring. Before she turned away in embarrassment, he gave her a wink. She felt a strange flutter like butterfly wings in the pit of her stomach.

There is no greater invitation to love than loving first.
—Augustine

THE RICHLAND RECORD

More Than a Newspaper—a Community Service
<u>A Weekly Publication Serving the Greater Richland Area</u>
Richland, Texas   Thursday May 11, 1967
<u>Winston Randolph Prichard, Editor and Publisher</u>

News and Views of a Tactless Texan

With the passing of a birthday last week, this columnist also commemorated another milestone in this life I've lived just passing through. Sixty-five years ago as a youngster of just ten years old, I began my career in the newspaper profession. I sold the *Atlanta Constitution* news on a corner in Atlanta, Georgia.

You may question the wisdom of allowing a child to hawk the morning news in a large city before dawn. May I humbly point out that it was a different world in the early 1900s. There was less crime toward children as we, unfortunately, see today, and it was also before labor laws. The Fair Labor Standards Act which placed restrictions on child labor was signed by President Franklin Roosevelt in 1938.

Since yelling the headlines on the street, I've worked as an all-round printer, typesetter, editor, and publisher. In other words, all positions of the printing industry. I can't deny that printer's ink flows through my veins. I am proud to proclaim that I come from a breed of true "journeymen" printers who worked in shops all over the country. When a newspaper came on hard times and could no longer use us, we roamed by rail, bus, or hitched rides on the roadways as means to find employment. We picked up new ideas and methods, then as circumstances changed or wanderlust urged, we moved on and passed innovative skills to other shops in need of a temporary "tramp printer."

Those old-time printers were common throughout Texas in the early part of the twentieth century before the mechanical typecasting machines started spewing out full lines of reading matter. Linotypes had an output of at least three to four times the master typographers when newspapers were put together one symbol at a time.

That era is in the past, but was a vital part of our country's rich history. The lead spouting typesetting machines which replaced all around printers are being replaced in turn by "cold composition" techniques using a punched tape. As stated earlier, the world is a different place than the one in which I was raised and will continue to change with each generation for the betterment of mankind.

It seems the wings of time have been flying mighty fast. I've witnessed many newfangled inventions and in my advanced age had to make adjustments accordingly. But one thing has remained constant in my life—my love of the newspaper profession. If we have to work by the sweat of our brow, it's a good thing to love what we are doing.

That's -30- for this week.

4

After picking up the mail, Miss Adkins smiled all the way from the post office. She went directly to Hope, who was hand-setting type for business cards. "We received quite a bit of mail today, could you help me sort through some of it?"

Hope set her composing stick down at the unusual request. "Certainly, Miss Adkins."

The older woman's grin was barely suppressed under her serious expression as she doled out an envelope. "Here, why don't you start with this one?"

Hope was puzzled until she read her name in flowing calligraphy, *Miss Hope Davidson, c/o The Hempstead News, Hempstead, Texas*. With a quick intake of breath she glanced at the return address, *Winston Prichard, c/o The Liberty Vindicator, Liberty, Texas*.

"Oh, Miss Adkins." She pressed the missive to her chest. It had been a week and three days since they met and though hopeful, it was beyond her imagination that Winn would actually write to her.

Miss Adkins giggled with delight at her part of what she suspected to be a budding romance.

Orville moseyed over from a work table, "What's going on? Y'all are so excited; it must be a letter from President Coolidge."

"Almost as important, Orville." Miss Adkins's face masked mischievousness. "It's from the young man who came in asking for a job."

"Humph, y'all stopped work 'cause a drifter wrote a letter? Ain't y'all got nothing better to do?" Scratching his head, he went back to the galleys of type on a work table.

Miss Adkins fanned her face with one of the unopened letters. "He's been here so long, he thinks he's boss. Go sit down, Hope, and read your letter."

"Thank you, ma'am. Mr. Prichard is most likely just asking about his suitcase."

"If that's all it is, Hope, he could've written to me." She walked toward her desk.

Hope sat on a wooden stool beside the open back door of the shop and turned the envelope over in her hands. She couldn't remember ever having received a letter.

Dear Hope,

I am certain your prayer for me was answered. I was hired immediately upon my arrival at the Liberty Vindicator. Thank you, and if I happen to cross your thoughts, pray for the Lord's guidance to the place where I can establish a newspaper of my own.

My impression of you, Hope, was one of utmost admiration, not only in your achievements at the Hempstead News and desire for a worthwhile profession, but also the refreshing honesty in expressing yourself.

I need to pick up my suitcase there and plan to ride the bus to Hempstead on my day off next Saturday, the eleventh. It would give me great pleasure to see you again if I may.

The bus scheduled arrival at the depot is eleven a.m. I can meet you at the newspaper office and take you to dinner. I hear Sophie's is pretty good if you like chili powder.

If it is not possible to meet with me, I will just pick up the grip and be on the next bus back to Liberty.

With kindest regards, your admirer,
Winston (Winn) Prichard

Hope read it through quickly, then again slowly. Her excitement made it difficult to remain balanced on the three-legged stool. She looked out at the dirt alley in back of the building and then her gaze swept to the cloudless sky. *My first letter, my first real admirer, and my first dinner invitation, all at once. I'm glad Miss Adkins gave me Saturday off for my birthday.*

She sighed and held the letter to her bosom. *Dear Lord Jesus, please let Papa allow me to see Mr. Prichard.* The priceless archive was carefully folded and placed in her skirt pocket.

Miss Adkins watched Hope approach her desk. "Well, Hope, your face is so bright I think I'll turn off the lights and save electricity."

Hope's broad smile revealed the jubilation inside. "He's coming Saturday to pick up his suitcase and wants to take me to Sophie's."

"How perfect, a birthday lunch with a handsome young man."

Hope's smile faded. "I don't know if Papa will let me meet with a perfect stranger. Anyway Mama's planning a big dinner with all the family at noon. My brother, Buford, is coming down from Texarkana."

"Maybe you could ask Mr. Prichard to come to your house. I'm sure he would understand, since it's a special occasion. He seems a friendly sort who would fit right in."

Hope's hand went to the letter in her pocket. "You don't know Papa, Miss Adkins, he's very strict. I told you what a terrible time I had convincing him to allow me to work here. He thinks a woman's place is in the kitchen or in the field." She sunk into the chair by the desk. "This is probably what he was afraid of—my falling in love with someone he doesn't know." She didn't mean to say that part about falling in love, but there it was, her deepest feelings tumbling out of her mouth.

A questioning look flashed across Miss Adkins's face. "Falling in love? Do you think you love him already, Hope?"

"I don't know how I feel really. I've never been interested in the boys at church." She hesitated to find the right words. "It's silly I know, but I think Winn is . . . is special."

"I can't see why your papa wouldn't allow Winn to come to your house and have dinner with the family. That way Mr. Davidson can size him up, and you can examine your feelings as well."

"I'll talk to Papa tonight and read the letter to him. I'll pray on the walk home for the Lord to work it out." She stood. "I need to finish setting the type for Mr. Plumber's cards so they'll be ready to go to press first thing in the morning."

"I'll say a prayer too, Hope. It's almost closing time; you can set the copy up in the morning."

"No, ma'am, if you don't mind I'd like to finish. I can lock up." She walked toward the type cases and then turned. "Thank you, Miss Adkins."

There is no medicine like hope, no incentive so great, and
no tonic so powerful as expectation of something tomorrow.
—Orison Swett Marden

5

Hope locked the wooden door of the print shop and headed toward home. She prayed and thought about how Papa might take the news that she had a suitor, at least that's what she hoped Winn to be. Walking slowly past the courthouse, she looked across the street and saw Sophie locking the café door. When Sophie turned and saw Hope, they both waved a greeting.

A smile remained on Hope's face as she thought about how much she loved working in town at the print shop. *As much as Papa hated it, I just had to get a job when we moved to town. It's like I'm being pulled by an invisible cord to improve myself. I hope the desire has been placed in me by the Lord. I sure would hate to think it's pride.*

The pavement stopped abruptly making a statement that the town had come to an end. She stepped onto the worn path by the school house. *I'm glad Betsy and Pearl can go to school.* She held her skirt as a breeze meandered across the familiar dirt road. *I loved school. My fourth grade teacher was as sad as I was when Papa said I had enough schooling.*

Thinking about Papa making her and her sister, Iris, quit school in order to work in the fields conjured memories of her childhood. She would never forget those hot, humid days when she toiled row after row dragging the cotton sack behind her. On winter nights, she huddled under quilts with her sisters in the sharecropper's shanty. Mama tacked newspapers over cracks in the walls when frigid wind howled across the Brazos River.

The bicycle repair shop came into view. It was where her oldest brother, Alonzo used to work. He saved every penny to buy the old house across the street where the Davidsons now live. The ramshackle place was so rundown, the owner was glad Alonzo took it off his hands. Her family might still be living in the sharecropper's house if her brother hadn't gotten a job at that shop. Her mind floated in a sepia haze remembering her brother. *How I loved him. Dear God, I'm still wondering why he had to die.*

Slowing her pace, a wave of sorrow poured into her heart. Alonzo's death made a bitter mark in Papa's abundance of ill traits. Buford couldn't take living at home anymore. Thoughts of Papa's mean streak clouded her mind as she arrived at the gate. Hollis was sitting on the dilapidated porch in his usual cane chair.

The "eek" of the leaning gate announced her arrival. Hollis looked up from his whittling. "Hi, Shug."

"Hello, Papa." She avoided the precarious step onto the porch. Her father kept at his carving task as she melted in the cane chair beside him and leaned back, studying him. His thick mustache and full head of hair were pure white. Hope noticed the redness of his skin under the white hair on his muscular arms. She knew he favored her over her siblings, maybe because she was expressive of her love toward him. The gruffness that soured his personality was hard to understand, but she decided it was mostly fear. Fear of change and appearing ignorant because of his lack of education. His large, rough hands were expertly wielding a jackknife, forming an unusual design on a walking cane.

"You've been carving canes with cut out designs ever since I can remember, Papa. It must take a lot of patience. Have you ever just whittled a solid wood cane?"

"Goodman's store wouldn't sell plain walking sticks as well as these, now would they?" He stopped his task and looked at his daughter. "It's something to talk about."

Her heart cautioned with the wisdom of allowing him to talk for a few moments before delving into the topic foremost on her mind. "They're truly a conversation piece. I can't figure out how you shape balls within the open squares. What made you think to carve a design like that?"

"When I was a young'un, an old timer tried to show me how to do it, but I couldn't sit still long enough to get the hang of it then. Later I got a hankering to do it, and after a while it come to me. And you're right, it does take patience. But if you ask Mama, she'll tell you I ain't got much."

Hope didn't have to ask Mama, she had witnessed his impatience and temper many times. Aromas filtering through the front screen door assured Hope that her mother was preparing supper. *I know Betsy's helping, but Pearl probably has a stomach ache or some other excuse.* Her hand went to the letter; it was a warm sensation in her pocket. Finally, her thrill about the letter from Winn took precedence over dread of talking to her father about it, and he did seem to be in a good mood. "Papa, I need to talk to you about something."

His knife stilled, he turned to her. "What is it, Sugar?"

"I met a man last week and . . ."

"Where did you meet a man?" Hollis's face turned into a thundercloud. His instant reaction was a loaded pistol of negative suspicion.

Octavia fairly flew out the door, wiping her hands on her apron. "What's the matter?"

"Mama, I'm trying to tell Papa about the gentleman who came in the newspaper office asking for work. You remember, I told you about him." She faced her daddy. "Miss Adkins couldn't hire him so she recommended the newspaper plant in Liberty." She stood and walked to the porch railing.

Betsy and Pearl came onto the porch. Hearing about Hope's interest in a man, they began to giggle. The warning from Papa stifled their girlish frivolity.

Hope explained about the letter and lunch invitation. Hollis stood and flipped his jackknife closed. If you didn't know he never raised a hand to anyone, his big frame could be intimidating. "You mean to tell me this feller talked to you for a minute and wants you to go somewheres alone with him?"

Though short of stature, Octavia was big on speaking her mind. She seemed to sense when to stand up to her husband, yet remain silent until the time was right to approach him. "Now Hollis, you know how it was with us. We knew right off we loved each other."

He turned to his wife. "But Tave, Sugar's only sixteen."

Mama put her hands on her hips. "Seventeen come Saturday, and do I have to remind you I just turned sixteen when we got married?"

Putting the knife in his pocket, he tilted his head with the realization. "Oh, I know how old you was, but that was different. It was for the best 'cause you didn't have nobody when your folks died 'cept your grandma and she was too old to take care of you." With renewed resolve, he said. "I ain't gonna have it. Hope can't go 'round town with no stranger."

Behind her husband's back, Mama gave Hope a wink. The tumultuous years with Hollis had not dimmed Octavia's memory of a young girl's heart. She took Hollis's arm and pulled him inside. "Come on, supper's ready. We can talk about this later." She knew her cooking was the oil to sooth the gears of his disposition, if only for a short time.

Hope watched them walk inside. The thought struck her—and not for the first time—what a startling contrast they are. Papa was fair with a Swedish background and Mama's complexion dark, telling of her Tejas Indian heritage. Octavia's mother from the Nacogdoches area tribe had shocked her family by marrying a white man.

Pearl followed her parents inside, but Betsy took Hope's hand, holding her back. "Is he handsome?"

Her big sister bent down and whispered, "As handsome as the prince in Cinderella." Betsy's box of giggles popped open again, but she covered her mouth as Hope shushed her with a finger to her lips.

It continued to amaze Hope that only of late Papa sat quietly at the table while Mama prayed before meals. She could remember times when he made disapproving noises while serving his plate and began eating before Octavia's humble "amen." His wife never faltered or failed to thank God and ask His blessing upon the provision though at times servings were scant.

Hope thought it best to wait until Papa ate his fill. She remained quiet during the meal. Octavia knew the wisdom of delaying the discussion. The young girls were antsy, but kept silent.

After he sopped the last bit of beef gravy with his bread, Mama already had a slice of spice cake with black walnuts on a saucer for him. He finished the cake in four huge bites, set his fork on the plate, and slapped both hands down on the wooden table. The fork jumped up and landed back on the platter with a clatter which captured everyone's attention. "Okay, Shug. This man . . . whaddya say his name is?" His voice was almost a normal volume.

"Winston, Winston Prichard, but his friends call him Winn." *Maybe my news is digesting with his meal.*

"So he wrote you a letter and wants to see you on Saturday?"

Hope nodded. "That's right, Papa. He's coming in on the bus at eleven o'clock and wants to pick up the suitcase he left at the print shop. He asked to take me to Sophie's, but if it's all right with you I could ask him here to meet everyone."

She tried to read her daddy's thoughts, but his face was contorted in an expression too deep to discern. She continued. "I'll read his letter to you if you want." *It's too bad he can't read to appreciate the perfect script of Winn's hand.*

Mama's eyes danced with interest. "I'd like to hear what the young man wrote."

Hope pulled the letter from her pocket and unfolded it with shaking hands. Enunciating every word clearly, she read it to her family. When finished, she looked at Papa who was intensely studying his empty saucer.

Mama said, "My, he writes purdy. I liked the part about God answering your prayer for a job. He sounds right nice; don't you think so, Papa?"

All eyes turned to him. He was still looking down. The ticking of Mama's clock in the next room reverberated against the thin walls like it did in the dark of night when Hope lay awake praying about her future.

Hollis huffed and wiped his shirt sleeve across his bushy mustache. The very air they breathed was thick with anticipation. Papa's face was etched with determination like all the times he kicked up a stubborn fuss. "This is how it's gonna be, Shug. I'm goin' with you to the depot. Then we'll walk back to the house together."

Hope didn't realize she had been holding her breath; his answer was more than she had expected. "That's fine, Papa. But we have to stop by the print shop on the way back to pick up his bag because Miss Adkins closes at noon on Saturday."

Heaving a sigh of resignation, he nodded and pushed away from the table. All was silent as he walked out the back door.

With laughter, Mama hugged Hope. Not able to sit still any longer, Betsy ran to her sister, "Can I go to the depot with you?"

Hope pulled her into the embrace with her mother. "That's 'may' I go, remember? Anyway, of course you may."

Pearl said, "I'm going too."

Mama released her arm from around Hope's shoulder. "Well, if everybody's going, then I guess I will too."

Children, obey your parents in the Lord,
for this is right. Honor your
Father and Mother which is the first commandment with a promise,
that it may be well with you and that you
may live long on the earth.
—Ephesians 6:1-3 NASB

6

March 11, 1928—

Sitting on a wooden bench in the Houston depot, Winn waited for his connection to Hempstead. Leaving the boarding house in Liberty at dawn, it was too early to enjoy Mrs. Emerson's usual hearty breakfast. He ate at the Houston station café where the plate of bacon, eggs, and grits was greasy and the coffee downright undrinkable.

While his stomach was making a valiant effort to digest his breakfast, the unsettling emotions in his mind gave Winn enough anguish to take a bus back to Liberty. *What am I doing? I can't lead Hope on and I sure as hell can't get involved with anyone.*

A man with several bags and a woman with a bundle in her arms headed toward his bench. Winn realized the bundle was an obviously distraught baby. He stood to allow them ample seating room. The man nodded his thanks and Winn moved across the crowded waiting area. He leaned against the wall studying the little family. *Lucky man—I could've had a family by now. I hope she's more loyal to him than Darlene was to me.*

A Greyhound bus came roaring into the loading area and stopped with an enormous *poosh* from the brakes. With no luggage to hinder his boarding, Winn located a rear seat. His mind was still questioning his intent to meet with Hope. The bus pulled out and took command of the streets lined with multistoried buildings.

There were stops along the way at the Washington Avenue station and the communities of Cypress and Waller. The heaviness of his heart lifted somewhat as the bus made its way into Hempstead. He checked to make sure his white shirt was tucked in and congratulated himself for buying new shoes with his first paycheck in Liberty.

It was surprising how anxiously he was looking forward to seeing the girl who couldn't seem to leave his thoughts. Winn craned his head above the seat in front of him to get a glimpse of Butch's filling station. There was quite a crowd waiting, but he picked her out immediately. She was wearing a blue and white polka dot dress, and her light brown hair was shining in the sunlight, a vision of loveliness indeed.

Upon seeing Winn, Hope experienced a new and exciting happiness. He was wearing a tan suit with stylish flare leg trousers. He was lean and clean-cut as she remembered.

Winn kept his eyes on Hope. When she moved toward him, the crowd moved with her like they were attached. It became apparent the group he saw from the bus window had come to meet him. He didn't care how many people were with her, it only mattered that she did meet him. "Hello, Hope. It's good to see you."

"Hello, Winn. I want you to meet my family. Papa, Mama, my brother Buford, my sister, Iris and her husband Delbert, and my sisters, Betsy and Pearl." She eyed him closely to detect any ill feeling. She saw none.

Winn's eyes lit up at such a reception, and he immediately warmed to the occasion with handshakes and greetings.

Hollis said, "Hope wanted us to come on down here to meet you."

Hope was amused. *I wanted no such thing, but I'll let Papa say what he likes, I just pray he'll be pleasant.*

Octavia Jane stepped beside Winn and tilted her head upward. "You know it's Hope's birthday, and I've got dinner already set back at the house. We'd be plum pleased to have you come eat with us and have some birthday cake."

She slipped her arm around his and began to walk, leading him onward as if they hadn't been strangers moments before. She said, "Buford made it down from Texarkana and Iris and Delbert drove in from the country." She pointed in the direction of her son, then the others. "Anybody around here can tell you I put on quite a feed, better than what you'd get over at Sophie's. So you'll be missing out on some good eating if you don't come on home with us."

Buford noticed an anxious look pass across Hope's face and quickened his step to walk beside her friend. "Winn, we don't mean to horn in on your plans, but Mama always makes a fuss over us on our birthdays."

"Why no, Buford, I'm glad to be here to help celebrate. I didn't realize it was her birthday. This is much better than any plans I had." His face didn't reflect otherwise, he was truly pleased to be swept away. "It's been a while since I've been a part of a birthday dinner." He looked over his shoulder to see Hope walking beside her father and gave her an infectious smile. "Happy birthday, Hope, sorry I don't have a gift."

"Thank you and don't worry about that. There wasn't time to answer your letter and invite you to dinner at my house . . . with all my family."

Winn was steered toward the printing office where they made a brief stop to pick up his suitcase. The publisher greeted the group enthusiastically. Winn said, "I'm beholden to you Miss Adkins, for allowing me to stow my suitcase here. You were correct about Mr. Spencer at the *Vindicator*; he did need a linotype operator and hired me."

"That's wonderful, Mr. Prichard. And keeping your bag was no trouble at all. It's good to see you again." She bid birthday wishes to Hope, and after pleasantries, the group continued on their merry way. Miss Adkins stood in the doorway watching and thought it quite comical. It appeared that Winn was pleased to be whisked away by his captors.

Never shy, Iris managed to squeeze beside Winn. "Hope told us about how you thought she was Miss Adkins. That was something."

Winn usually had good recall from introductions, but the oldest sister's name didn't come to mind. He thought it was a flower, but he didn't want to take the chance of calling her Daisy if it was Rose. "You're right. I was sure surprised when Miss Adkins blew in with the wind that day." They laughed, which seemed to be the order of the day.

Betsy ran ahead, then turned and skipped backwards. Pearl did the same. "I hope you like chocolate cake, Mr. Winn."

"It just happens to be my favorite . . . Betsy is it?"

The girl snickered. "That's right, I'm Betsy. And this is Pearl."

Hope noted how easily Winn chatted with her siblings and Mama. Even the usually reserved Delbert joined in the merriment as they strode along as a unit. Knowing Papa would not easily cater to the situation, Hope hung back to walk with him. *I hope he's tolerant. I do so want his approval and can't imagine a thing he would find at fault about Winn.* Her admiration was growing for the handsome man who suddenly appeared into her life.

As they neared her home, Hope's throat constricted with a rush of embarrassment. She looked at the rundown property anew with an outsider's eyes. *Dear Lord, let Winn overlook the shabbiness.* Her gaze drifted to the ground. *Forgive me, I know it's the best Papa and Mama can do.*

As if reading her mind, Mama said, "Hope worked like a beaver last night cleaning up around here, but the clutter is more than a body can handle. So just excuse the mess, Winn, and make yourself to home."

Before he could respond, the little girls opened the creaky gate and chorused invitations for him to come in. The procession made its way to the porch where Octavia offered Winn a seat.

He sat in one of the cane chairs. "This is a wonderful welcome, but please don't go to any trouble on my account."

Betsy said, "Mama made the chairs out of willow cane. She sells some at Goodman's store. We go down to the river bank and chop 'um for her."

Looking at the short, stocky woman, Winn said, "That's quite an art."

Pearl swayed back and forth as she stood close to Betsy. "Mama can do anything."

Winn heard a snort from Hollis, who was seated in a large cane chair which had arms and a high round back. *With his striking white hair and beard, he could look rather kingly if not for the overalls.*

Mama batted an unseen gnat. "Pshaw, Pearl, that ain't so. I made sweet tea, go fetch the pitcher and glasses, girls. I'll get dinner on the table."

Dreading to make conversation with Hollis, Winn was relieved when Buford and Delbert remained on the porch.

Hope's brother sat on the railing and leaned forward. "Say, Winn, have you seen the new Ford Model A Roadster?"

He liked Buford's friendly manner. "No, can't say I have, Buford. How do you think it compares with the Model T?"

"Ah, the Roadster's a humdinger, got my eye on one in Texarkana. 'Course I'll have to wait 'til after the wedding."

Before Winn could inquire about nuptials, Hope arrived with glasses of tea on a tray for each of them. "Dinner will be on the table soon." She lingered for a moment at Winn's side. Reading an apology in her eyes, he answered with his wickedly sly wink. The unspoken assurance ushered relief to the crevices of her concern.

Entering the home, Winn observed the poor living conditions of the Davidson family. He noticed immediately the floorboards were warped and the entire house seemed to slant. In the front room was an old couch with sagging cushions and in a corner he saw a lumpy bed covered with a faded quilt. To the right was a door leading to a bedroom and directly ahead was the doorway to the kitchen which extended across the length of the two front rooms. They had the barest of necessities, but the delectable aroma from the kitchen filled the modest home with warmth and goodness.

Winn was offered a short bench at one end of a long wooden table laden with heaping platters and bowls of food. Hollis sat at the opposite end and the others crowded around. Winn looked at Hope beside him and caught her smile as she bowed her head. He also bowed expecting Hollis to offer thanks, but it was Hope's mother who prayed.

Octavia Jane's voice rang out with sincerity. "Our Lord, we thank You for this day that we have never seen, but You have and no matter what lies ahead we know You are with us." During the prayer, Winn glanced up and cringed when he saw Hope's daddy glaring at him. He quickly resumed his bowed position. *Hollis is sizing me up or maybe he barely tolerates his wife's praying.* His face reddened when Octavia included him in her prayer. "And Sweet Jesus, I ask a special blessing for Winn, the guest at our table today. Please guide and keep him close to You. Bless Hope on her birthday and give her many more of them filled with goodness. Thank You and it's in Jesus' name I pray. Amen." Hollis stared at the table while the family members echoed Octavia's "amen."

Mama picked up the large serving platter stacked with roasted chicken and offered it to Winn. He was about to take a wing when Mama said, "No, no. Here take a bigger piece." She picked up a leg with the thigh and put it on his plate.

"Well thanks, but I don't know if I'll be able to eat all of that." He held the platter for Hope to serve herself.

Octavia said, "Of course you can, and I sat another piece on the stove for you to take back with you on the bus."

"Mama." Hope squirmed involuntarily.

Winn smiled at Hope and gave her mother a reassuring nod. "I appreciate that and I'll make good use of it before I get home."

Mama continued talking while passing potato salad, creamed corn, stewed okra and tomatoes, and homemade bread. "You know we're as tickled as can be that Iris and Delbert are expecting a baby."

Buford's head jerked in surprise. "You don't say. Hot dawg!"

"Congratulations," Winn said. "Are you hoping for a boy or a girl, Delbert?"

With a mouthful, he said, "Aw, it don't make no never mind."

Iris laughed. "Just a healthy one, that's what we're praying for." She looked across the table at Buford. "Yep, the family's growing like rabbits in a coop now that Brother's getting married."

Hope would have pinched her sister if she weren't sitting at the opposite end of the table.

Winn sensed Hope's discomfort with Iris' crude manner of speech. He purposely brushed against her arm as he reached for the butter. She visibly relaxed.

Facing Buford, Winn said, "Congratulations to you too, Buford. You mentioned that on the porch and I wanted to ask you about it."

A broad grin brought a beam to Buford's cheeks. "Yes, sir, believe it or not, I found a peach of a girl. Figured I better snatch her up before she gets to know me better."

Betsy, with a milk mustache, sat her glass on the table. "Why can't she know you better, Bubba?"

Sitting beside her, Buford gave Betsy a playful poke in the ribs. "'Cause she might find out my bad habits and change her mind."

Hope saw the worried look on her sister's pudgy face. "He's teasing you, Betsy girl. We know Brother doesn't have any bad habits." Giving Buford a sly look, she said, "Or do you?"

"Wouldn't you like to know?" Amusement twinkled in his eyes.

Winn took a swig of sweet tea to conceal his uneasiness. *That's what I fear. I won't stand a chance with Hope if she found out about mine.*

Mama passed the bowl of potato salad to Buford for a second helping. "I'm sorry you and Fayella can't have the wedding here, but I know her kin wants to have it up there. You know we won't be able to make it, Son."

"I know—it's okay. Her mama and sisters have it all planned down to what songs are going to be played on the organ. I'll be glad when it's all over and we can get settled." Buford scooped a large spoonful of potato salad on his plate and passed the bowl to Papa. "We can live in my little rent house for a while, but I've got my sights on a few acres outside of Gilmer."

There was lively chatter around the table; Winn's participation and interest was genuine. Glancing at Papa, Hope was dismayed at the look he gave her. That look and his body language spoke volumes.

Hollis finished his meal and without thought of others, he said, "Okay, Tave, I'm ready for some of that cake."

His wife laid her fork down and jumped up. "Okay, just let me get it cut."

She was cheerful, but Winn could see she had not finished eating. He was glad in a way for the meal to end, thinking he may have a chance to spend some time with Hope. While the others hurried with their last bites, Iris and Hope began to clear the table for the cake cutting and serving.

Setting his fork on the empty saucer, Buford patted his stomach. "Mm good Mama, I sure love your cooking."

Winn stood when the others did. "Yes ma'am, Mrs. Davidson. I surely did enjoy this. Thank you."

"Now none of that 'Mrs.' stuff, everybody just calls me Mama. Glad you're here to share the Lord's bounty with us." She turned to the smallest girls. "Now y'all stay in here to help Iris and me."

Iris gave Hope and Winn a little shove. "Shoo, birthday girl and Winn." When they turned to go, Iris gave Hope a playful swat. "Don't think you're ever too old for a birthday spank from me, Sister."

Winn witnessed true sibling devotion as both girls laughed and Hope gave her sister a hug. *I can't imagine having an encounter like that with Luther. He would more likely swipe my wallet from my back pocket.*

Buford and Delbert were already sitting on the porch steps talking. Papa was engrossed with his whittling. Hope sat on the cane settee and Winn ambled toward the chair beside her. She felt strained with conversation at first, but Winn set her at ease. He began talking about his job and the paper in Liberty.

Hope leaned forward with interest. "You mentioned you were an editor at one time."

He was impressed that she remembered. "Yes, when I was just seventeen in Powder Springs, Georgia." He went on to tell her how it came about when the minister who owned the paper felt called by God to help build a mission in Mexico. "I'd been working for him and the townsfolk asked me to continue running it."

"That was quite a responsibility for one so young, I can't imagine running the *Hempstead News* if Miss Adkins wasn't there."

It hadn't occurred to him that he edited the paper when he was her same age. It seemed eons ago, eons filled with bad decisions and consequences he would rather not think about. "Now that I look back, I wonder if I really did the job and the town justice. But there was a wonderful old gent and an eager young boy who helped me on press day."

Buford and Delbert turned to hear the story. She knew Papa was listening though he didn't look up. Before long, Betsy and Pearl quietly sat at Winn's feet and Iris found a place on the steps by Delbert. Mama joined Hope on the settee.

Winn continued. "It's amazing how the timing worked out. My parents decided to move to Texas around the same time the minister returned to take over his position at the paper."

Mama nodded. "That was surely the hand of God looking out for you."

"I felt that too, Mama." He was surprised how easily he said "Mama" and went on. "My Uncle Foster had moved to Texas years before and urged my family to move here. Then a few years ago, my Aunt Katy and her family moved to Bandera from Georgia." The entire group on the porch was in rapt attention as he continued. "I'm pretty close to Aunt Katy. I lived with her and Uncle John for a while in Atlanta."

Betsy's eyes grew big. "What was it like living in a big city, Mr. Winn?"

He related how he sold newspapers on the street corner when he was ten years old. When they wanted to hear more, he told them about the busy streets with trolley cars. "They run along the street by long wires attached to cables overhead. Sometimes sparks fly and crackle. A trolley moves around like a giant praying mantis." He reached out to playfully poke Betsy and Pearl in the ribs as he made a hissing sound. The girls squealed with laughter and Mama clapped her hands. A reluctant smile hinted under Papa's bushy mustache.

Winn felt completely at ease with congenial banter on the rustic porch midst the sincere, humble family. He was surprised when he heard four chimes from the clock. "The afternoon has sure gone by fast. My bus leaves at five. It won't be long before I'll need to mosey on to the depot."

Hope smiled nervously; Papa had not given Winn the least sign of approval. It was evident that Mama liked him and everyone else did too, but she was most anxious to know the impression he made on Hollis. *Iris had an easy time when Delbert came courting because Papa knew him from our farming days. I so want to believe I'm being courted by Winn.*

Presently Winn stood and thanked Octavia again for the meal. He shook hands with the rest of the family. "Sure has been a pleasure meeting all of you, I can't remember a more pleasant day."

Winn thought Hope's daddy had the traits of a polar bear with his fair, pink-toned skin covered with white hair. His thick mustache had an upturned twist on each end. His look was fierce as though the safeguarding of Hope had to be defended, and he was here to do it.

I imagine Hollis's tough exterior is a cover up of his fear that I might take his daughter away. I can't blame him for wanting to protect her. Well, I've faced other intimidating bullies. Winn stepped near Hollis and extended his hand. The older man stiffened but grasped it like an inevitable dreaded doom.

"Mr. Davidson, I appreciate your hospitality." His handshake was firm. "I'd like to ask your permission for Hope to walk with me to the bus station, sir."

Hollis looked at Hope who stepped beside Winn. "I'd like to walk with him to Butch's, if it's okay with you, Papa."

The entire group waited for his answer. Hollis dodged their direct look and stood. The thought hung in the air that he wasn't going to respond. Hope was mortified until Papa said, "Only if Iris and Delbert walk with you." He went into the house allowing the screen to slam behind him.

Patience is the companion of wisdom.
—Augustine

7

Later that evening after Buford, Iris, and Delbert left, Hope sat on the porch with Hollis. She came right out with her harbored agitation. "Papa, you didn't seem very friendly to Winn."

Hollis's overalls had a stain on the front from gravy that tumbled down to his chest at supper. He sighed. "Shug, you don't know this man. You know nothin' about him."

"You're right, Papa. I don't know much about him." Facing him directly, she spoke with confidence. "I've been praying for God to give me direction for my life. When I turned around and saw Winn Prichard that day, I knew in my heart the Lord brought him across my path for a reason."

He shifted in his chair. "Confound it. You and your Mama—answer to prayer my foot! He just needed a job and happened to walk in off the street. Aw, Shug, can't you see he has citified ways? He's all show like a medicine man in fancy clothes. Did you see his shoes? Probably paid a week's wages for 'um." His face reddened and even the hearing impaired would have no trouble grasping his words. "You . . . you've always been so smart and made so much sense. Think." He looked into her face and was surprised that it held an expression of sympathetic compassion. His eyes turned watery, he lowered his voice. "Don't you see he's not our kind, Sugar?"

The ache around her heart throbbed with conflicting emotion. She understood Papa and his fear, yet she was determined to stand firm in defense of Winn. "I'm sorry you feel that way, Papa. I see him differently. He's a man striving for a place to settle and start a newspaper. He has worth and ambition." Heat hovered in her chest. "It's not right for you to judge him because he's lived in the city and knows how to speak properly." As soon as the words were out of her mouth, guilt flung the hurtful words back to her.

Hollis looked down at the gravy stain on his overalls, and the shame he felt for being uneducated slammed against his obstinacy. *I'm going to lose her, sure as shootin'.* "Don't get your dander up now, Shug. I just want you to watch yourself." He leaned forward with his elbows on his knees, head in his hands. "It's just that . . ."

The door slammed behind Octavia, her dark eyes were bright with anger. "It's just that you're scared. You're scared to death that Winn's going to take her away from you. That's why you sat around all afternoon like a puffed up toad."

Papa's agitation flared anew. His eyes were icy blue chunks meeting Mama's fiery black ones. "Maybe somebody 'round here needs to take stock before this thing goes too far." He stood. "All y'all were pert near dancing a jig 'round him." Hollis bowed from the waist and mimicked in a sing-song manner. "Oh, Winn, need more chicken? How's living in the city? We're sure honored you came to woo Hope."

Hope's arms went around her stomach as a nauseating wave swam through her insides. She hated when her parents went at each other, especially when she was the subject of dissention. Hollis was a big man and had a voice that could rival the train whistle streaming into town, but short Octavia could hold her own with him when she had a mind to. And it appeared she had a mind to right then.

Fury engulfed Mama. "Now you listen to me, Hollis." With a finger wagging upward, toward his face, she said, "You just settle down. It makes no difference if you believe whether or not our prayers are answered. God ain't waiting around to see if Hollis Davidson has a better idea about Hope's life. He's going to work it out the best way for her—not you. So there's no need to get all fired up."

Papa stepped to the edge of the porch and pounded his fist on the weathered post. "Yes, there is. I'm saying maybe he ain't all he looks to be. I just want Shug to be careful about getting too close, too soon to a . . . to a city slicker." He turned toward Octavia with a face set in conviction.

Mama placed her hands on her hips and leaned toward him. "You mean he ain't poor folks like us." She brushed back the strands of graying hair falling across her face. "And another thing—what makes you think out of the clear blue Hope's going to do something foolish? You even said yourself she's sensible and thinks through everything she ever does."

Hope stood. "Mama, let's not talk about it anymore." She put her hand on Hollis's thick arm. "I'm sorry about all of this, Papa. I can understand your concern. But you needn't worry. You know I won't do anything impulsive." She looked at her mother. "Maybe we're jumping to a conclusion that's not going to happen." She turned to go into the house and added, almost in a whisper. "Who knows, maybe I'll never hear from him again."

Liberty—

Sunday morning, Winn was awakened by sunlight beaming through his window's lace curtain. Lying there for a few minutes, he relived the visit with Hope and her family. Though he didn't have time alone with her, Iris and Delbert stayed out of earshot during their walk to the depot, allowing them some privacy.

He untangled his legs from the sheet and walked to the window and pushed the curtain aside. Painful memories suddenly entered his thinking like something as fragile as a lace fabric had held them back. *Why did I have to get mixed up with Darlene? She didn't really love me. Hope's the kind of woman I should've married. Now it's too late.* He heaved a sigh and focused on Mrs. Emerson's neatly trimmed yard and rose garden. A couple with two children was walking on the sidewalk. *They must be on their way to the church down the street. All dressed up in their "Sunday-go-to-meeting" clothes as Grandma used to say. Grandma's prayers haven't kept me out of trouble, but guess that's my own doing . . . or undoing.*

He dressed slowly and washed up in the bathroom at the end of the hall. *Poor Davidsons, they don't have indoor plumbing or much of anything else. They all seem happy, except for Hollis, but maybe he was out of sorts because he doesn't cater to strangers visiting his daughter.*

Seven days a week, his landlady cooked a bounty for breakfast and supper and a noon meal on the weekends. She was setting the table when Winn entered the dining room. "Good morning, Winn."

"Morning, Mrs. Emerson." He helped himself to a cup of coffee from the pot on the side table. "Your coffee is a good sight better than that stuff at the bus depot."

"Well, I should hope so." The middle-age lady had a mirthful look about her. "How was your visit to Hempstead?"

"Fine, Mrs. Emerson, it was mighty fine. I brought back my suitcase and had a nice dinner with the family of one of the paper's employees."

The landlady's smile crinkled the lines around her eyes. "How nice. Is he someone you knew before?"

"No, ma'am, actually, we just met the day I applied for a job there. And . . . she's a she."

The stocky woman stopped with a handful of silverware midair. "Oh, it's like that is it?" There was a mischievous twitch of her mouth. "No wonder you were anxious to go."

Winn smiled back, enjoying her interest in him. "Well, I'm not sure how it is . . . exactly." *I don't know how it can be anything.*

Thoughts of Hope and the past plagued his mind as he entered the work week. *Hope's a sweet girl and she's going to amount to something someday. The man who marries her will have a true helpmate by his side. I told her I would write, but I can't, it would be wrong, I shouldn't have written in the first place.* In his room each night he looked at his writing pad, but words would not form to put them down on paper.

Hempstead—

Each day when Miss Adkins returned from the post office, Hope anxiously looked her way to see if there was a letter from Winn. Cratered by disappointment, she was thankful for a busy week with an advertising insertion of early spring specials in the paper. Hope's creativity was stimulated as she helped Orville place ad copy in the forms between symbols such as flowers or a woman in a hat.

Working at the *Hempstead News,* she felt as if she was making a contribution to the community, not just earning wages. To her, being a part of the newspaper business was something worthwhile. It provided means for the readers to find out what was happening around them and the world beyond their little town.

Miss Adkins was elated with the amount of advertising she managed to sell. Holding a new layout for Taylor's Dress Shop, she stood by the work table. "I think things are on the upswing for most of the merchants. With all these ads we won't have to insert many fillers in the columns to complete this week's edition."

Hope looked over her employer's notes. "I'm glad. Hempstead needs a boost, and I'm happy to see a bigger issue for the paper this week."

The owner said, "Look here, Hope. Taylor's is having a sale on Saturday. We ought to go and get a new dress."

"Oh, that would be nice, but I make my clothes." *And the ladies at church give me their hand-me-downs.* She bent and rubbed the calf of her leg.

"Are your legs aching, Hope?"

"A little, but it's okay, really." She didn't want to admit it, but her feet and legs did hurt after standing all day.

"I know something that helps me. Try putting an old powder puff in the heel of each shoe; it will give you a little cushion."

Hope briefly pondered the suggestion. "Thank you, Miss Adkins, but I don't have any powder puffs, new or old. It's all right."

"Oh, I'm sure I can come up with some for you." She studied Hope's porcelain skin under the smattering of freckles, void of make-up. "Your skin is so lovely, you certainly don't need any powder, but have you considered a touch of lip rouge?"

Hope was embarrassed at the scrutiny. "Oh no, ma'am, Papa wouldn't approve." *He'd come after me with one of his canes if I walked in with a painted face.*

Time is too slow for those who wait, too swift for those who fear,
too long for those who grieve, too short for those who rejoice,
but for those who love—time is eternity.
—Henry van Dyke

8

The Liberty printing office was six short blocks from Mrs. Emerson's boarding house. Prichard felt fortunate to find a place within walking distance. Not like when he worked at the *San Antonio Light* and drove his car to work from the neighborhood where Darlene wanted to live.

Walking to work Monday morning, a Model T Ford claimed the road beside Winn. With thoughts of the past racing through his mind, the sputter of the vehicle's exhaust incited his ire. *If I hadn't been such a fool, I'd still have my Tin Lizzie.*

Thinking of the house in San Antonio and his car stirred up glimpses of Darlene. The memory edged his teeth. *Wonder where she disappeared to and what of the baby she claimed was mine? Or was that another one of her lies?*

Entering the shop early, Winn squared his shoulders and presented his usual smiling face to his co-workers. He knew he was liked for lighthearted banter with a joke or two as the day progressed. The shop was small, but well equipped. He stopped for a moment at the editor's desk. "Morning, Mr. Spencer."

"Morning, Winn. But it's Raymond, remember? Mr. Spencer's my ole man's moniker." Raymond stood and walked to the end of the front counter where a coffee pot sat on a hot plate. "We haven't had much chance to get to know one another. Sure been pleased with your typesetting." He poured a cup of coffee and handed it to Winn, then filled a cup for himself.

"Thank you, Raymond—for the coffee and the encouragement." He raised his cup simulating a toast and cautiously sipped the steaming brew. "I look forward to sitting down at the linotype and seeing the copy form into metal. Sure beats hand setting like I used to do."

Raymond leaned an elbow on the counter. "Yeah, tell me about the paper in Georgia."

"I was only seventeen when the folks in Powder Springs put enough faith in me to carry on publishing while the editor, who was also a minister, went to Mexico to build a mission. As it turned out, he was gone for almost two years. The shop was a decade behind times. That's when I learned to write copy, sell advertising, and hand set type. I was able to get out a four-page paper every week on an old Washington Hand Press."

"Holy smoke, I've seen one of those hand cranked presses that can only print one page at a time. You started on the very basic machine that newspapers were printed on from way back."

"Guess that's why I appreciate the linotype so much, it sure has made the printing industry more efficient."

Winn took a drink from his cup and felt Raymond studying him. The editor said, "You know, it's been awhile since I've talked to someone who takes such pride in their work."

This was exactly the conversation that got Winn's juices flowing. He sat his cup on the counter to talk with his hands in motion. "It's not just my work that I take pride in, Raymond, it's the entire newspaper profession. We're broadcasters of current events locally and across the nation. A publication is as much a vital part of the community as the people who live in it."

A young columnist casually stepped closer to listen while Winn went on. "When we strive to keep our readers informed, we're forming a bond bringing together the merchant, the laborer, the housewife, the rich, and the poor. Have you ever thought about how we stimulate discussions over dinner tables, in offices, and in classrooms?"

Realizing several employees from the back shop and a customer had gathered around, he smiled and picked up his cup. "Sorry, guess I get a little carried away on my favorite subject." The coffee was tepid.

Raymond said, "Winn, you ever thought of running for office? If you have that much enthusiasm for one industry, you could represent all of them."

The customer nodded. "I'd vote for you for sure. It sounds like we'd be better off with you in office than some of those fellers running now. They're all full of hot air."

Winn laughed. "No, sir, I'm staying clear of mudslinging contests. I'll stick to what I know."

The news writer said, "Winn, I'm utterly inspired. I never thought my job was so important." She turned to leave with her notepad and pencil. Before reaching the door, she said, "Mr. Spencer, you're going to have the best report on the Four-H Club prize hog winner since they started handing out blue ribbons."

Laughing, Winn walked to the back shop and sat at the linotype. *Okay, ole girl. Let's see if you can spit it out as fast as I can type it. With city and county elections coming up there are extra editorials. Editorials—how I'd love to sink my teeth into the issues and candidates to say what I think about them. People are reading the articles I type now, but someday they'll be reading the articles I write.*

Looking at the keys, he chided himself. *Ah, I need to be content as an employee working for my weekly paycheck. I just need to concentrate on my job, save my money, and keep my ears open for an opportunity. I've got to get my mind off Hope and what cannot be possible.*

A month after he began working in Liberty, he received a letter at the shop from his daddy. Not taking the time to open it at work, Winn waited until he got to his room. Untying his shoes, he slipped them off. Remembering Mrs. Emerson will be serving supper at six o'clock, he didn't bother unfastening his socks from the garters.

Sighing, he leaned back in the wooden rocker beside his bed. He turned the envelope over in his hands. The familiar handwriting summoned the pain of old wounds, coiling tighter the rope of contention around his chest. *Since I've met Hope, it seems everywhere I turn, something reminds me of things I wish I could forget.*

Gazing out the window, Winn was beset with the same unanswered questions. *Was Darlene involved with someone else besides Findley? My best friend—humph. Where could she have disappeared to? Someone had to help her empty the house of everything I worked for, and I don't think it was Findley.*

Mrs. Emerson's call for supper snapped him from the frame of mind that always took him into a crazy carnival house of mirrors. He tossed the envelope on the bed and put on his shoes.

Besides Winn, there were only two other boarders, a couple awaiting the building of their home nearby. Meals with them were enjoyable. Well-traveled, the Peabodys took an interest in hearing about Winn's ventures. As they lingered over dessert and coffee, Mrs. Emerson joined them as they expounded on the subject of talkies in the theaters.

"I predict talking movies will completely take over the flickers." Mr. Peabody forked his last bite of cherry pie.

Shaking her head, Mrs. Emerson stirred a teaspoon of sugar in her coffee. "Will wonders ever cease?"

Prichard sat his delicate cup in the matching saucer. "No, Mrs. Emerson, I don't think they ever will. Mankind will continue moving ahead, changing the world as we know it."

Mrs. Peabody nodded. "You're right, Winn, just look at aviation and Charles Lindbergh flying across the Atlantic Ocean. I don't doubt people will soon be flying like birds flitting all over the world. I would sure love to."

Presently Winn felt the pull of his pillow and the comfort of the feather bed awaiting him. He bid good night and trudged heavily upstairs, the weight of his restlessness had sunk to his feet.

*If our inward griefs were seen written on our brow,
how many would be pitied who are now envied?*
—Pietro Metastasio

9

In his room, Winn glanced at the envelope on the colorful quilt. Sitting on the bed, he placed a pillow against the wrought iron headboard and leaned back to finally open his Daddy's letter. For the first time he realized how thick the envelope felt and decided there must be a lot happening at home.

> *Dear Winston,*
> *We are as usual and hope this finds you well. I realize this will be a shock, but I feel obligated to let you know, I have news of Darlene.*

"What?" He said aloud. "This is a bolt out of the blue." He lowered the letter to his lap. *How strange that this should come up now. I've thought of Darlene more than I have in years.* He looked back at his daddy's writing.

> *When I got to my office this morning, Findley came from the press room. As you know, my work doesn't take me to that part of the plant, so I haven't seen him in quite a while.*
> *He asked about you and then told me he ran into Darlene at the Buckhorn Saloon last night. They evidently had a long conversation where she revealed she has been in Colorado and is married.*
> *Now this news floored me, she filed for divorce from you as soon as she arrived there fourteen years ago claiming desertion.*
> *Since you were not to be found (according to her) it was uncontested and therefore granted. She didn't have the consideration to let us know. You have legally been a single man all these years.*

Winn sprang out of bed at this astounding news. Pacing the floor, he went back to the beginning of the letter and reread it before continuing.

> *There is more. Darlene told Findley about her fifteen-year-old daughter she says is your child and was born before the divorce was granted. Her name is Marsha Prichard.*

He stopped pacing and mumbled. "This is unbelievable. I have a daughter? How could a woman keep this fact away from the father of her baby?" He sat on the edge of the rocker. "Maybe I'm not really the father." His eyes went back to the letter.

> *Darlene admitted to Findley that previously she and her present husband were in a longstanding relationship, but had a falling out. That's when she moved to Texas. After marrying you, she realized she was still in love with the man in Colorado and took up a correspondence with him.*
>
> *Darlene reunited with the old flame even though she was expecting your baby. They married immediately after the divorce was granted and her husband vowed to raise the child as his own.*
>
> *The woman was heartless not to let your family know about any of this, even news of the child who bears our name. I want to get this letter off to you right away, but will try to contact Darlene and request a visit with the granddaughter we didn't know we had.*
>
> *Since Findley doesn't know how to contact you, he felt obligated to tell me about seeing her and his part in the situation. The man deeply regrets his actions. He said Darlene was packing to leave the night he went to your house. Findley was red-faced in relating this to me, but explained that he thought you were home with that miserable head cold. He stopped by your house to give you a western magazine. She met him at the door scantily dressed and well, there is no other way to say it, she presented herself to him while you were at work.*
>
> *He said Darlene was troubled and had been drinking. He was a fool to be seduced by her. Later he realized you must have seen them together and surmised it was the reason you left that night without an explanation.*
>
> *Findley makes no excuse and is truly contrite to have caused such turmoil and pain. He says it was the only time it happened and wants to ask for your forgiveness in person.*
>
> *I now understand why you drove away after witnessing your wife and best friend together. I see why you were adamant about not letting him know your whereabouts.*
>
> *Winston, I can only speculate what you must be feeling about the information in this letter. My hope is for you to forgive Darlene and Findley. Some thoughts of gratitude should be given to her husband. He took on the responsibility of raising a daughter his wife claims is yours.*
>
> *The best road for you to take is to press on with your aspirations and leave the past in the past. You know that is what I had to do when alcohol took over my life and the Lord delivered me from it. Jesus will do the same for you, my Boy.*

I will keep you informed as to what success I have in any communication with Darlene.

Mother sends her love, Eddie also.
Your Daddy, Francis M. Prichard

Winn threw the stationery across the room. Bile of hatred stung in his throat—hatred for the first woman he loved. *She never loved me; she used me to try to forget the man in Colorado. I refuse to believe the daughter is mine; Findley could even be the father.* Despite the heaviness of the letter's contents, his thoughts went to Frank's signature and he almost laughed. "He always signs his letters so formal, *Your Daddy, Francis M. Prichard,* as if I don't know his name. Now he knows the entire nasty mess, guess I should've told Daddy before, but he probably figured it out. It was simple enough—my wife disappears, I get drunk and wreck my car and on top of all that, I refuse to talk to Findley. Ah-h, here I am in this lonely room talking to myself. I honestly don't know whether to cry or laugh."

"I need some fresh air." Snatching his hat from the stand, he flung open the door. On his way through the foyer, he saw Mrs. Emerson in the sitting room and gave her a perfunctory wave. "Just going for a little walk."

She opened her mouth to respond, but he was already out the door. Heading in the opposite direction of town, he sprinted at first and then slowed his pace when his heart pounded with exertion. He was standing in front of the church with the bell tower housing the peaceful chimes he heard on Sunday mornings. Feeling drawn to the red brick building, he ambled to the front steps and sat.

It was quiet. The church was surrounded by small homes. *I guess families are settling down for the night, wonder if I can ever settle down.* Resting on the brick step, he looked at the sky's dark expanse, a breathtaking backdrop for the brilliance of twinkling stars.

A familiar gnawing inside began to distract him beyond reason. "I have to stay away from the bottle, can't let this drive me to drink. I've got to keep this job." The mumbling elevated into a prayer. *Dear God, help me through this, help me to stay strong and sober. Don't let Homer at work tempt me again with his bootleg whiskey.*

Winn stiffened as a slight chill mounted the air and filtered through his limbs. Slowly he stood and retraced his steps to the boarding house. A light by the stairway guided his path.

Lying on top of the coverlet, he gazed out the window at the blue, black sky through the lace curtains. A star occasionally made its presence known.

For the hundredth time, he envisioned the words in his daddy's letter. As his mind succumbed to slumber, the words ran together on the stationery and blended into ink blots, then slid down the paper.

In that illusive expanse of time between sleep and wakefulness, Winn tried to solve the puzzle as to his whereabouts. Opening his eyes, he was surprised to see that dawn had been draped over the night sky. He was still dressed and lying on top of the quilt. Rising quickly, he moved to the desk under the window and began writing.

> *Let the past sleep, but let it sleep on the bosom of Christ.*
> *Leave the irreparable past in His hands and step out into*
> *the irresistible future with Him.*
> —Oswald Chambers

10

On Saturday afternoon, Hope helped Mama weed her flower garden in front working their way around to the back vegetable garden. She toiled silently. *I know God sent Winn into the printing office that day. Why hasn't he written since his visit? We must've scared him away. Papa was so gruff and rude.* She yanked at crabgrass with a vengeance.

Octavia, tired of the heat, walked to the shade of the huge oak. "Get out of the sun, Hope. Come sit a spell." She patted her face with a handkerchief. Her waist-long hair was twisted lightly in a knot at the crown of her head with a few fallen strands sticking with sweat to her neck.

"In a minute, just let me pinch some suckers off the tomato vines. *Mama and Iris made such a fuss, even Pearl and Betsy acted like they'd never seen a nice looking man from the city. Well, maybe they hadn't, but still, it was embarrassing.*

Mama looked at Betsy playing with stick figures by the back steps. "Go fetch us some water, Puddin'."

Hope joined her mother and sat cross-legged on the grass. Her hair was covered with a bandana and she wore a faded shirtwaist dress. They rested for a moment and Mama seemed to read her daughter's thoughts. "You know, Shug, we're poor country folks and don't know how to put on airs. If that young man is the right sort, it wouldn't matter one whit if he truly cared about you." Picking at the grass, Hope nodded. Mama went on, "My Grandma told me that it's a bad thing to be poor, but what's worse is to be ashamed that you're poor when you can't help it."

Hope pulled her knees to her chin. "Oh Mama, I know. It's not that. Guess I'm trying to figure out why he seemed so cordial, then not write like he told me he would."

Betsy carried a full glass of water in each hand placing her bare feet carefully so as not to spill a drop. Handing one to Mama and the other to Hope, she sat on the grass beside them. "Pearl's not coming outside 'cause she's afraid she'll have to do a chore."

Mama said, "Don't you worry your sweet head about Pearl. If I have a chore that fits her hands, I'll find her." She took a long drink. "Ahh." Her attention turned again to Hope. "Shug, you made Jesus the Lord of your life, didn't you?"

"You know I did, Mama, at the tent revival."

"He's Lord of my life too." Betsy piped up and was pleased with the smiles of approval.

Mama continued to make her point. "Well then, we have to trust that Jesus is working for us all the while. We can think maybe we have something all figured out, but then maybe it ain't God's way or time. Could be Winn's not ready to come courting just yet, then could be you're not ready, even though you think you are."

Betsy gave her sister a puzzled look. "Y'all thinking Mr. Winn ain't gonna come see us no more?"

It had now become Hope's habit to correct her younger sisters. "Isn't going to come see us any more, Betsy." Smiling, she gave her empty glass to the girl. "Thank you for the water. I think Mr. Winn is taking his sweet time, but I'm not giving up, it's only been a few weeks." *Three weeks today to be exact.* Unfolding her legs, she stood to finish her task while remembering how wonderful she felt when Winn touched her arm as he said good-bye at the depot.

Sunday at church, Hope absorbed Pastor Wright's sermon about Jacob's love for Rachel. *Oh, what would it be like to be loved so much? Poor Jacob went through a lot for her. They both waited a long time for each other.* She straightened in the wooden pew. *Don't make me wait long for Winn, Lord. That is . . . if it's Your will for it to come about.*

Later, Hope washed dishes and Betsy dried. Pearl avoided helping by staying in the outhouse. Betsy said, "Rachel's papa was mean to Jacob wasn't he?"

Hope scrubbed the last of the pans. "It seems like it, but Laban must've had his reasons. The oldest daughter usually married first back then, so maybe he was just following the custom. But then again, maybe Jacob was such a good worker, Rachel's papa wanted him to work seven more years before giving his permission for Jacob to marry Rachel." She rinsed the pan and put it upside down on a towel to drain. "Main thing to remember from the story is—we obey our parents and wait for love, no matter how hard that may be." *No matter how hard it is to wait for Winn and get Papa's approval.*

Never think that God's delays are God's denials.
Hold on, hold fast; hold out. Patience is genius.
—Georges-Louis Leclerc de Buffon

11

Monday brought sunshine riding through Hempstead on a promise of warm weather ahead. Walking to work, Hope's spirit was lifted as she consciously released her concerns about Winn. *I trust You, Jesus. I've made up my mind. If I don't receive a letter, then he's not in Your plan for me.*

She brought her lunch and ate while sitting at a worktable proofreading copy. In the afternoon, she printed letterheads and completed the matching envelopes. Hope looked over her work with satisfaction, and after five o'clock, she walked home.

Hollis was sitting on the porch in his usual spot, but he wasn't whittling. "Hello, Shug, been waitin' for you."

She hurried up the steps. "Is something wrong, Papa?"

"Nothing 'cept me being ignorant and can't read when the mailman hands me a letter."

"I'll be happy to read it for you."

Hollis reached in the pocket of his overalls and pulled out a crumpled envelope. "Figured you would. When I showed it to Mama, she told me who sent it and wanted to read it. I told her I want you to tell me what it says." He held it out for her. "It's from Winn Prichard."

Hope took in a breath; she looked at the beautifully formed writing. *Mr. Hollis Davidson, 701 Hickory Street, Hempstead, Texas.* "He knew our address."

"Well, I reckon so. Ain't it on the sign Buford made out there by the gate?"

"Yes, it is. He's quite observant. What in the world could he be writing to you about, Papa?"

"Well, shoot fire, that's what I've been wonderin' about. Come on; let's see what he has to say. Mama's been pesterin' me all afternoon to let her read it."

Hope sensed someone at the open window behind Papa's chair and began reading with a clear, strong voice so Mama could hear.

> *Dear Mr. Davidson,*
>   *I trust this finds you and your family well.*
>   *It is with great admiration for your daughter, Hope, that I ask your permission to court her, if she so desires of course.*

Stunned, her eyes were wide as she searched Papa's face.

He said, "Is that all the words on that paper?"

"Oh no—I'm just so surprised." She continued to read.

> My intentions are honorable, and my request is to have your blessing if our friendship leads to marriage.

Hope began to cry. The sound of a sniffle came from the window. She grabbed the hem of her dress, wiped her nose, and continued in a shaky voice.

> I realize it must be difficult to accept someone you just met briefly as a suitor for Hope. May I assure you, I will abide by the rules you set for courtship.
>
> My job here in Liberty is good, and I am a man of Christian principles. I can offer devotion, loyalty, and respect. It would bring me great pleasure to provide for her and share my life with her.
>
> I will await your reply, sir, hoping it is in the affirmative.
>
> > Respectfully,
> > Winston Prichard

Hollis was leaning forward, staring at the knothole in a plank by his oversized, mud encrusted work boots. Hope knew her Papa would not respond soon—if ever.

Sleep eluded Hope as she listened to her parents through the paper-thin wall. It was an unusually quiet discussion as Hollis and Octavia lay in their bed. No ranting. Her mother's voice was calm. "We've known Hope was going to up and leave us someday, Hollis. She's a hard worker, always reading and thinking about bigger things than just getting by, like we had to do."

Hope waited for Papa's response, but Mama wasn't finished stating her case. "Winn's done what's right by asking for your blessing. He said outright what he's thinking. I do believe he's a good Christian man. He says he'll take care of her."

"Hope don't need no takin' care of."

"Well, you're right about that, Hollis. She has gumption. Maybe that's why I don't let myself get all worked up about her going away. But I'd be comforted knowing there's a good man by her side. Somebody she loves and who loves her."

"We'll see, Tave. If he's a skunk she better see his stripe before it's too late." The springs groaned under Hollis' turn to face the wall.

> *The soul would have no rainbow if the eye had no tear.*
> —John Vance Cheney

12

April 1928—

The bus dwarfed Butch's filling station when it screeched to a stop beside it. Winn wiped smudges from the window to search for the Davidson family. With a singularly sweet smile, Hope stood alone. She wore a lavender dress and a straw hat with a small bouquet of dried flowers on the wide, upturned brim.

The thought crossed Winn's mind that the bus door was the gateway to what he had been waiting for since receiving the letter from Hollis. Stepping down from the bus, he grasped Hope's outstretched hands.

Her heart was fluttering. "It's good to see you, Winn."

"Likewise, Hope." He glanced around as they stepped away from the bus depot. "Did your family come with you?"

"No. You so impressed Papa with your letter, he said you're a man of honor and could be trusted." Happy anxiety came through in her manner and voice. "I'm allowed to go to Sophie's if you want. But Papa said he'll come looking for us if we're not back in due time."

"We'd better hurry then, I wouldn't want to get off on the wrong foot." He held her arm lightly as they crossed the street.

Settling at a table by the window in Sophie's Café, Hope was practically dizzy with elation. Winn wasn't wearing a suit, but was stylishly dressed with striped suspenders over a white shirt, the sleeves rolled to the elbow.

Now that they faced each other, Winn took in her appearance anew. "That's a very pretty dress, Hope."

Her face beamed. "Thank you, I just finished making it last night." Her hand fluttered across the top of the dress and then touched the brim of her hat. "Mama pinned on these flowers we dried last year." It was impossible to hide nervousness in her chatter and quick smile.

Laughter was in Winn's eyes. "A girl that can operate a job press can also run a sewing machine? That's something."

She simply smiled, not telling him the Davidsons didn't have a sewing machine and the dress was hand sewn.

With unconcealed curiosity, Sophie came to the table and gave Winn the once-over. "You new in town?"

"Just visiting Hope here."

She tossed her attention toward Hope. "Well, Honey, wherever you found him, I think I'll send Effie there to find one just like him."

The man at a table nearby said, "Aw, Sophie, you're always trying to find a son-in-law."

"Hush, Elwood, you missed your chance." She looked at Winn. "What'll it be?" She pointed the end of her pencil toward a blackboard behind the counter. "The special today is fried pork chops, mashed potatoes, and fresh mustard greens."

Winn nodded. "Sounds good to me, with a Coca-Cola, please."

"Yes, I'll take the special with a Coca-Cola also, Sophie. Thank you."

Sophie pushed her pencil over an ear and turned. Passing Elwood, she playfully tapped his head with her order pad. He swatted and missed his target as she scurried by.

The couple laughed with the other diners. Winn said, "The pork chops won't have chili powder will they?"

Hope's effervescent joy shone on her expressive face. "Or the mashed potatoes or greens?" *Well, that sounded silly.* After a moment, she spoke again. "I hope you didn't think it too forward of me to invite you here when I answered the letter you sent to Papa. You know he doesn't read or write."

"No, I wasn't aware of that." He studied the red and white checkered tablecloth and then raised his eyes to hers. The light in her brown eyes was mesmerizing. "So . . . you must've read my letter to him."

She blushed and suddenly felt shy. "Yes, he asked me to," then quickly added, "before we knew what it was about, of course."

"Well then, I'm an open book. You know how I feel about you."

She wasn't sure how to respond. "I guess we can spend some time getting to know each other better."

He could see the conversation was making her uncomfortable and changed the subject. "What have you been working on at the print shop?"

She brightened with interest as she told him that Miss Adkins gave her the responsibility of handling classified ads for the paper. Conversation came easy over their meal.

After Sophie cleared the dishes away, Winn said, "Guess I better get you home before your daddy sets out looking for us." He stepped to the cash register on the counter and paid the check.

As Hope walked beside Winn to the Davidson home, her steps were never lighter. Relief washed over her to see that Papa didn't appear riled when they entered the yard.

Winn stepped toward him to shake hands. *Wonder if he ever does anything at home except whittle.* "How are you, Mr. Davidson?"

"Tolerable."

Octavia bustled out the door as if her skirt was on fire. "Oh, you're back so soon, did you have a nice dinner?"

Winn and Hope answered at the same time, agreeing that they did. He laughed. "But not as good as your cooking. It's good to see you again, Mama."

"Come on in the house, I just made bread pudding." She tapped Hollis on the shoulder. "Your favorite, Papa."

Betsy squealed with delight to see Winn. "Can you tell us some more stories, Mr. Winn?" Although Pearl hung back, joy outlined her features.

He rubbed his chin in thought. "In order to think up a story, I'll need something to pry open my memory box."

Disappointed, Betsy said, "What might that be?"

Winn sat on one of the benches by the table and put his arm around the child. The younger girl stood just out of his reach. "Well, let's see." He wrinkled his brow as if in deep contemplation. "Maybe a pineapple from Hawaii?"

Betsy was utterly sorrowful. "We ain't got none of that."

Hope quickly corrected. "We don't have any, Betsy."

Winn looked thoughtful. "Hmm . . . how about a Japanese bonsai tree?"

Betsy shook her head, devastation swept through the kitchen and wrapped itself around her.

Winn was willing to carry on his little game, but the look on Betsy's face made him decide to end it. "Okay . . . maybe a bowl of bread pudding will do the trick."

She giggled, and it was contagious. They all laughed, except Hollis who was standing in the doorway. Mama served large portions with a creamy lemon sauce for the topping. Papa joined the rest of them when the aroma of the warm sauce was too flavorful to resist.

Wanting to pull Hollis out of his silence, Winn said, "You sure whittle some interesting looking canes, Mr. Davidson. I saw several leaning against the wall by the front door."

The man's countenance took on a semblance of pleasantry. "Yep."

Winn nodded. *Don't think I've ever had to work so hard at making conversation. But at least it seems the edge has been trimmed off his gruffness.*

Hope filled in the gap of awkward silence. "Goodman's store sells them."

Before Winn could come up with a comment, Octavia dominated the conversation over the sound of spoons scraping the pudding bowls. She talked about Buford's job and Iris's preparations for their baby.

Hope interrupted when her mother began to relate a story about her as a youngster. "Mama, I don't think Winn is interested in family history." Color rose to her cheeks.

Winn's smile was mischievous. "On the contrary, Hope, I'd like to know all about you."

Octavia said, "Oh don't mind me. Hollis says I can talk 'til the cows come home and then some. Would you care for more pudding? There's plenty."

"Whew. No, ma'am. It was mighty tasty, but I'm so full I'd have to put any more in my ear." His response was met with laughter. Even a slight chuckle escaped Hollis's lips before his resolve to remain solemn prevented it.

Hope stood to stack the dishes, but Mama whisked her and Winn out of the kitchen. "Now you two go on out to the porch. We'll take care of the dishes." She gave a meaningful look toward Betsy and Pearl. "Won't we, girls?"

On this visit the family provided more privacy for the couple. Their dance of courtship began. It started with a lovely slow waltz of exchanges as they became acquainted on a deeper level. Their mutual love of the publishing business was the favored topic.

Winn spoke again of his desire to have his own newspaper. "I picture a small community where there's good potential for growth. My paper will progress with the town, and I can be a part of it with my editorials."

Hope embraced his vision. "I can understand the longing to start a printing business and see it grow. Every community needs a newspaper."

Later, Hope broached the subject of faith. "Winn, do you go to church in Liberty?"

"There's a church a few blocks from my boarding house. I've been meaning to attend, but haven't as yet."

"Will you go tomorrow?" Unwavering, her brown eyes gazed into his soul.

"You're a direct little lady, Hope. No beating around the bush."

"I seem to recall a 'no beating around the bush' letter from you, Mr. Prichard."

Impasse. He took her hand. "Hope, I was fortunate to live with my Aunt Katy and Uncle John in Atlanta as a youngster. They took me to church and I professed my faith in Jesus when I was ten years old. Later I lived with my devout Christian grandparents in Powder Springs. They were a wonderful example of living for the Lord."

He patted her hand before releasing it. Leaning back in the chair, he sighed. "I'm ashamed to say that when I got out on my own, I drifted away from attending church." Pausing, he looked for any sign of disapproval.

Hope nodded, realizing Winn was sharing the depths of his heart with her.

Relieved, he wanted to make his point. "Before meeting you, I was beginning to see that walking without direction is a dead end. I know God is the answer, but I need to work out some things in my mind. I won't promise, but I'll consider going to church. Is that okay for now?"

"You know it's not a building we need, it's fellowship with Jesus. But He did tell us not to neglect gathering with believers, to draw strength from each other."

"I think that's what I'm doing now, Hope. I'm drawing strength from you, your insights, and your positive outlook. I'll go back to Liberty feeling your encouragement and I bet it will last all week." Wanting to divert her train of thought, he said, "Will it be all right if I come next Saturday?"

"Of course. But you don't have to buy my dinner. Mama always cooks a noon meal."

Hope was allowed to walk with him to the depot. He found a seat on the bus by a window and stuck out his hand to wave good-bye. He was surprised when she stepped under his window and reached for his hand. "You'll be in my prayers, Winn." She didn't let go until the bus started to roll and she walked along side for a moment.

In Houston waiting for his connection, the drab surroundings, unsavory smells, and seedy passengers dampened Winn's spirit. Doubts began to plague his mind, and his elation of being with Hope plummeted. *What is it about her that attracts me so? She's been like a magnet from the moment I saw her walking so carefree on the sidewalk. Maybe that's it, her innocence. She's wholesome—good to the core. Wonder how she'd feel about me if she knew I'd been married before and may even be the father of a girl almost her age. Hope's so young, too young for the likes of me. She may think I'm in my late twenties. Yes, that's what I'll tell her if she asks.*

The depot bustled with the unnerving cacophony of several buses arriving at the same time. Winn sought the one that would deliver him to his destination. Leaning his head back on the seat in the rear of the bus, thoughts betrayed his longing for a future with Hope. *I can't allow her to find out about Darlene. Then there's the drinking. Oh God, help me control the urge. There are so many things to cover up, the binges and all the rambling around I've done.*

Their parting rippled across his mind. *Daddy was right in his letter, it's best to put all the heartache brought by Darlene behind me and press on. I'm ready to settle down with Hope by my side, there's no reason for her to find out anything about my past.* Just outside Houston, it began to rain. He dozed listening to the hum of the tires on the pavement. Visualizing the image of her smiling face, doubts became raindrops drizzling off his window.

> *Truthful lips will be established forever,*
> *but a lying tongue is only for a moment.*
> —Proverbs 12:19 NASB

THE RICHLAND RECORD

More Than a Newspaper—a Community Service
<u>A Weekly Publication Serving the Greater Richland Area</u>
Richland, Texas   Thursday March 7, 1968
<u>Winston Randolph Prichard, Editor and Publisher</u>

News and Views of a Tactless Texan

It was forty years ago that I breezed into the *Hempstead News* office seeking employment as a linotype operator. The chance meeting of a lovely employee there changed my life, for the better, I'm happy to add. My wife, Hope, was the young lady working in the shop. Since the small printing plant offered no positions, I continued my quest and found work at the *Vindicator* in Liberty, Texas. Hope and I began our short courtship through frequent letters and weekend visits as I rode the bus to Hempstead every Saturday.

I've heard said that history is just gossip well told. I, for one, am not interested in gossip, but I do love history. I trust the accuracy of legitimate accounts which are researched through several sources before passing my findings on to you. Hempstead has quite a colorful reputation, and at one time was known as "Six Shooter Junction" because of the many murders that took place there. In 1905, a county judge and three others were shot and killed in the courthouse.

Being an editor, I've been especially interested in the chronicles of the town's newspapers. For years, Hempstead had one fire-eating editor after another. Most of them had an axe to grind with slavery, Civil War reconstruction, crooked politicians, and the Ku Klux Klan. [Which is also spelled Klu Klux Klan.] Back in 1859, the Civil War halted publication of the *Hempstead Courier* as it was named at that time. In 1880, the editor was shot and killed by a disgruntled reader opposing the paper's political view. His successor also met a violent end, shot in a saloon. There were numerous editors over the years with threats and various civic uprisings to deal with. In the early 1920s, there was much feuding and fighting when the KKK was in full swing in the Waller County area.

In my editorial years there have been a few readers who contradicted opinions cited in our newspapers, but with a nod of thanks toward the Heavens, I've not encountered gunfire.

When I stopped by the *Hempstead News* in 1928, Miss Anna Louise Adkins was editor. She only managed to stay afloat for a few years through the depression and sold out in the 1930s. Of course, my taking away her loyal employee couldn't have helped matters in publishing her fine paper.

Every editor I've known has coped with their conscience to stand up for the principles they believe in. We feel an obligation to print the truth, recount activities, and inform readers of events which affect our community. As my column title says, I'm a tactless Texan and at times may expound upon affairs as I see them. At the *Richland Record*, we strive to report current newsworthy issues and welcome your views as well.

I cannot end this week's column behind page one without saying how grateful I am for favorable comments expressed by our readers about this family-owned and operated newspaper. The publication of which would not be possible without my wife, Hope.

May I leave you this week with an encouraging word to pursue your dreams and continue on the path for a better tomorrow.

Ending with my usual -30-.

13

Mid May—

Buford surprised his family with a visit on Friday night. "Fayella's sisters and aunts have wedding showers and doings all weekend. They have her as busy as a barn cat in a nest of field mice. They told me I'd just be in the way, so figured I'd head on down to see y'all."

He was the only brother now, all the love Hope held for him was double since Alonzo died. "I'm glad you came, Brother. Winn's coming tomorrow."

"He's still hanging around, Shug?"

"Just every Saturday." A blush of joy colored her cheeks. "He wrote the most beautiful letter to Papa asking to court me and has written to me almost every day since."

Sitting, relaxed at the kitchen table, Buford took a swig of his R.C. Cola. "Sounds serious. Mama, you may have a new son-in-law." He looked at Hollis. "Whatcha think of that, Papa?"

Hope could hardly wait for a comment from her daddy.

Papa leaned forward. "Well Son, I have to admit, I didn't like his looks right off. But he don't put on airs like I thought he might." Aiming at the spittoon on the floor beside him, he made a direct hit. Hope cringed when he wiped his whiskers on his shirt sleeve. Hollis gave her a long look. "I can't find no fault with him. He's a right nice feller. I reckon if Hope's gonna marry so young, he'd likely take care of her." His breath came out sharply as if it couldn't decide to be a groan or a sigh of resignation.

Mama and Hope exchanged looks of astonishment. Hope rushed to give him a hug around the neck. "Oh, Papa, thank you." He stiffly patted her shoulder.

The next day, Hope met Winn at the depot. Saturdays became the highlight of the week as they stepped into the now familiar routine of courtship, Victorian style as Papa demanded.

Arriving at the house, Winn greeted her brother. "Hey there, Buford, it's good to see you again. Did you get cold feet and decide to run away while you had a chance?"

Buford laughed as they shook hands. "Not on your life, I can't wait to marry that girl. She's a peach. I'll be glad when I can bring her down to meet everybody."

It thrilled Hope to see Winn and Buford get along so well. "I'm sure we'll fall in love with Fayella just as you did, Brother."

"Well, not exactly like I did, but you'll love her all right." He winked at Winn.

Hope noticed the sly look between them. "I don't think I want to ask what you mean by that, so I'm going to help Mama get dinner on the table."

Along about mid-afternoon, Buford came up with an idea. "Winn, you've been riding the bus back every Saturday, why not spend the night and go back tomorrow?"

Hope's fine, silky eyebrows raised a trifle as she attempted to decipher Winn's face.

Betsy's excitement erupted with jumps up and down. "Oh please, Mr. Winn."

Mama nodded. "Why sure, you can bunk down in the kitchen with Buford."

Winn took in the shocked expression on Hollis's face and quickly said, "That would be fine, Buford, if I would've known, but I didn't bring extra clothes."

Buford sat his empty bottle of cola beside his chair. "Aw heck, that don't matter. Your clothes will still be okay tomorrow, and I got something you can sleep in. It'll be like old times with Alonzo." Suddenly lines indented his brow. He rarely spoke of his brother.

A silence came over the family at the mention of Alonzo. Hope had related to Winn the tragedy of her oldest brother who was killed when a train hit the truck he was driving. Winn looked down at his shoes, trying to think of something to say.

Papa stifled a sob by making a point of clearing his throat. "Reckon it'd be all right since Buford's here. That is if you don't mind beddin' down on a cot in the kitchen, Winn."

Hollis was the last person Winn thought would want him to spend the night in such close proximity to his daughter. He was definitely without excuse. "Much obliged, Mr. Davidson. I don't mind one bit. I could even put the cot out here on the porch. It's going to be a nice night." *It's really not that much further away from Hope than the kitchen, but the screen door will be a decent barrier.*

Buford stood. "Hey, that's a great idea."

Ready to make preparations, Mama said, "Buford, go get the other cot from the shed."

Winn stood. "I can get it, just tell me where."

Buford placed his hand on Winn's shoulder. "No you don't. I know right where to look, and besides, it's covered in cobwebs. You might have a granddaddy longlegs crawling on you tonight." He laughed as he jumped over the porch steps and headed around the corner of the house.

Winn felt a tug on his trousers and was surprised to see Pearl. He leaned to hear what the shy girl had to say. "Can you go to church with us tomorrow?"

"I . . . I suppose I can, Pearl."

Hope's head was swirling with everything that had just taken place. *I never thought Papa would agree for him to spend the night. It'll be an answer to prayer for him to go with us to church. I don't think I'll sleep a wink tonight.*

After supper, a comfortable peace settled as rays of sunset's pastel colors played on the flowers in the front yard. Buford, Hope, and Winn remained on the porch when the rest of the family retired. They sat quietly for a while, each in his own thoughts. Winn, beside Hope on the settee, dared to put his arm around her shoulders. Hope thought of the many times she spent alone on the porch. *Winn sitting beside me is pure heaven—never have I been so content.* She saw her humble surroundings in a much different light; everything appeared dreamlike in her eyes.

There was exquisite beauty in the evening as crickets chorused a nocturne serenade. Moonbeams softly floated where the sun had warmed the front yard before descending to its nightly hiding place.

Buford broke the quietude and unknowingly drew his sister from her fanciful state. "Boy, I sure wish Fayella was here."

Hope looked at her brother, who was leaning back in Papa's kingly chair. "Tell us about Fayella, Buford. What does she like to do when she's not working at the telephone company?"

Buford talked comfortably with them as if he had known Winn for years. "Well, I know you'll like her right off. She's sweet and purdy." He paused, listening to the gentle coo of a dove in the sycamore tree. Buford smiled thinking of his soon-to-be bride. "She teaches Sunday School at the First Baptist Church. Fayella's something; she's even got me going to church."

"I know that pleases Mama. I'm truly happy for you, Brother."

Buford's speaking of church brought to Winn's mind the commitment he made with little Pearl to attend services in the morning. *It seems a lifetime ago since I've been to church.* He gazed at Hope. *It was a lifetime ago . . . Hope's lifetime.*

Keeping their voices low, not to disturb those in the house sleeping nearby the open windows, the threesome solidified their relationship. Hope loved her brother for suggesting Winn spend the night. "I hate for this night to end, but I'll need to get up early to help Mama. I know she'll be getting things ready so we can eat when we get home from church."

When she stood to bid goodnight, Buford suddenly decided a trip to the outhouse was necessary. "I'll be back in a minute." He rushed around the side of the house reminding Hope of their childhood days when he always outran her in their games of tag.

Winn appreciated Buford's willingness to allow a moment alone with Hope. He put a finger to his lips and took her hand as he led her down the porch steps. They walked in silence on the path to the front gate.

Hope gave him a quizzical look, but waited for him to speak. "Hope, I just wanted to move away from the house a bit, in case there are any listening ears inside." She nodded with understanding and waited for his soft southern drawl that she loved. Her eager face couldn't hide her love for him any more than the starlight could prevent its gleam this special night.

He took both her hands. "I know it's awfully soon really, but we've packed so much in these Saturday afternoons that I know you better than I've ever known anyone."

Hope was filled with anticipation of what Winn might say. "And we've written almost every day."

He nodded. "I've fallen in love with you, Hope." His voice was filled with emotion, barely above a whisper. "Will you be my wife?"

With a catch in her throat, she didn't hesitate. "I love you, Winn, and prayed you would ask me. Yes, I'll be proud to be your wife." It took great effort to maintain a whisper; she could have shouted her answer. Leaning closer to him, she felt his arms around her; it was the couple's first real embrace. Hope knew this was right, she felt strength and assurance in his caress.

Winn held rein on the kisses he desired to smother her with during the past weeks. The feeling he had at that moment was one of complete peace. He wanted to be her protector, her all. He longed to walk with her through that squeaky gate to their own place. He wanted their life as man and wife to begin immediately.

He glanced toward the house; its outline in silhouette appeared lifeless against the sky, like a cardboard façade. He had been in Hollis's good graces and this was not the time to overstep his bounds. He released his hold as they walked back onto the porch.

Buford joined them. His timing was perfect, or more likely he had waited from a distance until they returned to the porch. It didn't matter to Hope if he had been watching. It didn't matter if the entire town of Hempstead was watching.

Her brother sat on his cot. "Those tree frogs are as loud as a herd of bleating sheep." He pounded his pillow into an acceptable lump. "See y'all in the morning."

"Good night, Buford." Hope turned to Winn and gave his hand a squeeze. "I hope you sleep well." She quietly opened the screen door and stepped into the house.

Before it closed she heard Winn say, "Sweet dreams, Hope."

The grand essentials to happiness in this life are something to do, something to love, and something to hope for.
—Joseph Addison

14

The proposal brought about a release, an astringent of sorts to Winn's soiled and sordid thoughts. There was no doubt of his love for Hope and the decision to make her his wife. Letting go of his past was a major step toward the future.

Behind the outhouse, in the clear illumination of the moon, Winn slipped out of his clothes and donned the nightwear. *My clothes will look like I slept in them if I sleep in them. Guess I have to change. But I want to get up early before anyone sees me in these striped pajamas.* Settling down on the cot, he listened to Buford's light snoring. He had slept in more uncomfortable places, like a wooden seat on the train from Georgia.

His circumstance this night reminded him of another time when he slept on a porch. He was a youngster at his grandparents' grist mill beside the Chattahoochee River. He smiled remembering the night he woke to see Grandpa's work clothes hanging on a nail by the door. They were covered with flour from the mill. Winn hollered with fright thinking it was a ghost. The comfort Grandma gave to him was never forgotten. She soothed his fears and rocked in the chair beside him singing a hymn until he fell asleep.

Stretched out on a cot within a few feet of his beloved, he was surprised when a tear collected in the corner of his eye and brushed it away. *Grandma and Grandpa would've loved Hope. Can I be all she needs? She loves me and will depend on me to take care of her. We won't have much, but if I wait until I can support her, who knows how long that could be?*

He turned onto his side and looked out into semi-darkness as a cloud meandered across the moon. *I know I'm doing the right thing for my benefit, but what of Hope's? I'm going to do my best to be all she expects starting with church in the morning. That's where I should've been all along.* He sighed. *Between the tree frogs and Buford's snoring, I may not get any sleep tonight.*

After the huge breakfast, Winn wasn't surprised when Hollis became scarce while the rest of the family rushed to prepare for church. Hope's happiness bubbled from every pore making even her freckles glisten. On the walk to church, Hope turned to Buford. "I still laugh when I think of Pastor Phillips baptizing you in the Brazos River."

When her mother and sisters laughed, Pearl said, "What happened?"

Betsy skipped beside her brother and said, "He almost got drowned 'stead of baptized."

Hope explained to Winn that Buford was a gangly, tall youngster and the old preacher was a small man. "When he dipped Buford in the river, he couldn't pull him up and fell forward on top of Buford. The men on the bank rushed to rescue them both."

Winn laughed with the group. "I would love to have seen that!"

Buford said, "Yep, I figured if I was going in the drink, all the men better be baptized with me, whether they wanted to or not."

Assuming that everyone there had been baptized, Betsy said, "Mr. Winn, how old was you when you got dunked?"

Hope yanked her sister's puffed sleeve. "Betsy, that's not the way to ask and it's disrespectful to call the sacrament of baptism 'dunked'."

They were near the church and Winn stopped to kneel beside the child who was embarrassed by her sister's rebuke. His voice was soft and kind. "Betsy, not everyone has made the decision to give their life to Jesus. Sometimes it's best to just ask about a person's faith and then let them share what they want."

The family formed a small circle around them, listening as he spoke gently to her. "I gave my heart to the Lord when I was ten. As a young teenager, I wanted to follow the teaching and example of Christ. My grandparents' church was near the Chattahoochee River, so that's where I was baptized."

Betsy wrinkled her nose. "The chachawhoche?"

He laughed and stood. "You almost said it—the ChattaHOOchee. And it was very cold."

Mama hurried the family along, but Hope and Winn hung back. "Thank you, Winn. I shouldn't have snapped at her, but I'm glad Betsy asked so I could learn about your baptism."

Again he noticed the slight overlap of her front teeth under her smiling lips and the freckles dusted across her nose. *Charming, she's just charming.* Winn took her arm and walked into the plain wooden church building. Octavia grabbed his other arm and persuasively pulled him from person to person, proudly introducing as they went. He was glad Hope managed to hang on.

At the first strands of organ music, the threesome found the pew with Buford. Iris and Delbert had taken charge of Betsy and Pearl. Mama whispered to Hope. "I feel like a proud hen with feathered wings tucked around my chicks."

Hope smiled. She was enveloped in a warm, glorious aura of her own.

Winn never heard so much singing and praising in all his life. A stout couple joyously led the congregation, who mostly sang to their own timing. The church in Georgia wasn't quite as exuberant, but he followed Hope's clear voice and clapped, exchanging loving glances with her. As Pastor Wright brought his message, Winn became engrossed.

The preacher based his sermon on the last few verses of chapter eight in Romans, where it promises that nothing can ever separate us from the love of the Father. Winn must have heard it before, but digesting it now was an astounding realization of God's love for him even through the years of drifting and disobedience. The words dug deep into his spirit.

Pastor Wright ended by affirming that, "Nothing or no one above or below can separate us from the love of Christ when we have professed Him as our Savior. The power of the Lord is stronger than any force that could keep His love from us."

Afterwards, as they walked to the Davidson's house, Winn was deep in thought. The profound knowledge that from the moment he prayed to receive the Lord's salvation, his name has been in the Lamb's Book of Life for all eternity. In looking back at his foolish ways of binge drinking and keeping company of ill repute, even then he was a child of God.

Hope said, "Winn, you look distracted. Was the service livelier than you're used to?"

"Actually it was, but . . . but good. Well, the singing was a bit long; I have to admit, for my liking anyway. But your pastor presented a strong message." They were lagging behind the rest of the family. Mama was in a rush to get dinner on the table for Hollis.

Winn placed himself between Hope and the road as a car whizzed by. "I can't fathom a love so great for us."

Hope wasn't sure what "fathom" meant, but quickly decided it must mean we can't imagine the depth of God's love. "We can't compare our meager capacity of love to the Lord's. We just have to accept it. Then it's easy to obey His word because we want to please Him."

He gave her a sideways look and smiled. She was lovely in the brightness of the sun wearing her lavender dress with the jaunty straw hat. *She's pure, delightfully pure and trusting. She sees the best in me; I hope I don't fail her.*

With a house full, Winn wasn't sure how he would manage to have a moment with Hollis. After the bountiful meal, the women rushed about the kitchen while Buford and Delbert were deep in conversation at the table. Hollis headed to his favorite oversized "throne" on the porch, and Winn followed him.

"Mr. Davidson, may we talk for a few minutes?"

"Why sure, Winn." Over the weeks, the man's initial animosity had melted away. Hope was right in knowing that Winn's likable personality would break through Papa's rough exterior.

Winn pulled a chair closer to Hollis and sat down. "In the letter I sent to you asking for permission to court Hope, I expressed that my intentions are marriage."

Hollis nodded. "I remember." His icy blue eyes looked directly into Winn's brown ones unlike the way they avoided him on the day of their first meeting.

"I proposed to her last night and she accepted." He waited, wondering what the reaction would be.

Davidson nodded. "Yep, I seen it comin'. Reckon you two done talked more than me and Tave ever have." He reached for the cedar stick he was forming into a cane. "I was put out at first 'bout how young she is and you being a good deal older." Winn held his breath and the question came that he dreaded. "How old are you anyway?"

"I'm twenty-eight, sir." *Another lie to hide behind.*

"Figured about that. It's better to have someone to take care of her than a young whippersnapper she can't depend on."

"You know I'll take care of her." His breathing had returned to normal.

Hollis pulled his jackknife out of his pocket. "She's always been my Sugar, 'cause she's a sweet girl, 'cept when she loses her temper that is. You ain't seen her when she's riled, have you?"

He blinked with surprise. "No, sir, I haven't."

"Hoowee, it takes a heap to get her peeved, but all I got to say is—get outta the way." His stomach bounced with a chuckle.

Family poured out of the house one after another until everyone was present. Papa said, "Y'all listen here. Winn's got somethin' to say."

Surprised at the prompting, Winn looked at Hope who was already blushing. He stood, walked to his intended and put his arm around her. "I've asked Hope to be my wife and she's agreed."

They were smothered with approval in a blanket of love. Betsy couldn't contain her joy; it burst through her limbs inciting jumps and spins. "Mr. Winn's gonna be my brother!"

> *The feller that puts off marryin' till he*
> *can support a wife ain't very much in love.*
> —Kin Hubbard

15

A heat wave hit Hempstead like a sudden tornado. Octavia and her girls carried bucket after bucket of water to the gardens. The morning glories could barely raise their heads and proclaim all was right with the world.

All was very right with Hope's world, however, as she sent and received a letter every day. Winn wrote about his hopes for the future and his life in Liberty, saying as little as possible about his past.

Liberty—

> June 14th
> Sweetheart,
>
> Mrs. Emerson loves our song as much as we do, judging by how many times she plays it on her phonograph in the sitting room.
>
> Hearing it makes me miss you all the more. Have you given any more thought about the wedding? I'll let you make all the decisions, just let me know when to show up.
>
> In your letter yesterday, you asked about my family. Well, as I mentioned, Daddy works for the San Antonio Light newspaper. My youngest brother, Edward (Eddie), lives with Mother and Daddy. He has a paper route and has to get up early every day to distribute them.
>
> Since my other brother, Luther, was discharged from the Army, he hasn't stayed in touch very often. He is a good linotype operator. Not as good as me of course, but fair enough to keep him working when he runs out of money.
>
> Mother keeps to the house. She was used to having a housekeeper all her life until we moved from Georgia. I have to hand it to her; she has managed to become a pretty good cook. Eddie does most of the cooking, however, and seems to enjoy it.
>
> My parents have had to overcome the grief of losing three sons. Two died in infancy and then my brother, Robert, died when he was twelve. I told you about him. I was ten and took it pretty hard too. That's when I went to live with my Aunt Katy and Uncle John in Atlanta.

> *When I was around thirteen, my folks allowed me to move to Grandma and Grandpa Prichard's farm and grist mill near Powder Springs. That's where I started working for the newspaper.*
>
> *I bought the sheet music to "Let Me Call You Sweetheart", I'll bring it to you Saturday. The lyrics express what I want to say to you. "Let me call you Sweetheart, I'm in love with you. Let me hear you whisper that you love me too."*
>
> *Until Saturday, Winn*

Sitting at the small desk in his room, he scanned the letter hoping the scant details about the Prichard family would suffice in answering Hope's questions. What could he say about his complicated family? He had no desire for Hope to discover the ongoing personal battles of his parents and both of his brothers.

Winn's mother, Priscilla, was born with the notion that God created her a notch above everyone else and never hesitated to let it be known. She had an affluent upbringing with an indulgent father. Her critical nature and inability to demonstrate emotion caused marital problems and the development of character flaws in her sons. Since girlhood, Priscilla suffered depression and "sick headaches" more often than not. Any upset from the trivial to the tragic sent her to her room where she remained cloistered for days on end. Years ago, Frank attributed her behavior to the loss of their three sons and disappointment in a lifestyle much less than she expected. But her melancholy was evident before those events, and continued though she lacked for nothing. Her seclusion and indifference to Frank and her sons reaped ongoing unhappiness.

Winn walked to the window. Thinking about his family conjured the deep hurt when his brother, Robert, contracted pneumonia and died at age twelve. Winn's ten-year-old mind couldn't understand why his confidant and best friend was taken away. His sorrow was intensified with being left alone to cope with his devious younger brother, Luther. His daddy was drowning his sorrows in whiskey, and his mother seldom entered his world. The Prichards had a faithful housekeeper who took over household duties allowing Priscilla to indulge in her self-imposed confinement.

Looking out the window, but not focusing on the view, Winn's mind continued to wander. *Thank God I was rescued by Aunt Katy when she took me to Atlanta to live with her and Uncle John. She was so full of joy—the complete opposite of Mother. I suppose she still is, I haven't been to visit her and Uncle John since right after they moved to Bandera. If it weren't for them, I don't know what would've happened to me. They introduced me to a new outlook on life.*

He turned back to the desk and stared at the letter. *I was fortunate to see how a loving couple live. I'll never forget their happiness when I accepted Christ in their church and how Uncle John cared for many poor patients free of charge.* He sighed aloud and sat in the desk chair. *It was a sad time when I had to go back home when Eddie was born. Luther was a handful and Mother's demands were too much for the housekeeper to handle. It was up to me to keep Luther out of trouble—an impossible task for anyone.*

Luther's rebellion became more severe in his teens. His daddy pulled him out of more scrapes than Priscilla ever knew about. His drinking, carousing, and even petty theft was swept under the carpet to keep his mother from spiraling into one of her "spells." Luther was a disappointment to the family, he only showed up every couple of years or so. About the time his parents began to wonder if Luther was still among the living, he popped up on their doorstep asking for money.

Poor Eddie, the youngest, got short changed in mental capability in some ways; anything other than menial tasks rattled him. A sullen, quiet boy, his childhood traits were manifested in manhood. He was a sensitive and caring individual who loved to read and could fill out crossword puzzles like a scholar. Eddie's mission in life was to please others and he catered to his mother's whims without question. He adored his daddy and Winn, but his relationship with Luther had always been strained.

Winn's daddy, Frank, a soft-spoken, compassionate man, lost his profession in Georgia as an attorney because of a dangerously increasing infatuation with alcohol. His drinking began as an escape from belittlement on every count as he tried to please Priscilla. Realization of the damage to his mind and body broke through Frank's haze of addiction when he appeared in court rip-roaring drunk. Along with humiliating Frank, for public intoxication, the judge also threatened him with disbarment. Retreating to his parents' farm, Frank endured the painful process of drying out. With the urging of Foster, Priscilla and Katy's brother, the Prichards migrated to Texas where they sought a new beginning.

Winn folded the letter. *I greatly admire Daddy. I don't think he's touched a drop since we left Georgia seventeen years ago. Circulation manager of the San Antonio Light is a good enough job, but beneath his education. I've got to hand it to him for staying by Mother's side. She can cut him to ribbons, but he handles her with love and understanding. It's beyond me.*

He sighed again and pulled an envelope out of the letter holder on the desk. *Hope's family is dirt poor, but I feel love when I'm with them. I see love and hear it—oh, maybe sometimes Hollis is rough around the edges, but it's plain he couldn't do without his family. How can I expect Hope to comprehend my relations who are so abstract in comparison with hers? I have to gloss over so much about them and keep my past hidden.*

Correspondence to his family didn't include anything about Hope or his intentions of marriage. He reasoned that keeping them apart would cancel or at least postpone chances of Hope getting an inkling of his secrets.

Turning down the quilt and fresh white sheet, he couldn't seem to shake the pessimistic feeling concerning his family and his own drinking battles.

So far I've managed to steer away from Homer. He's so ready to share his bootleg whiskey. I can't give in to one small slip. I don't understand how some people can have a nip or two and walk away. If I let my defenses down, it's no stopping until I pass out or end up in a fight and get knocked out. Thank God my mind has been occupied with thoughts of Hope and on my days off I'm in Hempstead.

> *Love is not an affectionate feeling, but a steady wish for the loved person's ultimate good as far as it can be obtained.*
> —C. S. Lewis

16

Stepping off the bus, Winn was cheered by the exuberance written on Hope's face. Her enthusiasm was contagious, and he laughed at the buoyancy of her floppy hat as she ran to meet him. With the assurance of his love and promise of marriage, Hope didn't hesitate to give him a quick hug. "Oops, I hope there are no busybodies around who will report that to Papa."

He was swept away by her ardent display. "Well, can I expect a welcome like that for the rest of my life?"

She tucked her arm through his. "When I have good news you can."

He chuckled. "You look like a school girl at recess. What's the good news, besides the fact that I'm here, that is?"

She gave him a playful punch. "Well, that's always good news, but what do you think of the Fourth of July?"

"I love the Fourth of July—the parades and picnics."

"No, you big tease. I mean for our wedding."

He stopped short and she stood in her tracks. Studying her face, he said. "You mean next month?"

Smiling, she bobbed her head up and down. "Of course. Why wait? Aren't you tired of riding that bus every week and writing every day?"

He resumed walking, slowly now. "Riding and writing. Well, yes, that can become tiresome and I'd rather have you with me. The fourth would suit me fine, but what about you, that's awfully soon."

Her pale yellow dress fairly danced around her calves as she kept pace with his long strides. She was barely five foot three and loved the way his arm easily slipped around her shoulders. They stopped walking as a wagon rambled on the road beside them. Her eyes met his with serious intent. "I'm ready to become your wife, Winn. Pastor Wright can come to the house and marry us. I don't want a big 'to do', just a simple ceremony and that doesn't take much preparation."

He had hoped she would want to wed soon and this was ideal. Encircling her waist with his arms, he lifted and twirled her around. "The sooner, the better."

She held on to her hat and laughed with pure joy. "Now a busybody would really have something to tell Papa."

A canning jar of colorful zinnias in the center of the Davidson's table matched the joyful mood at the noon meal. Winn was pleased beyond simple pleasure that he was treated as one of the family.

Before anyone else was finished eating, Hollis cleaned his plate and stood. "Got to head on down to the cemetery. Me and Abner gotta fill in Hinley's grave. The funeral's probably about over by now. The Fourth of July sounds like a good day as any to get hitched, Winn."

"Yes, sir, looks like I'll lose my independence on Independence Day."

Hollis laughed. "That's a good one. I'll tell it to Abner. I'll be back in a little while."

Hope stood and gave him a peck on the cheek. "Bye, Papa, see you later." She grabbed the dog-eared *Farmer's Almanac* and sat on the bench beside Winn. "See, here's the fourth. I thought you might be able to get a few days off work." She blushed at the thought of being alone with him.

He put on an exaggerated woeful expression. "I don't know if the *Vindicator* can get along without me."

Hope's balloon of happiness deflated. "Oh, . . . well then. I guess we can . . ."

"I'm joking with you, Hope. I'm sure a few days off can be arranged."

Hope laughed with everyone else and swatted him on the shoulder with the book. "Oh, you."

Octavia waved them out of the kitchen as if they were pesky children. "Y'all go make your plans. Betsy and Pearl are going to take a basket of vittles to Widow Sloane."

Hope filled water classes to take to the porch. "Has she taken a turn for the worse, Mama?"

Filling a basket with a large canning jar of homemade soup, fresh baked bread and half an apple pie, Mama said, "No, thanks be to the Lord. She's a good sight better."

"Probably due to all the food you've been fixing for her."

Winn had witnessed Octavia's generosity each time he was there. "You're mighty kind, Mama."

She waved her hand at an invisible gnat. "I do what I can, when I can, while I can. I pray to be the hands and feet of Jesus in bringing a bit of comfort to those in need." Her plain features radiated genuine love. "After all, that's the least I can do for all the Lord has done for me."

Winn took the glass of water Hope offered and walked through the humble home to the front porch. He was struck with the enormous difference between Octavia and his selfish mother.

Hope tucked her skirt beneath her as she sat on the porch steps. Winn's lanky legs were stretched out in front of him as he leaned back on his elbows beside her. Mama's abundant flowers were in full bloom now, a butterfly flitted its dainty wings in and around the snap dragons. The sun had reached the top of the sky, making a path toward the west affording shade on the front of the Davidson's house.

Hope's fervor had not waned in the least. "Do you think your parents can come?"

Winn couldn't picture his mother in the Davidson home. He knew the moment she stepped out of their car her face would explode with disapproval which would last the entire ceremony. No, he did not want his mother to stick up her nose at these sincere folks and their modest surroundings. He said, "I doubt it. Mother's uncomfortable meeting new people. I'd rather have you meet her when it's just the two of us."

There was a small crinkle in Hope's forehead. "Do you think she'll like me?"

"She'll love you, Hope, don't you worry about that. Daddy and Eddie will too." He swatted at a fly. "And when Luther meets you, he'll be so jealous; he'll ask you how I ever talked you in to marrying me."

Hope giggled. "I love your sense of humor."

"I learned a long time ago laughter is better than melancholy. When I was a kid, our house was pretty placid. My brothers and I had to remain quiet to allow rest for Mother's nerves." He hadn't planned on telling Hope about his Mother's malady, but there it was. He looked at Hope's face which had a frown of concern. He went on. "Guess when I got out on my own, I developed a sense of humor to enjoy laughing and cutting up for a change. Besides, it makes people feel comfortable if you share a funny story with them."

"You're right. I'm very comfortable with you."

Winn couldn't resist the desire to kiss her. He barely touched her waiting lips when Hollis gruffly cleared his throat behind them. They weren't aware he had returned through the back door.

They do not love that do not show their love.
—William Shakespeare

17

July 4, 1928—

Sunrise beckoned Hope from a night of peaceful rest, like that of a child spent from play. Preparations complete, her spirit held no qualms about the decision to become Mrs. Winn Prichard. She stole past her sleeping sisters to the porch with a cup of coffee in hand and gratefulness in her heart. Hope witnessed the primrose sky transform to the dazzling white blur of a typical Texas July sky. The sun took pleasure in representing God's resplendent presence on this her wedding day.

Jars and pots of flowers were on all flat surfaces of the Davidson's front room. Betsy and Pearl had picked every bud and bloom that exhibited any color whatsoever in Mama's garden. To allow more standing room, the bed had been moved out. Octavia and Iris wore the dresses they had been sewing for weeks. Hope worked late into many nights making pastel colored frocks for her little sisters. Betsy's was pink, and Pearl wanted pale blue.

For the most important day of her life, Hope had a store-bought ensemble including dress, hat, stockings, and shoes all purchased from Taylor's Dress Shop. As a wedding gift, Mrs. Taylor gave her a special price.

Getting dressed in Mama and Papa's bedroom, Hope was fidgety. "Oh Mama, what if I snag these stockings?"

"So what if you do, Sugar, the wedding will go on as planned and you'll be just as happy with Winn." Mama peeked out the window. "I thought Buford and Fayella would be here by now."

Gingerly fastening a stocking to her garter, Hope said, "I wish they'd get here soon so we can have a chance to meet Fayella and see what she's like." *Guess I should feel guilty, but truth be told, I'm single-minded today. I'm going to become Mrs. Winn Prichard, that's all my thoughts will hold. If it's just the preacher with the two of us, that would be fine with me.*

Delbert and Iris met Winn at Butch's Filling Station when his bus streaked in right on time. No one could doubt the man was dressed for a special occasion. He was wearing a light brown, three-piece suit with a dark brown bowtie on a blindingly white shirt. His brown shoes were polished to a high sheen. The best part of his attire was a silver ring with a tiny diamond setting tucked inside his vest pocket.

When he saw the couple, Winn removed his stylish straw hat. Delbert extended his hand for a hearty handshake and took Winn's valise. Iris gave him a hug and gushed about his appearance. "You're dressed to kill for sure."

"I'd rather be dressed for a wedding. Guess Hope is busy with all the last minute things."

"You know you can't see the bride before the wedding." Iris walked beside him. "Mama's having a fit because Buford and Fayella ain't here yet, but Hope's cool as a cucumber. Her dress is so beautiful— it's store bought. Her shoes and stockings are too. Oh, guess I oughtn't be telling about her leggings." She laughed at her purposeful discretion. "She even got her hair cut. What do you think about that, Winn?"

"Well, I think if she likes it, I'll like it."

Iris picked up her pace to match Winn's. "Papa said it was a brazen thing to do."

A man of few words, Delbert surprised them both. "I like it."

Laughing, Iris said, "You never pay me a compliment, Delbert. Guess I'll go get my hair bobbed."

Octavia hurried to meet Winn, Iris, and Delbert at the gate. Her salt and pepper, mostly salt, colored hair was in the usual bun. But today the style was softer around her face instead of pulled straight back. She gave Winn a motherly hug and took in his courtly appearance. "You look fit as a fiddle, Winn." Her eyes searched the road. "I'm worried, Buford and Fayella ain't here; they should be here by now."

Walking along the dirt path, Winn asserted a positive response. "They wouldn't miss the wedding. I'm sure they'll be along." He noticed the lack of flowers in the garden. "Looks like a swarm of locusts plucked your garden clean, Mama."

Her worried expression was replaced by a smile. "Not a swarm, just two little locusts by the names of Betsy and Pearl."

Betsy pranced to meet him twirling around in her frilly pink organza. "Winn, look at my new dress. Hope made it for me."

As usual, Pearl hung back on the porch with her arm wrapped around a post. "You're s'pposed to say 'Mr. Winn', Betsy." She relished in the admonishment.

"Not anymore." Betsy hollered at her sister and then looked up at him. "Ain't that right since you're going be family?"

Before he could respond, Octavia said, "Only if it's okay with Winn."

"Sure it's okay with me." Again, he warmed to the idea of being a part of this loving family. He stepped onto the porch to greet Hollis. His usual attire of overalls was replaced by a pair of dark blue pants that looked as though they just came off a shelf, probably in Goodman's store. Creases in the sleeves of his denim shirt told of its recent folds, also a new purchase, no doubt.

Mama anxiously wrung her hands. "Oh, I wish Buford and Fayella would get here."

Iris swept her mother away. "Come on Mama, Preacher Wright's going to be here directly."

Just as they were about to walk in the house, they heard the exuberant duck-quack honking of a horn. The entire family, except Hope, was on the porch to see Buford and his bride drive up in a Ford Model A Roadster.

With wings on their feet, the children scurried out first. And the others were on their heels. Even Hollis was compelled to join the excitement. The commotion brought Hope to the window of the bedroom. *My stars, it's Brother and he has a car.* Her eyes found Winn, and then the joy of seeing her beloved surpassed the elation of Buford's arrival. While everyone looked over the vehicle, she thought of honeybees swarming around a hive. Unbridled happiness rose within, what joy she felt seeing her loved ones together and so happy. *Will there ever be a more blissful day than this?*

Betsy wrapped her arms around Buford's legs. "I wanna ride. Can you take me for a ride, Bubba?"

He rubbed her head. "Oh, all right. I know you won't let me even say 'hello' to everybody if I don't take you for a little spin. Jump in. You too, Pearl." The girls rushed by Fayella and squeezed into the two-seater.

As Buford drove off, Iris hollered over the noise. "My turn is next." She finally looked at Fayella, who was being showered with Mama's welcoming hug.

"Mama, let her catch her breath." Iris pushed her way in to give her new sister-in-law a crushing hug.

Octavia introduced her husband. "Honey, this here's Papa."

Hollis was taken aback when Fayella lunged at him with a big bear hug. "I'm so glad to meet you, Papa. I hear you're pretty handy with a jackknife and make some beautiful walking canes." He was speechless, but she didn't notice as she turned her attention to Winn. "Well now, this handsome man must be the groom. I can tell by that nervous look—the same one Buford had on our wedding day."

Winn liked her immediately and laughed. "I was hoping it didn't show." He held out his hand, but Fayella stepped closer and gave him a sisterly hug. "Guess you and I are the 'out-laws' in this family, we better stick together."

Iris said, "There's one more 'out-law', Fayella." She pulled Delbert by the hand. "This is my husband, Delbert."

Fayella ignored the man's awkwardness and grabbed him for a hug. "Oh, that's right, there are three of us. You just let me know if Iris gets sassy, Delbert, and I'll set her straight." She wrapped an arm around Iris and everyone in the circle laughed. It seemed especially funny because Fayella was such a tiny little thing, and apparently full of fun, like Buford.

Along with the rest of the family, Iris was charmed by Fayella. "I know Hope is just dyin' to come out to meet you, but she's stuck in the bedroom before she gets hitched to this nervous fellow here." Iris nodded toward Winn.

Octavia was overcome with meeting her daughter-in-law and seeing her son drive up in an automobile of all things on Hope's wedding day. Looking at Winn, her face radiated pure love. Mama dabbed at her eyes with her ever-present hanky as she, Iris, and Fayella turned toward the house.

The men lingered, watching the road for the car. Buford drove a short distance before turning around promising a longer ride later. When the car was parked, Buford shooed the girls out. "Now don't y'all go messing with anything, I don't wanna be wiping off little fingerprints." He was finally able to properly greet the men.

Winn slapped him on the back and laughed. "Well, looks like a lineman brings in pretty good wages."

They ambled to the porch out of the sun. "Not enough to pay for a car, but I've started doing some carpentry work on the side." As he placed his foot on the step held by the shim, it wobbled, causing Buford to stubble.

Hollis chuckled. "Did you have a nip or two, Son?"

Buford stooped to pick up the piece of wood by the slanted step. "Oh no, Papa. You won't find me nipping when I'm driving my beauty on wheels." He held up the shim. "Guess I have a little carpentry job right here."

Hollis said, Aw, don't worry about that. I'll get to it directly."

Buford smiled and kicked the shim back under the step.

Hope's best friend, Dora Chapman, walked briskly to the gate and rushed by the car as if it were a common fixture in the poor neighborhood. Breezing across the porch, she said, "Hi, everyone. I can't wait to see Hope!" Her greeting was punctuated by the slamming of the screen door behind her.

The men laughed to hear squeals and lively chatter from inside. Pastor Wright arrived and stopped to admire the Roadster.

Breathless, Octavia hurried to meet him, "Brother Wright, you're here." She proclaimed it as if he wasn't aware of the fact and ushered him into the house so briskly, he barely had time for a nod to the groom and others.

Mama took charge placing him across from the closed bedroom door where Hope would enter. Octavia called to those outdoors and literally pulled them to what she considered proper places to stand. She placed Winn beside the preacher. Moving around in hurried purpose, she stopped in front of her husband. "Hollis, you're not supposed to be here."

"Well, Woman, this is where you shoved me."

"No, no. You need to be in the bedroom to walk in with Hope."

Like a scolded child, he walked to the bedroom door and reached for the knob. Octavia hollered, "Nooo, Hollis don't open that door."

He jumped back as if it were on fire. "You just told me to go to the bedroom." His confusion was comical.

When the children snickered, Mama realized everyone was enjoying the interaction between them. As if the others in the small room couldn't hear, she whispered. "Go through the kitchen." Waving her hand, she signaled for him to go around to the kitchen door leading to the bedroom.

It amused Winn to see the large man, so gruff in appearance, silently obey his wife's orders. He had witnessed it during his visits and it completely reversed his first impression of Hollis. However, he had also seen Papa flare up with his blustery voice and reddened face, but it was apparent he listened to his little Tave.

The bedroom door opened to a waiting group in the living room. Pearl was first in line, but seeing all eyes on her; she pulled Betsy forward and walked closely behind. Iris entered, then Hope with Papa. Winn's eyes were only for his intended; her face radiated a deeper dimension of beauty than he had seen before. The loving gaze between them was unfaltering as she took the few steps to stand at his side.

Hope listened intently to Pastor Wright's words and spoke her vows with sweet sincerity and Winn did the same. When he slipped the ring on her finger, it was her coronation. There was a sweet edge in Dora's voice singing "Let Me Call You Sweetheart." Listening to the words, Hope studied the bouquet of fresh flowers in her hand with glimpses at the delicate wedding band. It felt strange hearing the intimate words of their song surrounded by her family. Winn gently leaned toward her, touching shoulders. Indescribable happiness was at the center of her being. *Thank you, Lord, for Winn. Help me be the wife he needs.*

As Winn felt Hope's shoulder on his, the thoughts filtering through his mind were similar to hers. *This feels so right, I love her more than I thought possible.*

When the pronouncement came that they were husband and wife, Hope turned to face Winn with a smile. He softly brushed his lips against hers half expecting to hear Hollis clear his throat. Again she felt the flutter of butterfly wings deep within. She was too soon drawn from the pleasing experience when the family clapped and shouted best wishes. A "serve yourself" wedding dinner had been prepared. With jubilation, food was piled on plates and balanced on laps.

As time drew near for the newlyweds to catch the bus to Houston, Fayella ran to the car. "I almost forgot about our new camera. We got it for the wedding."

She snapped a picture of the newlyweds. Winn with his straw hat tilted in his usual jaunty manner and Hope in her brimmed cloche. Her ivory color dress was street length; the stylish low waistline was belted with a fringed sash that hung to the hem. Her mid-heeled, bronze-tone shoes were tied with wide matching grosgrain ribbon.

Buford planned to drive them to the bus depot and hurried the couple along; he knew their departure would bring on Mama's tears. Octavia pushed her way through the well-wishers to grab Hope and her new son-in-law. "You're family now, Winn. Come see us every chance, you hear?" Before he could answer, Octavia pulled Hope to her for an all-encompassing squeeze. "It'll be so strange without you, Hope, but you have your own life now. May God grant you and Winn every happiness." Hope returned the embrace. Mama briefly held a hand to Hope's cheek before she turned away blotting tearful eyes.

The new bride sought Papa. He was on the porch standing by the railing. Hope hugged him. "I love you, Papa."

His throat was tight with uncharacteristic emotion. He gave a nod and croaked the words, "You too, Sugar."

With the bags tucked in the rumble seat, Winn and Hope squeezed into the roadster. Before Buford drove away, Hope suddenly thought of all the thanks she forgot to say. She called out, "Dora, thank you for singing. It was beautiful. And Iris, your cake was so good, thank you." The car was slowly moving away from the gate. "Bye, Betsy girl, and Pearl. Oh, Fayella, I didn't get to talk to you."

Shouts were flying back and forth with no discernment. Both Buford and Winn laughed. Winn said, "If this keeps up, Buford, we'll miss our bus. Hope and I may have to spend our wedding night on those cots on the porch."

Buford stepped on the gas. "Not if I can help it."

At Butch's station, they untangled from the two-seater. Winn turned to his new brother-in-law who was retrieving the suitcases. "Much obliged, Buford, and best wishes to you and Fayella. You're right, she's a peach."

Hope gave Buford a hug. "Thank you, Brother. Wish I could've spent more time with Fayella, she seems perfect for you."

"That she is, Shug. And you take care of this ole feller right here." The men shook hands and then pulled closer for a hearty slap on the back.

> *Then the Lord said, 'It is not good for the man to be alone; I will make him a helper suitable for him.*
> —Genesis 2:18 NASB

18

She placed a hand to her heart; it was racing as the bus pulled on to the road. To say Hope was overwhelmed is as understated as saying Texas might get a little sunshine in July.

Suddenly she remembered the envelope in her handbag. "Oh, I almost forgot, Miss Adkins gave this to us." Handing it to him, she said, "Since it's to both of us, I want you to open it."

"Still sealed? I would've torn into it with curiosity as soon as she gave it to me." Tapping the blue envelope on end, he tore the other and blew into the slit. A note was wrapped around a crisp twenty dollar bill. Hope gasped as Winn gave a low whistle. "Here, you read her note."

Miss Adkins's initials printed in dark blue ink were centered on pale blue onionskin paper. Hope held it delicately. "Oh, isn't her stationary lovely?"

Winn chuckled. "Only a printer would admire the stock and printing before reading the contents. What does she say?"

> *Mr. and Mrs. Winston Prichard*
> *My Dear Hope and Winn,*
> *I wish you both God's utmost blessings now and always.*
> *Hope, you will be sorely missed, not just as a loyal employee, but as a friend I have come to admire.*
> *Winn, I'm sure you know that you have a treasure in your bride, and from the little I know of you, she has found the perfect mate for a lifetime.*
> *Please stop by the Hempstead News when you are in town.*
> *Sincerely, Anna Louise Adkins*

Overcome, Hope's eyes became moist. "I'll always remember her. She believed in me when I hardly believed in myself." Leaning her head on Winn's shoulder, he held her close.

Rereading the note, Winn focused on the words, *"the little I know of you"*, and he thought, *I hope to keep it that way.*

The landscape changed from fields of grazing cattle enclosed with barbed wire fences to more businesses and congestion. After a few scheduled stops in small communities, Houston's skyline came into view. Winn pointed ahead to the tall buildings of concrete and glass standing against the clouds making way for dusk. From a distance they reminded Hope of Pearl's handmade wooden blocks stacked as high as possible. Disregarding the warm wind blowing across her cheeks, she breathed deeply. "Mmm, I smell coffee."

Winn savored the aroma every time he rode through the area. "Smells good doesn't it? We're passing Bright and Early Coffee Company on Washington Avenue."

The bus entered the city and threaded its way through paved streets perfectly lined with cement curbs. A cloistered feeling pushed its way around Hope; she shivered when the shadow of the buildings hid the sky. "It seems like everything is so close together. Is Liberty like this?"

"No, nothing like Houston. This is a big city with over twenty-eight thousand people."

"You have a good memory for numbers and history, Winn."

"I don't know about numbers, but I do love history. I'll probably bore you with facts and details every now and then."

"Never, I love learning new things and you make it so interesting. Tell me more about Houston." Her eyes explored the cityscape.

"Well, let's see. The national Democratic convention was here at Sam Houston Hall just a few weeks ago." He tilted his head to peer out the window at one of the tall buildings. "Liberty is a small town just a little bigger than Hempstead. You'll like it."

Relief swallowed her anxiety. "I guess people get used to it, but even as hot as it is, there's a cold feeling in the middle of all these buildings."

"It's not going to feel cold as long as I'm around." He gave her shoulder a squeeze as the bus pulled to the curb of the Greyhound station.

With luggage in tow, they walked a short distance where Winn surprised her by hailing a taxi. *I can't embarrass him and gawk at everything like I'm a country girl and never been to the city. Just so happens that's exactly what I am, but I can adjust to anything, even riding in a taxicab.*

Racing through a maze of streets surrounded by skyscrapers, she imagined herself in the bottom of a deep canyon. The cab stopped in front of the fanciest building Hope had ever wished to see. Winn held his hand out for hers as she stepped onto the sidewalk. *When I write Betsy, I'll have to remember to tell her that Winn is truly my Prince Charming, and I hope I'm his Cinderella. I certainly feel like it.*

The Rice Hotel on Texas Avenue was so tall she almost fell backward trying to see the top. While Hope was looking up, Winn quickly grabbed her before she tumbled into the street. The lobby was elegant beyond her imagination. The chandelier seemed as big as her parents' entire house. Underneath it, a flower arrangement was sitting on a gilded table displaying more flowers than bloomed in Mama's garden all summer long.

Winn walked to a long counter while Hope slowly pivoted and continued to stare. When a bellman took the suitcases and led them to an elevator, Hope stepped in with the most composure she could muster. It was obvious to her new husband that Hope had inborn grace and elegance. She could have ink on her face feeding a printing press or enter opulent surroundings and carry herself with assurance in either circumstance. They stood behind the bellboy and elevator man who wore red and gold uniforms. Hope's eyes grew big when her tummy felt a tickle as they came to a sudden stop at the seventh floor. She glanced at Winn; he smiled with pride because he was able to show her a new world.

Walking in the hallway behind the bellboy, she whispered to Winn. "I've read about luxurious hotels, but this is beyond expectations. A room must cost a lot, Winn. Are you sure we can afford it?"

He winked—that wonderfully amusing wink that always took her to a place where butterflies dance.

The bellboy unlocked their door and placed the suitcases on stands. He exchanged the key for a tip from Winn. Hope turned to take in the yellow and green floral wallpaper and matching bed cover. She rushed to the window and looked out. Street lights had pushed away darkness midst their allotted corner. People rushed as if being chased by the minutes of the clock on the side of the building across the street.

Her freckled face flushed with excitement. "Oh Winn, everything is so wonderful. Thank you." Taking off her hat, she shook her head, allowing newly cropped hair to fall into place with curls forming around her temples and cheeks.

"There's no need to thank me, Hope, I see it in those wide eyes of yours."

"They're wide because I don't want to miss a thing." For the first time, she gave him a wholehearted hug. He returned her embrace with a kiss of full abandonment as he had longed to do ever since their first meeting.

There was a distant booming sound and when they turned to the window, fireworks lighted the sky behind buildings blocks away.

Winn laughed heartily. "How's that for timing. Must be a fireworks display down at Hermann Park."

"I thought it was just for us." Hope matched his laugh. "You realize there will be fireworks on all our anniversaries?" As more rockets splashed across the darkness, they stood with fingers entwined and watched. "Now you know why I wanted to be married on the Fourth of July." There was a mirthful lilt in her voice.

Electricity sparked between them and he hugged her. "Well, Mrs. Prichard, I figure we can always make our own fireworks."

Adoration for Winn superseded all Hope's apprehensions about her wedding night as they consummated their marriage. Hope remembered the words from the ceremony *"God has put them together"*. The divine plan of God for man and woman in the Biblical words, *"become one flesh"* held reverence in her heart. Being away from home for the first time felt strange yet seemed so right being with Winn. The tenderness of Winn's touch spoke of his love and consideration for his sweet Hope.

Later that night, Winn said, "I'm sure glad Buford got us to the bus so we didn't have to sleep on those cots." Hope giggled and pushed a pillow in his face.

The next afternoon, they took in the sights downtown and window-shopped before going to the new motion picture, *The Jazz Singer*.

Slowly walking to the hotel afterwards, Hope said, "I never imagined there could be talking in films. I wonder how it's done?" Her eyes sparkled. "And that Al Jolson, he's so . . . so . . ."

"Flamboyant? Entertaining? Talented?"

"He's all of that, and more." She tucked her arm around his. "Oh Winn, I have so much to learn."

He held her arm tightly. "I do too; we'll learn new things together for the rest of our lives."

That evening they ate in the hotel's Flag Restaurant. Hope felt weighted down midst the elegantly dressed clientele, uniformed waiters, rich linens, delicate china and silver. The words of Papa came back to her. *He's not like us, Shug.*

Again she questioned the expense. "Winn, isn't all of this costing a great deal?"

He looked across the table at her furrowed brow and reached for her hand. She pulled it from her lap under the white tablecloth and placed it in his. He said, "It's more than I normally spend on a honeymoon, but you're worth it." He made the joke before realizing what he said and wished he could retract the words. *I hope she never finds out this is my second honeymoon.*

She laughed and pulled her hand away when the waiter brought their entree concealed under a silver domed cover. A magician revealing a white rabbit couldn't have exhibited more flair than the white-gloved hand that lifted the cover. Hope salivated upon seeing a charbroiled steak garnished with a spiced apple slice on a lettuce leaf.

When the waiter was out of earshot, she lowered her voice and said, "I mean this is so . . . so high on the hog. Should we be spending your hard-earned money like this instead of saving for your newspaper?"

Winn loved her practicality. "Hope, stop worrying. We have time to save for our future. I set aside funds for this because I want to give you something you've never had and want to enjoy it with you. It's true, I'm out of my realm here also, but this will be a time we can look back on in the years to come and talk about our wonderful honeymoon."

Hope cut a piece of the juicy steak and took a tentative look at it on her fork. "I'll always remember our honeymoon, and maybe we can come back on our fiftieth anniversary." She placed the bite in her mouth, savoring the tender meat. As he watched her eat, his smile reached clear to her heart. Resting her fork, she said, "What?"

"Sugar, you're pure delight. I love seeing you enjoy everything."

Softly, she said, "I hope you always feel that way and I never embarrass you."

The newlyweds watched dancers in the extravagantly appointed hotel ballroom. Winn invited her to dance, and Hope haltingly took his hand. "I've never really danced, Winn. Iris and I used to try some steps on the sidelines at a pavilion where Mama and Papa used to go when we were kids."

"Come on, just follow me." He took it slow, but wasn't an accomplished dancer himself. They laughed and sat out the next few orchestrations.

Later they stood looking out the window of their room as they did their first evening there. The predictable streetlights formed circles of amber illumination along the avenue as darkness fell upon the city. Standing behind her with his arms wrapped around hers, he gently kissed her temple. *I'm thankful to be the one introducing her to things she's only dreamed about.*

Consequently they are no longer two, but one flesh.
—Matthew 19:6a NASB

THE RICHLAND RECORD

More Than a Newspaper—a Community Service
A Weekly Publication Serving the Greater Richland Area
Richland, Texas   Thursday, July 11, 1968
Winston Randolph Prichard, Editor and Publisher

News and Views of a Tactless Texan

The times through which we are now living will probably be referred to fifty years from now as the "good old days," as old timers say when reminiscing about yesteryear. Folks may differ on which times were truly good according to the events and conditions of their circumstances. But most of us can agree, (enthusiastically or regrettably), that time or tide waits for no man.

My wife, Hope, and I went on a jaunt to Houston recently and drove by the Rice Hotel where we spent our honeymoon forty years ago on the Fourth of July, 1928. Rice Hotel is located on the historical site of the Capital of the Republic of Texas which was from 1837 to 1842.

The magnificent seventeen-story structure, founded in 1913, has hosted numerous celebrities and six presidents. Politicians congregated there during the Democratic National Convention in the spring of 1928. More recently, President John F. Kennedy napped there on a stopover in Houston the day before he was assassinated in Dallas on November 22, 1963.

On our outing, we parked the car across from the hotel and reminisced a bit. Hope talked about her impression of the grand two-story lobby and her first ride in an elevator. Back then, I marveled at the comfort of air conditioning in the hotel cafeteria which was the first public room in Houston to acquire such luxury. We laughed at the remembrance of my feeble attempt to teach her to dance in the "Rice Roof Dance Pavilion."

The good Lord said that man needs a helpmate. God's provision for me has been met in Hope, who has been by my side through times so lean we weren't sure we could make it. We started our life together with only a couple of suitcases. With Hope's unwavering belief in me and the Almighty, I have been blessed with much more than the eye can see.

My lifelong dream of owning a newspaper came to fruition many years ago. There were saints along my journey who contributed to my obtaining that objective. They hold my gratitude, but none were as tenacious and faithful as Hope to see that ambition fulfilled. My obsession became hers. She caught my vision and committed it to prayer on the first day we met. Without Hope's faith, prayers, hard work, and longsuffering the aspiration would not have been achieved.

Some memories are soothing to the soul to recount. Our honeymoon is definitely considered the era of "good old days" for us. But more importantly, my advice is: strive to make each day one to be remembered as "good."

That's -30- for this week, my friends.

19

Mrs. Emerson greeted Winn and Hope at the boarding house door with an embrace to them both. "I feel like my own son is coming home with his bride. Welcome, my Dears."

Winn was touched by her regard for him. "Thank you, Mrs. Emerson. This is Hope."

The woman's warmth reminded Hope of Mama. She was just as Winn described. Motherly with a bit of whimsy wrapped around her caring soul. "Winn has told me so many good things about you, Mrs. Emerson. You're making me feel right at home already." This home, however, was large with tasteful furnishings and colorful décor, nothing like her home in Hempstead.

The landlady said, "I do want you to feel at home, Dear." Hope glanced toward a cozy room off the entry. Mrs. Emerson directed her toward the open double doorway. "This is our sitting-room, Hope; feel free to come here anytime you want."

Hope was drawn to one entire wall of bookcases and stepped closer to gaze at the collection of reading material. Running her hand along the shelves, she had the feeling of a child in a sweet shop. "Mrs. Emerson, you have so many books."

"Yes, Dearie, I've had many given to me through the years. Help yourself to any of them." She turned and realized Winn was still holding their suitcases. "Oh, Winn, you look like a young boy standing there." She held her arm out to guide Hope toward the staircase. "Ah, it does my heart good to see such happiness. Come on, I'll show you to your room. I have it all ready." She had prepared the larger room across the hall upstairs.

Mrs. Emerson led the way. Hope followed with her hand lightly on the polished oak banister as she took in the floral still life paintings stair stepped along the wall. Walking behind Hope with her skirt swaying with each step, Winn was reminded of the first day he saw her in Hempstead wearing a floral print dress.

Entering the light, cheery room, the older woman ushered her new boarder to the double window and pointed out her roses. She then fussed about, acquainting Hope with her surroundings including the bath facilities at the end of the hall. "Now, you just let me know if you need anything. Supper is at six and breakfast is at seven, but you can come to the kitchen and help yourself anytime, Dearie." She gave a sweet little smile and hurried down the stairs to see to the pork roast in the oven.

Relieved of the bags, Winn opened the chifforobe and saw that his clothes had been placed there from his old room. Hope opened a drawer in the chest to see flowered wallpaper lining the bottom. She pulled out each drawer and found his folded clothing in the last one. Hope was impressed with Mrs. Emerson, the room, the books, the rose garden, indoor plumbing, and especially her husband. Exhaustion and gratefulness enveloped her at the same moment; she sat on the bed to ponder the sudden changes in her life.

Winn grabbed a hanger and placed his suit coat on it. "Mrs. Emerson asked if she could move some things for me. I was working overtime and making plans for the honeymoon. Now I feel badly that I didn't take care of this before I left. She's the best landlady I've ever had." He turned when he heard a tiny sniffle and saw Hope wiping her eyes with a handkerchief. "Sugar, what's the matter?" His arm went around her as he sat on the bed beside her.

"Oh, Winn, everything's so nice. I can't believe it's happening to me."

"Well, that's nothing to cry about. You should be happy."

"I am happy." Her tear-stained face wasn't very convincing and Winn laughed which coaxed a smile to her lips. "I'm sorry, it just hit me how the Lord is blessing me. He brought you into my life and has given me a wonderful place to live."

"Us—the Lord is blessing both of us. We are one, remember? Tears don't belong in those big, brown eyes. Come on now, go wash that pretty face, it's almost six."

At supper, Hope met the Peabodys who were lively and talkative, exactly as Winn had told her. A pleasant looking couple, Hope surmised them to be in their mid-forties. Mr. Peabody was barrel-chested with dark hair losing residence to a gaping bald spot. With a cordial manner, the man held Hope's chair for her. "Welcome, welcome, Hope, call me Dexter. Winn has told us so much about you."

Mrs. Peabody was vivacious, her joyful aura almost visible. "No, he hasn't. Not nearly enough." She was bubbly to the point of too much suds if Hope was to give an opinion, which she wouldn't. Mrs. Peabody greeted her with a pumping handshake. "I'm Alice, and I know we'll be great friends." Hope thought she had never felt such soft skin. Winn held the chair for Alice as she continued her welcoming chatter.

Hope was a little fed up with all of the chair pulling like the waiters at the hotel. *For goodness sakes, I'm able to sit down by myself.* But the thought was quickly forgotten as she eyed the table so beautifully set with every plate, bowl, cup, and saucer in a matching floral design with not a chip in sight.

The aroma of pork roast made Hope's mouth water. There were bowls of mashed potatoes with gravy, lima beans, carrots, and a side dish of sweet corn relish. The meal was spiced with conversation and laughter. Winn related how he met Hope and his deviousness in leaving a suitcase as a means to see her again.

Later, sitting in the front room, a bond with the Peabodys began to develop when Hope witnessed the couple's affection for each other. Alice didn't seem quite as flighty when she came down to earth and related the hardship of losing her first husband in the Great War.

Dexter stood beside Alice's chair and put a hand on her shoulder. "I knew her first husband from church; he was a good man. Alice and I became friends through a Bible study when I lost my wife. Bless her soul, she caught the Spanish influenza when the epidemic hit and it took her down quickly."

Alice's hand went to her shoulder and patted his hand. "Over the years we grew to love one another. We relied on God's word to get us through the grief and reach the place where marriage felt right for us." She changed position in her chair to focus on Hope. "So you see, we have something in common—we've only been married six months."

Surprised, Winn said, "I didn't realize that. Congratulations." He and Hope were seated on the horsehair sofa upholstered in chintz with large pink flowers between varying shades of greenery. He looked at Dexter. "Did you serve in the war, Dexter?"

"I served, but not in uniform. I helped the war effort working on sub chasers at the New Orleans Naval Shipyard. It was a rough time; I lost two of my best friends fighting in France." He tapped his pipe in an ashtray on an end table. "How about you, did you see any action, Winn?"

"Those 'I Want You' posters with Uncle Sam pointing a finger directly at me were tempting. I was considering signing up while President Wilson was vacillating on whether to get involved or remain neutral." He gave Hope an apologetic grin. "There I go with a history lesson for you, Sugar."

Alice laughed. "Well, did Uncle Sam entice you, Winn?"

He rested his elbow on the overstuffed arm of the sofa. "I figured I'd be called up, but unfortunately or maybe fortunately, whichever way you want to look at it, I came down with a severe case of pneumonia."

Hope swiveled her head toward him. "You never told me you had pneumonia, Winn."

"Well, it was a time I'd rather forget. Our boys were fighting the Kaiser and I was laid up in the hospital and later at my parents' home." A frown flashed across his face. "I had some complications and it took months to recuperate. For a while my folks didn't think I'd make it, it looked like they were going to lose another son. We lost my brother with pneumonia when he was twelve years old. It was pretty testy for all of us. By the time I gained my strength back, all but the shouting of victory was over."

The mood in the room was getting too somber. Winn's countenance changed with a laugh. "My younger brother, Luther, lied about his age and signed up. When he got to boot camp, he called my parents to get him out, but Daddy said he got himself into it at seventeen so he could just stay and let the Army make a man out of him."

The Peabodys laughed with Winn, but Hope was busy calculating. *He told Papa he's twenty-eight. That doesn't add up. I thought he said Luther was four years younger. If his brother was seventeen, that would make Winn twenty-one about fourteen years ago during the war.*

Hope managed to smile occasionally but grew quiet. Thinking she must be tired, Winn made their excuses to Alice and Dexter. When they reached the room and closed the door, Hope's demeanor was unusual as she sat in the wooden rocker. Feeling a cold spell had descended upon the summer evening, Winn casually walked to the window. "Mrs. Emerson recently put the glider under that shade tree; it'll be nice to sit out there sometime."

Hope wasn't listening. "Winn, you told Papa you're twenty-eight. I can't figure out how that could be right according to what you told Dexter about your brother's age."

I should've known I couldn't keep my age from her. He sat on the bed near the rocker and heaved a sigh. "Hope, I was thirty-five on May fifth."

She was confused and waves of anger began to flow, washing over her features. "You lied to Papa and let me believe it too." Her voice was several levels above normal. "You're what . . . nineteen years older than me?"

"Eighteen."

She stood and crossed her arms in front of her breasts. "What does that matter? I would've married you if you were a doddering old man. You didn't have to lie."

"If I was a doddering old man, my age would be obvious and I wouldn't have to lie." He stood beside her and reached out to touch her arm. She pulled away. He remembered what Hollis said about losing her temper. "I love you, Hope, and didn't think Hollis would approve if I was so much older."

Her arms dropped to her side. "I'm disappointed that you told Papa an untruth."

"I apologize." He waited. Her silence screamed in his ears. "I shouldn't have lied, can you forgive me?"

Ignoring his request, she leaned forward at the waist. "You didn't even tell me when you had a birthday in May."

"Because you would've asked how old I was or Betsy would have."

"You're almost the same age as Mama." Her voice was pensive. "I think Papa's about twenty years older than she is."

"See, it's okay to be older." He rubbed her arm, calming the waves. "Except when you're in your prime, I really will be a doddering old man."

Hope gave him a flirtatious look. "I thought I was in my prime."

He twirled her around onto the bed. "You are and will be for a long time and I promise to age slowly."

They laughed. Then her expression turned serious. "Promise you won't lie again, Winn. Whatever happens, don't lie to me."

He caressed her, burying his face in the curve of her neck. "I promise." Something lurched in his stomach as he made the vow he had already broken by keeping his past from her.

Sin has many tools, but a lie is the handle that fits them all.
—Oliver Wendell Holmes Jr.

20

Monday morning—

With bent knees, Winn peered into the dresser mirror to comb his hair. "Come to the print shop at noon today, Hope. I want to show you off to everyone, and we'll have lunch."

"I would love to. I'm glad you want to introduce me around." She jumped off the bed and shuffled through her meager selection of clothes. "What should I wear?"

He gave her a peck on the cheek. "Whatever you wear will be just right, but that flowery dress is kinda special to me. Got to get going, see you at noon."

"But Winn, I don't know where the shop is."

He was halfway out the door. "Straight on Orchard to Main, you'll see it on the right."

That evening in their bed, Hope cuddled next to him. "That was so nice of Mr. Spencer to take us to dinner today. He seems like a good Christian man."

"No doubt about it. I didn't know he was going to buy our meal, but I'm glad he did. I could tell he was sure impressed with you. Most women know diddly-squat about the printing business, but you two carried on a conversation like veteran printers."

"I want to know all I can about the trade, Winn. After all, if you're going to publish your own newspaper someday, I'll be right beside you."

He caressed her. "That's where I always want you to be. And it will be our newspaper, not mine alone."

Several weeks later on Friday afternoon, they took their books outside to the glider. The summer sun was still high, reluctant to close the day. Before sitting, Hope made a circle around the rose garden, bending occasionally as a full bloom beckoned her to embrace its aroma.

After perusing a bit, Winn closed his Zane Grey book, *The Vanishing American*, and watched Hope. *I've never seen anyone with such interest in learning.*

Hope felt his eyes upon her. "What are you so deep in thought about?"

"Just you. How you're so eager to learn. You've been like a lion in an eating frenzy devouring Mrs. Emerson's library. What have you read so far?" He brushed an unruly curl from her temple.

She placed a paper on the page to mark her place. "I've read some of *The Encyclopedia of Etiquette*, most of *The Art of Writing Social Letters*, and now I'm scanning *Good Manners for All Occasions*. I want to be proper when I meet your parents." Dread zigzagged across his eyes when she mentioned his parents, but in her enthusiasm, she didn't notice. "I want to learn all I can, and I do love books."

He nodded. "So do I. Mark Twain said, 'The man who does not read good books has no advantage over the man who can't read'."

"Maybe the reason I love to read is because Papa can't, and I realize how much he's missing." She propped an elbow on the book and rested her chin in the palm of her hand. "But I'm feeling guilty." Winn raised questioning eyebrows. She went on, "I keep thinking I should be doing something. I've asked Mrs. Emerson if there's anything I can do to help out, but she shoos me away."

"You are doing something, Hope. You're doing a very good job of making me happy, and you certainly aren't wasting time by reading."

"Thank you, Winn. I'm glad I make you happy."

He took on a boyish grin. "How about me? Do I make you happy?"

"In every way." She snuggled closer. "I love waking up with you beside me and look forward to your coming home from work. Our weekends have been wonderful, and I feel so good about us going to church together."

Winn tightened his arm around her. "Hmm. Me too."

He hadn't balked at her urging to attend the small church in the neighborhood. Each time they approached the steps, Winn remembered the night he sat there and made the decision to begin his life anew. Many other things, like the contents of his daddy's letter that evening, were tucked away without sharing them with Hope.

They were just about to go in to freshen up for supper when the Peabodys strolled to greet them. Winn rose and offered Alice his seat in the glider.

Alice didn't release her hold on Dexter's arm. "Keep your seat. We just came out to invite you to ride with us to Galveston tomorrow."

Hope jumped up. "Galveston. I've never seen the ocean."

Dexter chuckled. "Well the Gulf of Mexico isn't quite like an ocean, but it's the biggest Texas has to offer. We thought it would be a nice outing. We could do some sightseeing—maybe take a walk along the beach."

Hope looked eagerly at Winn. He laughed. "If I don't say we'll go, Hope might just burst with disappointment. I usually work half a day on Saturday, but I can make up the time. Sure, sounds like fun."

The four of them walked toward the house making plans for the next day. Winn called Mr. Spencer to let him know his plans for Saturday with assurance that he would be in early Monday morning.

It was one of those sunny days artists attempt to capture on canvas. The sky was the bluest of blue background for the smattering of clouds balanced just right to depict a perfect setting. Dexter had the top down on his 1928 Franklin.

Hope settled in the comfortable back seat. "This is wonderful. I know it's going to be a fun day."

Tying a scarf around her light brown hair, Alice said, "And it's just begun."

Hope's unrestrained hair tossed freely as she absorbed all the sights along the way. The drive from Liberty to Galveston was an adventure in itself for her. Winn literally had to hold her down when she got her first glimpse of the water. "Ohh, it goes all the way to the horizon as far as I can see."

The others saw it through her eyes, making it all the more spectacular. As soon as Dexter stopped the car on the solid sand of the beach, she slipped off her shoes and scampered out. "Come on, Winn, it's wonderful." The gulf breeze was intoxicating; she gathered her A-line skirt and ran toward the water, enticing Winn, Dexter, and Alice to catch her joy.

Winn quickly shed his shoes and socks in the car. On the sand, he hopped on one foot rolling up his pant leg and then hopped on the other making his way toward her. With the backlighting of the sun, Hope was a silhouette outlined by golden rays as she waded in the warm surf. Winn thought he had never seen a painting or read a verse as beautiful as this lovely sprite dancing in the tide.

Alice and Dexter ran their own race of frivolity with the gentle waves. There were few spectators; most people were in more popular spots near the main area of town.

Side by side, Winn and Hope raced from the incoming waves and then stood to watch the dizzying sand shift around their feet in the receding water. After a while, they simply walked hand in hand at the water's edge, making footprints together.

Hope stooped to pick up a shell. "I only imagined what the beach might be like, now I know. Isn't it grand that Alice and Dexter asked us to come with them?"

Winn nodded. The rhythmic sound of the water was calming as they walked a little further. "Hope, you're a jewel. I feel like I've discovered a diamond and am privy to watch as each karat within becomes more defined."

His words swelled in her heart, and her spirit soared higher than the seagulls overhead. "Why, Mr. Prichard, that's pure poetry." She stopped walking. "I'm finding out so much about how other people live. I do feel like I'm becoming more defined. I'm finding myself. And best of all, I'm discovering more about you—you made it possible for me."

As brazen as it seemed, Winn kissed her right there on a public beach. It was a long, deep kiss as their arms clung to each other standing in the surf. Their feet sunk deep in the sand. Hope pulled away in pretense of embarrassment. "Shame on you." She glanced at the Peabodys who were sitting a distance from them. "What if someone saw us?"

"What if they did? And what do you mean 'shame on me'? Seems you're the one to blame with your freckles popping out and your skirt hiked up around your thighs."

She immediately lowered her dress and laughed with the merriment of a carefree child.

A joyful heart makes a cheerful face.
—Proverbs 15:13 NASB

21

The foursome climbed in the car and drove closer to downtown Galveston. They found a food stand and ordered hotdogs and Coca-Colas. The Peabodys talked excitedly about their new home.

Alice wiped mustard from the side of her mouth. "You must come see it. I can't wait to start decorating."

Dexter smiled at his wife. "Yes, she's chomping at the bit to get the furniture in and curtains up. That's why we wanted a little diversion today; she's been driving the carpenters bananas to get a move on."

Alice could hardly sit still with the thought of it. "They say it will be finished this coming week, and we'll probably be moving next Saturday."

Winn held his Coke bottle up ready for the last sip. "I'll help you move; your furniture is stored in the back of Peterson's warehouse isn't it?"

"All except the things Alice has bought. I have no idea what's going to be delivered."

Hope's voice trilled with shared happiness. "I'll help too, Alice. This must be a dream come true for you."

They continued talking about the home and plans for the move. Later, while driving out of town farther along the beach, Hope saw an old wooden pier. "Dexter can we stop? I'd love to walk out over the water."

"Sure as shootin', Hope. Your wish is my command."

Laughter came easily in their lighthearted mood. She and Winn jumped out first. Still barefoot, they reveled in the warmth of the sunbaked sand between their toes.

Hope pointed at Winn's rolled up pant legs. "I see you're meticulously dressed for our stroll on the pier, my Dear. Oh listen to me, I should start writing poetry."

"This day could inspire anyone to write poetry." Winn followed her lead onto the dilapidated structure.

The combination of salty breeze, sound of seagulls swooping overhead and swishing tide highlighted by the blazing sun was a completely new experience for Hope. She leaned over at the edge to see the churning waves below them. "Just look, Winn. Can you imagine all the life swimming around under those waves?"

"With your imagination, I can try." He reached for her hand. "I love seeing the world through your eyes, Hope." They strolled toward the end of the wharf and turned to see Dexter and Alice hesitate.

Dexter hollered, "Do you think this thing is safe? Looks like it has seen better days."

Through cupped hands, Hope yelled over the pounding surf. "It's fine, come on."

In a terrible suddenness, a board gave way under Winn's foot. He yelled, "Ohh, noo."

Hope jerked around to see his leg plummet through rotted wood up to his lower thigh. Her smile gelled into shock. She thought he was going to be swallowed by the pier and fall into the water. "Oh, Lord Jesus." Immediately her adrenaline kicked in as she tried in vain to lift him. Dexter ran to them and saw the seriousness of the situation.

Winn's right leg had slid out to the side, leaving him in an awkward position with excruciating pain. Crying, Hope frantically grabbed Winn underneath his arms and yanked with all her strength. He pushed against the weathered planks.

As Hope and Dexter lifted, Winn yelled out piteously. "Stop, for God's sake. Stop!" As they pulled, the raw splintered edges ripped deeper into his flesh.

With no care to the blood on her hands and clothes, Hope wildly tore at the jagged wood. While Alice tried to help, Dexter's attempts to cut away the wood with his pocketknife were in vain.

It took all the strength Winn had to hold his torso upright as waves of grayness passed over him. *I'll be dead weight if I pass out.* His voice was raspy against the pain. "Dexter, maybe we can do it now."

Winn's anguished face caused Hope's stomach to lurch. She never felt so frightened—not even when she watched her house burn down when she was twelve or even when Alonzo was killed. Her adrenaline was pumping faster. "I'll pull this side, Dexter, you pull the other." She clasped her hands under Winn's arm and tugged with all the power within. "Help us, Jesus, please help Winn."

Alice ran to the road screaming over and over, "Help, someone help us!"

As he was lifted, Winn was able to get his other leg situated beneath him with bended knee until he was free of the jagged hole with sloshing water below. His resistance depleted, Winn's resolve to remain lucid was futile. With Hope and Dexter still holding him, the hovering blackness prevailed. They gently laid him on the pier. Hope cradled Winn's head in her lap. Shuttering, she gazed at the gaping hole. The waters below now took on a menacing cast.

Alice had flagged down a passing automobile and breathlessly explained what happened. Willing to aid, the two men from the car followed her to the pier. The sight was raw. Winn was sprawled on the planks, his pant leg in tatters. His leg was covered in blood. Hope was sobbing.

Dexter said to the men, "Can you help me carry him?"

One of the men pointed to the Franklin. "Is that your car?"

Dexter answered, "Yes, if you two can lift his shoulders, I'll take his legs."

Looking at Hope, the other man said, "Ma'am, we best hurry. I know where we can find a doctor."

Alice put a stabling arm around Hope as they walked behind the men. Hope whispered, "Thank you, Jesus, for sending those men. Please get us to a doctor quickly."

Winn's lanky body was too long to lie across the back seat. He roused for a moment and looked at what he would later describe as "a raw piece of meat". In words barely audible, he moaned, "Oh no, I'll get Dexter's car dirty." Hope got in to hold Winn's torso. There was a sick feeling in her stomach seeing bits of flesh hanging from his kneecap and shin. Alice gently placed towels brought from home under his leg.

They quickly made it to a doctor's office which was in the front part of a large house. Hope glanced at a sign swinging from chains on a post in the yard which read *Doctor Samuel Abrams*. She watched as the three men lifted Winn and carried him into the examining room. It was apparent his pain was intense. With forced composure, Hope explained to the doctor what had happened. The doctor's wife stood nearby, Dexter gave her their names.

As the rescuers turned to go, Dexter said, "Thank you. I don't know how I would have handled the situation or where I would've taken him if you two hadn't come along."

He walked with them to their car. One man said, "I'm just glad we happened by."

The other one agreed. "We don't usually go the beach route on the way home from work, but guess the good Lord had it planned." He shook Dexter's hand. "I'll pray your friend recovers quickly. His leg looks pretty chewed up."

Watching them drive away, Dexter reflected on the events that happened on their intended joyous outing. He said a prayer of thanks for the help they received. When he returned, Alice met him at the door with an embrace. They sat in the parlor which had been made into a comfortable waiting room.

Winn was given a sedative, and Hope held his hand as he wavered in and out of awareness. Presently he slept, allowing the tranquilizer to temporarily relieve the torturous agony. She watched as the physician cut away the tattered pant leg and examine the injury. He methodically cleaned wood fragments away from deep punctures over the entire leg. Disinfectant peroxide was liberally poured into the wounds. She grimaced when Winn's shriveled skin was pulled into place, but no stitching was done. An ointment was generously applied before Dr. Abrams tightly bandaged the entire leg to hold the severed skin in place.

The doctor motioned for Hope to follow him out of the room. She looked at Winn and back at the doctor, who said, "He'll sleep for a while."

When he and Hope entered the waiting room, Alice and Dexter stood. Alice put her arm around Hope's shoulders. "You all right, Sugar?" Hope nodded.

The doctor waved toward a settee. "Mrs. Prichard, please have a seat."

"No thank you, please tell me if Winn's leg is going to be okay."

"Muscle and ligaments have been punctured severely and he's lost a lot of blood." Dr. Abrams included the Peabodys in his conversation with Hope. "I've done all that is possible in my facility. There should be a great amount of suturing. He needs to be in a hospital where the same physician treats him through his recovery, which will take some time."

Concern filled Hope's face, but she fought back tears. Suddenly she began to shake so violently she felt her insides vibrate. The doctor saw her lips and hands trembling and gently led her to the settee. "Mrs. Prichard, your mind has been focused on what you could do for your husband. Now that he's resting, reality of the traumatic accident has set in. It's natural to experience some anxiety; you'll be all right in a moment."

The doctor's wife brought fresh coffee to Hope and the Peabodys. They nodded their thanks. Hope's hands shook as she sipped the hot liquid. Mrs. Abrams sat beside her and offered a sympathetic pat on her knee.

Dexter spoke up, "Doctor, I can get him back to Liberty within two hours' time. I know firsthand he'll receive excellent care at the hospital there."

Hope looked at Dr. Abrams. "Do you think he'll be okay to ride to the hospital in Liberty?"

Dr. Abrams was in thought. *She has had enough to handle today. I best not tell her that amputation is probable.* "All right then, I won't attempt to make a prognosis, but his injury is extensive. His hospital stay could be lengthy, and he will need family nearby."

Dexter looked at Hope. "You make the decision, Hope. Do you want to get him back to Liberty or go to a hospital here?"

Feeling the urgency to be on their way, she stood. "I want him in Liberty."

Dr. Abrams took Hope's hand. "The medication I gave him will last several hours, keep his leg elevated. If he wakes, keep him still. He's not going to have an easy time of it."

A hard fist of fear grew in Hope's stomach, but determination of purpose kept her voice calm. "Can you help me get him to the car, Dexter?"

The doctor said, "I'll help move him. I'm sure you would like to wash up."

Mrs. Abrams stood. "Ladies, come with me." She led them to a large tiled room with two toilet stalls and basins. "I'll get a pillow and light blanket for your husband."

When alone with her friend, Hope leaned against the wall. Her resolve to stay strong crumbled. A quivering chin was prelude to her sobs. "I'm so sorry this happened, it's all my fault."

"It wasn't your fault, Hope, or anyone else's. It was an accident."

"I know, but it was so foolish." She stepped to the basin where she washed her face and hands. Both attempted unsuccessfully to wipe blood stains from their clothing.

Before the women returned, Dexter paid the physician for his services. "Thank you, Doctor; I'm sure glad you were here today."

"I am too. Mr. Prichard needed urgent care. He's got a rough road of recovery ahead of him." Dr. Abrams prepared a sedative for the trip.

Dexter lifted Winn from under the arms while Dr. Abrams carefully carried his legs. Hope climbed in the car and the men gently laid him on her lap with his injured leg propped up with the towels.

Mrs. Abrams gave Hope the pillow for Winn's head and placed the blanket over his legs. Hope said, "I must pay you for these."

"Oh no, Honey. Just take good care of your husband."

"Thank you, ma'am. You've been so kind." She looked at Dr. Abrams and realized she had given no thought of payment. "Oh, Doctor, I need to pay you. Let me give you our address, can you send a bill?"

"Don't concern yourself. Your friend took care of everything."

She looked at Dexter and before she voiced objections, he said, "Goodbye, Doc. Thanks." He waved and slowly accelerated as not to jar the patient. "Hope, we have to get Winn to the hospital, so let's don't think about anything else right now. Let me know if you need for me to stop or slow down." Concentrating on the road, he pulled onto the main highway.

Hope felt a sob gather momentum in her throat. She allowed it to flow to the surface. Alice looked over her shoulder and gave Hope a look of sympathetic concern. Winn was pale, still as death. Hope was drained and filled with fear for him. A prayer was on her lips as they traveled. Not wanting to jostle him, she remained in the same position. The trek back was very different from the jolly mood that morning. Hope briefly took her eyes off Winn and looked out to see dusk surround the landscape. *The day had begun so picture perfect.* Only toward the end of the trip did he stir and groan but remained sleeping.

Two Liberty hospital attendants carried Winn into the emergency room where Dr. Yates was on duty. Alice and Dexter waited with Hope throughout the examination. When he became aware of his state, Winn was sedated again. The doctor in Galveston was correct; a large amount of stitching was required.

Finally Winn was taken to a room. When Hope saw that he was in deep sleep, she allowed Dexter to drive her to the boarding house to wash and change clothes. Gritty sand was on her feet and her clothing smelled of blood.

Mrs. Emerson was frantic when told of the accident and coddled Hope as if she were a child. "Now, my Dear, you let me know what you need."

"Thank you, Mrs. Emerson. What Winn and I need most is prayer."

"That I will do, gladly."

Dexter drove Hope to the hospital as she insisted. In a chair beside Winn's bed through the night, she had little sleep. Sunday was a blur of Winn's pain, nurses in attendance, and a morning and evening visit from Dr. Yates. At church Alice and Dexter requested prayer for the Prichards. The pastor visited after services and prayed with Hope as Winn slept.

Early Monday, Dexter reported the news of Winn's accident to the printing plant. Immediately Raymond Spencer went to the hospital with deep concern for his employee. Hope had just bathed Winn's face and he was able to briefly tell Spencer what happened with Hope filling in details he didn't remember.

Mr. Spencer said, "Looks like you're going to be laid up for a while. Homer wants to switch over to linotype from the job press; guess I'll let him have a go at it. The most important thing is that you take it easy and get well." He looked at Hope. "You have a pretty nurse, Winn, and looks like a good one, too."

Winn's eyes drooped from the last medication he was given, but managed a weak smile. "Yep, she's the best."

Hope thanked Spencer for coming. He assured her to call if she needed anything and he would be sending someone over with a week's paycheck.

"That's mighty kind of you, Mr. Spencer."

"He's the best linotype operator I've ever seen, he's fast and accurate. Men like him are hard to come by. Take good care of him and yourself, Mrs. Prichard." When he departed, Winn drifted off again.

The next few days, Hope lived at the hospital. Her fears were intensified when a fever developed. Winn was delirious at times and determined to get out of bed. It took the help of a nurse to assist her in holding him until medication took effect for another few hours. Alice and Dexter came every day. On one visit, Alice convinced Hope to get a few hours' sleep at the boarding house while Dexter stayed with Winn.

Plagued with fatigue, she relented and allowed Alice to drive her home. Mrs. Emerson greeted her with a letter for Winn from his daddy. Hope took the letter and gave the landlady a report which was the same as before.

In her room, Hope cratered on the bed and was overtaken with sleep right away. Upon waking, the letter from her father-in-law was lying beside her. *I wonder why Winn has been so silent, almost secretive about his family. It may be wrong to read his mail, I'm not even included in the address, but I'm his wife and he's in a bad way.*

She sat on the edge of the bed and opened the envelope.

> *Dear Winston,*
>
> *I hope this finds you well. Since not hearing from you of late, we have been concerned. Mother has been feeling poorly, she blames it on the heat. It happens every summer and is her excuse for not cooking, but then she usually finds a reason for staying out of the kitchen. It's a good thing Edward likes to cook and he does a pretty good job of it.*
>
> *We finally received information about Luther; he is in a Pennsylvania prison. This time is a more serious offense. He broke into a business and cracked the safe, stealing a large amount of cash. It looks like he will be there for a year or more before the possibility of parole.*
>
> *That is also part of Mother's illness, though we both have accepted the fact that Luther is troubled and until he turns his life over to the Lord he will remain so.*

Stopping for a moment to digest the words, Hope whispered. "No wonder he hasn't said much about Luther. At least his parents are believers. That's good to know." Her neck ached; she rubbed it while continuing to read.

In my last letter I told you that I would try to contact Darlene, but to no avail. Perhaps she was here in San Antonio for a visit and went back to Colorado. If you want the divorce papers, I will write the Public Vital Statistics Records there, it would be advantageous to know the date it was granted.

Write soon, it will cheer your mother to hear from you. She and Edward send their love.

Your Daddy,
Francis M. Prichard

Stunned beyond measure, she read and reread the last part stopping every time on the words *divorce papers*, thinking she misunderstood. Not grasping it, she shook her head for comprehension. *Surely there's a reasonable explanation.* But no, his daddy wrote about a woman named Darlene and asked if Winn wanted the divorce papers. Bone tired, she fell across the bed, numb, painfully hurt, and scared. *There was no mention of me. Winn hasn't even told his parents of our marriage.*

She responded to a light tap on her door. "Yes?"

Mrs. Emerson announced through the closed door that she was about to serve supper. Hope tried to think when she had eaten last and realized her stomach was empty. "Thank you, I'll be down in a minute, Mrs. Emerson."

Folding the letter and replacing it in the envelope, she set it on the desk. *After supper I'll write his daddy and let him know that Winn is in the hospital.* She walked toward the door and looked at the letter with disdain. *I'll also inform him that he's married . . . again evidently.*

> *Never does a man know the force that is in him 'til some mighty affliction or grief has humanized the soul.*
> —Frederick W. Robertson

22

Hope stood by Winn's bed a good part of the night as she applied a cloth to his face, chest, and arms. She repeatedly dipped the cloth in a pan of cool water and prayed for his temperature to go down. By morning he was lucid, and the fever was slight.

Removing the bandages, Dr. Yates closely scrutinized the leg. "Mr. Prichard, when you arrived and I first examined your injury, I was doubtful your leg could be saved. I've waited to monitor the healing, but I'm not pleased with the way it looks. You need to be prepared for the possibility of amputation."

Upon hearing the word "amputation", Hope became dizzy and quickly sat in the chair behind her.

Winn's face was set in determination. "No, Doc, you or nobody else is going to amputate my leg."

"You're subjecting yourself to infection. Right now it would be below the knee, later if fever persists and gangrene sets in, the entire leg may have to be removed. You're taking a big chance, Mr. Prichard. Gangrene can quickly spread throughout your body."

Winn threw back the sheet and sat up. "You never said anything about gangrene. And what difference would it make if my leg is gone below the knee or above? It would still be a stump, no sir, my fever's down, and I'm getting out of here."

Dr. Yates said, "Calm down, Mr. Prichard. Nothing drastic will be done immediately. But we don't want the possibility of gangrene. I've seen cases like yours get out of control overnight. Being a medic in the war, I've performed many amputations on wounded soldiers who may have died otherwise."

Winn's facial features hardened. "Or they may have lived a normal life with both legs. I've heard about medics as far back as the Civil War all the way to the Great War. All of you Sawbones have the mindset that it's best to just be done with an injured limb instead of dealing with complications which may never occur." His fury was surprising.

Hope got a grip on her faint feeling, sobering instantly at the dreadful possibility and Winn's reaction.

Dr. Yates had witnessed similar responses. "Wait, Mr. Prichard. I'm not saying it is certain for now, but you need to be prepared for the possibility."

"Okay, you prepared me. Now just give me a bottle of something to get me through the pain until it heals. I'm going home—I'm sure you can use an extra bed here." Now he was standing on one foot balancing against the bed, nerves at full stretch.

Hope needed someone to hold her up, but instead she grabbed her husband's arm to steady him. "Winn, you're too weak right now." Her eyes beseeched Dr. Yates. "Shouldn't he stay at least one more night?"

The doctor went around to their side of the bed. "Of course, let me help you back in bed, Mr. Prichard. We can discuss this tomorrow."

Winn's leg was on fire. He was dizzy almost to the point of nausea, but had made a decision and was not going to back down. "There'll be no discussion of cutting off my leg. I want to be in my own bed."

Hope regained her strength. "Doctor, I can take care of him at home. I've helped the nurse change the dressing, and I can do it."

Dr. Yates saw that further persuasion would only agitate his patient more. "All right, but please lie down, Mr. Prichard. I'll send the nurse in to bandage your leg." Reluctantly he added, "Someone will bring a pair of crutches, medication, and bandages you will need at home."

They helped him return to the bed. The doctor cautioned Hope to get Winn to the hospital if his fever went up or if there was change of color around the injury. "I'll stop by every few days."

She nodded. "Thank you, Doctor. I'll watch him carefully." When he left the room, she said, "Winn, you're a stubborn man. You had a 'do or die' look in your eyes. Now I know what I have to deal with when you make up your mind."

Winn was spent, but he matched her smile. "That's right, once I get something in my head, I'll do my darndest to do it. But I think I know someone else like that, and her name is Hope."

"I guess together we have enough doggedness to get us through this."

His smile was weak. "Grandpa Jim called it grit, and you're right. With you by my side, I'll make it with two legs to stand on."

"With the Lord by our side, we'll make it." She gave him a kiss on his whiskered cheek. "Once I get you home, I'm going to get rid of that beard. I need to go down the hall to call Dexter to come get us."

Winn's brow creased. "No, Sugar, don't call Dexter; he's done enough. I feel badly about making such a mess in his car. Call ole man Preston's cab service, it's bound to be in the phone book." For the first time he thought about his money pouch. "You do have the money out of my pocket, don't you?"

She assured him she did and went to call the taxi. She also called Mrs. Emerson to let her know to expect them home directly.

Mrs. Emerson was out of breath. "I'm getting a room downstairs ready for you. It's the one the Peabodys had before they moved into their new home. It's nice and large at the end of the hall right next to the bathroom."

"I'm sure it's very nice, Mrs. Emerson. We appreciate your thoughtfulness. Winn would have a difficult time getting up the stairs." Noting her breathlessness, Hope added, "But I can move our things. You already have so much to do."

It took all Winn's fortitude to make it from his hospital room to the taxi. Hobbling up the few steps from the sidewalk to the boarding house front door was quite a task, but Winn managed with his crutches. "It's mighty thoughtful of you to give us a room downstairs, Mrs. Emerson."

She held the door open. "I knew you'd have a hard time with the stairs. Besides, my rose garden is right outside the window."

Ready to catch him if he faltered, Hope stuck to Winn like glue. He said, "Do you honestly think you'd be able to stop me from falling?"

"Maybe not, but I could break your fall."

He was perspiring with the effort to maneuver the long hallway which led to their bedroom. "Break my fall and probably break your arm or leg also."

Finally in the room, he made it to the bed and fell across it, dropping the crutches on the floor. "I've never been so relieved."

Winn slept no better than at the hospital. He tossed and flailed through the night. The medication did little to relieve the throbbing. Hope's slumber came from exhaustion as she slept on the full-length sofa in their room.

She began transferring their belongings the next morning. Winn woke from a troubled nap as she carried a pile of his clothing into the room. "Sugar, I'm sorry you have to carry all that down the stairs." He looked at her bedding on the couch. "Guess I didn't leave room for you on the bed."

"I'm happy to be doing something." Hope put the clothes on the couch and sat on the edge of the bed. "There was room, but I didn't want to take the chance of kicking your leg in my sleep."

"I'm the one who kicks, but you never budge; guess that comes from sleeping with your sisters all your life."

She stood and picked up a shirt to hang in the chifforobe. "Pearl slept on one side of me and Betsy on the other. They both kicked, but I only get kicked from one side sleeping with you." Her smile was generous.

Winn looked out the window at a large oak shading a table and chairs beyond the roses. "Wonder how long it'll be before I can sit outside?"

Hope held the shirt to her bosom. "Well, let's see. You fled the hospital before old Doc Yates could cut your leg off." She ambled thoughtfully to the foot of the bed. "You made it up the porch steps and down the hall without help. I think with your tenacity, you'll be venturing outside in record time."

"Are you sure your name isn't Pollyanna?"

Later that day, Dexter and Alice stopped by. Alice was carrying a basket of baked goods. Placing it on the bedside table, she said, "My Sunday school class put this together for you and send best wishes for a speedy recovery."

Propped up on an elbow, Winn peered inside the basket. "So, I suppose I have to share this with Hope."

Alice said, "You better. The ladies said it's for both of you. After all, you're just lying around, and Hope is the one who needs energy." It was said lightheartedly and Winn laughed, but it struck a nerve. His pain had been edged with worry and guilt for the strain the accident had placed on Hope.

It had dawned on Winn that there must have been a doctor's fee in Galveston and concluded that Dexter had paid it.

Dexter said, "Now don't concern yourself with that, Winn. Just get well."

"Oh no, I pay my debts. You had the expense of getting your car cleaned also, I imagine. I want to pay for that too." It took some coaxing, but Dexter relented and accepted a portion of the reimbursement Winn offered.

"Well, all right, I'll accept it, just so you'll quit worrying about it."

"I'll get the rest to you in a few weeks, Dexter. I'm much obliged to you and Alice."

The ladies went to the kitchen to make a pot of coffee. Hope said, "How do you like your new home, Alice?"

"I love it. We'll come get you after Winn improves, and I'll give you a grand tour." Alice placed the creamer and sugar bowl on a tray. "Hope, I have to tell you that throughout Winn's ordeal, I was impressed with your calling out to the Lord. I'm so glad you know where to turn in a crisis."

"Not just in a crisis, Alice, we need him every day in each thing we do."

"You're a special lady, Hope. I'm glad I met you."

"Me too. See how God works in our lives? I came here to the boarding house just in time to meet you before you moved."

A few days later, Mrs. Emerson was about to serve supper when a man jangled the doorbell. "How do, ma'am. My name's Homer, I work with Winn at the print shop."

"Oh, come in." Mrs. Emerson pushed the screen door open. "How nice of you to stop by. Winn's had a rough time of it, bless his heart. I'm sure he'll appreciate a visit." She waved a hand toward the sitting room. "Just wait in there; I'll see if he's awake."

"Yes, ma'am, thank you."

Winn's attempt to bear his pain without concerning Hope was a constant struggle. She had just helped him to bed after a torturous trip to the bathroom when a knock came on the open door. Hope said, "Yes, Mrs. Emerson, I'll be there for supper in a minute."

"That's fine, Dearie. And Winn has a visitor waiting in the front room."

Winn plopped his head on the pillow. "Wonder who that could be?"

Hope stepped to the door. "Who is it, Mrs. Emerson?"

"He said his name is Homer and works at the newspaper office. Does Winn feel like seeing him?"

Hearing Homer's name, Winn remembered that the man had a source for obtaining whiskey. "Yes, Hope, I'd like to see Homer. Maybe he can fill me in on what's happening at the shop."

Happy to hear Winn felt up to receiving a visitor, Hope went to the sitting room. She recalled meeting Homer the day Winn introduced her to his co-workers. His prominent nose with a road map of broken blood vessels dominated his features. With a cordial greeting, she invited him to their living quarters. "I'll let you two visit while I join the new tenants. May I get a cup of coffee for you, Homer?"

"No, ma'am. I won't stay long; I just wanted to see if there's anything I can do for Winn."

She left the men to their shop talk and hoped Homer could bring some cheer to Winn. He hoped so too, but it wasn't the same kind of cheer Hope was thinking about.

"It's good to see you, Homer." Shaking his hand, Winn motioned for him to close the door. He didn't want to waste a minute of privacy with him. "You must've been reading my mind, Homer. You bet there's something you can do for me. The pain is intolerable. I need a bottle of hooch—bad."

The man's smile revealed several missing teeth. "That's what I was thinking. Ole man Spencer said you're in a bad way. I got a bottle in my car."

"Do you think you can sneak it in without anybody seeing it?"

"Slicker than a whistle. Been sneaking bottles around ever since it was outlawed."

Winn reached for his money pouch on the bedside table and handed Homer some bills.

Homer's face lit up. "Be back in a jiffy."

Winn hid the bottle in his valise at the bottom of the chifforobe where Hope wouldn't likely find it. Chances were few when his wife was not in the room with him, but he came up with reasons for her to leave so he could hobble to the suitcase and take a swig.

Calamity is the perfect glass wherein
we truly see and know ourselves.
—Sir William Davenant

23

Hope was in the front room seeking another book to read when the door ringer jangled. She paid it little mind until Mrs. Emerson ushered a tall, distinguished-looking man into the room.

Mrs. Emerson assumed Hope had met her father-in-law. "Hope, Winn's daddy is here to see him." The landlady walked toward the hallway, then turned back. "Mr. Prichard, I'll set a place for you to eat with us."

His head bowed slightly. "That's mighty kind, ma'am, thank you." When Mrs. Emerson left them, awkwardness hung in the air for a moment. Frank Prichard appeared uncertain with both hands folded around the brim of his hat which he held in front of his chest. Neatly dressed in a dark, pin-striped suit, he smiled at his daughter-in-law. It was a smile so much like Winn's; she would have recognized him without an introduction.

He and Priscilla had been shocked to receive Hope's letter. Frank felt compelled to see Winn's condition for himself and meet Hope. As usual, Priscilla feigned a sick headache when it was suggested they drive to Liberty.

With the same southern softness as his son, he said, "Hope, thank you for your letter. We didn't know Winston was married."

She was holding her book selection. "I gathered that from your letter to him. I apologize for reading it, but he was in the hospital and . . ." She felt the heat of embarrassment on her face.

Frank stepped closer but wasn't sure if a hug would be acceptable to Hope, so he kept a distance between them. "My Dear, you had every right to read my letter, and I regret omitting your name . . . if I would have known . . ." He studied her features. *She has a wholesome look about her, a refreshing change from the hardness of Darlene.*

Hope always found comfort in the sitting room; it was the perfect setting to finally meet Frank. His presence, though uncertain at first, brought calm to Hope's desperate heart. "Mr. Prichard, Winn has had a difficult time. It's been so hard seeing his pain. The doctor thought at first his leg might have to be amputated." She seemed compelled to pour out words quickly without considering how shocking they would sound to Winn's father.

Frank swayed slightly; a hand flew to his forehead. "It was that severe?"

She regretted blurting out the negative news. "It was bad, but the doctor said yesterday it looks a little better. The fever has subsided, but he's been restless and uncomfortable." She realized all of this may be too much for the man, he looked pale. "I'm sorry, Mr. Prichard, let me take you to him."

He followed her lead and was impressed with the well-appointed house. Winn had just crept back into bed from his stealthy visit with the hidden bottle. Seeing his daddy enter the room, the thought fleeted across his mind the liquor had caused him to hallucinate.

In his mild manner, Frank said, "Hello, Winston."

"Daddy, how . . . how did you . . ." Winn was so taken aback he would have fallen to the floor if he weren't in bed.

Frank walked closer and saw that Winn had lost weight. He looked drawn and pale. "Son, Hope wrote to us of your accident."

Winn's eyes were wide with complete surprise. Hope stepped to the bed opposite of Frank. "Winn, I apologize. I . . . your father sent a letter to you." Though nervous, her head was held high, and she spoke as if there was no doubt about the correctness of her actions. "You were in the hospital, and I felt your parents needed to know what happened."

Winn was confounded. His leg was aching, and the effects of the whiskey had made his thinking process numb. All he wanted was some sleep in hopes his nightmare would be a vague memory when he woke.

Frank sat on the chair by the bed. "She was right about informing us, Son. I only wish we would have known of your marriage. Hope and I only spoke for a few moments, but she has already gained my respect and gratitude for taking care of you."

Mrs. Emerson tapped on the open door. "Excuse me, dinner is ready. Winn, I can bring a tray for you if you like."

"No, thank you, Mrs. Emerson. I need to take a little nap." He slid further down in the bed.

During the meal, Frank interacted with the new tenants, but he yearned to have some time to get acquainted with Hope. He was awarded the opportunity after they ate and checked on Winn who was sleeping soundly. The two of them went outside and sat at the table under the oak tree.

Hope related how the accident occurred and how much the Peabodys had helped them. "And Mr. Spencer at the paper has been attentive and gave Winn a week's pay."

Frank could readily see Winn's attraction to Hope. It wasn't necessarily her physical beauty that drew him in, yet she was certainly pretty. It was the way she expressed herself, looking him in the eyes, completely sincere and forthright.

As they talked, admiration grew between them. Hope told him how she met his son and a little about herself and her family. In exchange, her father-in-law explained that his wife was frail and couldn't tolerate a long drive, but she was overwrought about the accident. He skimmed over family troubles and completely avoided any mention of Winn's first marriage. Hope didn't have the heart to bring it up and thought it best not to let him know it had been kept from her.

Mrs. Emerson kindly brought glasses of lemonade to them. Hope took a sip of the refreshment; she felt completely at ease with her father-in-law. "Mr. Prichard, I . . ."

"Hope, please call me Daddy or Frank. Mr. Prichard seems too formal for family."

She smiled and considered his suggestion. *It would feel strange to call him by his first name.* "How about Daddy Prichard?"

"Whatever you're comfortable with, Hope."

"All right, Daddy Prichard. I just wanted to say how relieved and happy I am to finally meet you. I've wondered about Winn's family."

Frank leaned forward in his chair with his elbows on his knees. "Hope, I want to make a suggestion, and please understand that it isn't my intention to interfere."

She liked his easy manner, so like his son's. His hair was dark with gray making an introduction at the temples. *If this is the way Winn will look when he reaches his father's age, I'll still have a handsome husband.* "I won't consider any suggestion from you interfering."

"I want to take you and Winston home to San Antonio with me." She leaned an elbow on the table, her hand holding the side of her head. He didn't know whether she was going to cry or balk, but he continued. "Now, before you say anything, think about it. I have no idea of Winston's finances, but no matter—a calamity like this plays havoc with anyone's plans and savings."

Contemplating a response, she straightened and looked at her lap. Seeing one of the buttons on her navy blue skirt was hanging by a thread, she made a mental note to mend it.

He reached out to lightly touch her arm. "Hope, we have an extra bedroom. It was built on the back of the house as an afterthought, I imagine. Anyway, it's private with its own entrance. We're using it as a catchall room of sorts now."

Exhausted, her defenses were down; it would be easy to readily agree. "You're kind to extend the offer, Daddy Prichard. Let me talk to Winn about it."

"Of course. Go in and see if he's awake. I think I'll stretch my legs and walk down the street." He wanted to locate a telephone and place a long distance call to talk privately with Priscilla. She needed to know the seriousness of their son's condition and Winn and Hope may be coming back with him. He also wanted to give instructions to Edward to clear out the spare room and put clean linens on the bed, just in case.

Winn awoke and the realization came that seeing his daddy had not been a nightmare. *I wonder what was in the letter he wrote. I should've told Mother and Daddy I was married, why didn't I? Still the fear of Hope discovering I'd been married before, I guess.* His eyes rested on Hope as she entered their room and closed the door behind her. It was warm; she opened the windows higher and pulled the sheers to the side.

She picked up some clothes from the back of a chair avoiding his eyes. "Your daddy went for a walk."

"Hope, I . . . I can't really explain why I didn't tell my folks about you."

She stopped at the foot of his bed with the clothes across her arm. "Were you ashamed of them . . . or me?"

"Neither." He pulled himself up and leaned on the headboard. "I wasn't ashamed at all, it's just that . . ."

"It's just that they might slip up and tell me of your previous marriage?" Her voice snapped with indignation.

"Oh no, Daddy shouldn't have told you."

"He never mentioned it."

Questions circled his reasoning. "Well, how . . . oh, I knew it would come out sooner or later." His eyes went downward, she waited. He dragged his eyes back to her and held out his arm. "Come here, Hope."

"No, I'm going to stand right here until you tell me about Darlene, or I'm going to ask your daddy when he comes back."

"You even know her name?"

"Yes, I know her name; it was in the letter which is in the desk drawer if you want to know exactly what I read."

Feeling his way on this uncertain path, Winn said, "I do want to read the letter; will you get it for me?"

Her feet were firmly planted on the braided rug. "First I want to know about the divorce and why you didn't tell me about it?"

He groaned and ran his hand through his hair leaving the front part sticking straight up. It would have made Hope laugh except for her mood. Winn looked toward the window for a moment. "Okay, please come sit here on the bed, you look like a school marm standing over me."

She threw the clothes across the footboard and sat on the bed, just out of his reach sending the message of her disposition. Since reading the letter, curiosity gnawed and anger festered. She had planned to approach him about it when his leg improved. With his daddy's arrival, her need for answers came up suddenly. "For the life of me I can't understand your dishonesty. Why didn't you tell your family about me?"

Winn briefly told her of his short first marriage and the reason he left which began to thaw the hard lump inside her. "Sugar, I guess I am ashamed. Not of you or my family, but of myself. Can you forgive me?"

His pitiful countenance and physical condition played heavily on her charitable nature. Moving closer to him, she couldn't allow anything less than her unconditional love. "I forgive you. And in a way I can understand your need to keep it inside."

"Hope, I thought I could never give my heart to anyone after seeing the woman I thought I loved in another man's arms—my best friend at that." He hugged her tightly. "You mean everything to me. I love you and trust you." They kissed. "Now will you let me read the letter? And while you're up, please hand me a dose of that medicine the Doc left."

"Can you wait just a little longer to read the letter? Your daddy should be back soon." She got the bottle of medication and gave it to him. "Do you really trust me, Winn?"

"Oh no, am I going to hear some sort of confession about your past now?" He took a swallow from the bottle without the teaspoon she handed him.

"Of course not. The biggest confession I could make is when Dora and I peeked through a hole in the school outhouse when Billy Sanders was in there. He was peeking right back at us, so we ran away and hid."

They both laughed. "No, Winn, this is serious, I want you to trust my decision." He gave her a quizzical look and she continued. "Your daddy wants to take us with him to stay until you can go back to work, and I think we should take him up on his offer." There, she got it all out in one breath.

This made him sit straight up; he winced and grabbed his leg. "What? You don't know what you'd be getting into. You've never encountered anyone like my mother. She's a nitpicking hen and will tear both of us apart."

"You think I'm so insecure that I can't take your mother's remarks?" She took the bottle of medicine and set it on the dresser. "Our savings is a pittance and the check Mr. Spencer gave me is going to pay next month's rent, then what? I could try to get a job, it might be enough to keep our heads above water, but someone needs to look after you for a while."

A gray omen of probabilities shot through his mind. Hope sat beside him and continued pleading her case. "We don't know how much the hospital bill is going to be, and you need time to heal. I think it's an answer to prayer. Surely you can see the wisdom of being with family at a time like this."

A hard knot grew in his stomach. "I haven't even mentioned Eddie; he means well but can be a real pest."

"I'm used to pests, there was one at home named Betsy. But she was a loveable one."

"Well, with your soft heart, Eddie would seem loveable to you, I suppose. But don't say I didn't warn you about Mother. She's tiny, but she could intimidate a stampeding elephant by telling him his ears are too big. She could turn him into a whimpering pup with his tail between his legs."

Hope laughed as he went on. "Then, as he's running away, she'd tell him his tail isn't big enough to tuck between his legs." She laughed harder.

Frank knocked on the door. She stifled her laughter and stood to welcome him. His eyes crinkled with an engaging smile. "I couldn't help but hear laughter. Does that mean my idea of coming home with me has been approved?" He looked at Winn.

Winn nodded. "Reluctantly so, Daddy. It's been a long time since I've lived under the same roof with Mother. I'm questioning how I can handle it. Remember how she was when I had pneumonia? You know she makes me crazy."

Hope was surprised he spoke so negatively about his mother to his daddy, it seemed disrespectful.

Frank walked to the side of the bed. "I fully understand how you feel, Winston, and will try to be a buffer of Mother's interference." He took a deep breath and seemed ready to mount the hills ahead. "Now, I think we best prepare to leave so we won't be late on the road. Hope, if you will show me where Winston's suitcase is, I'll pack his things."

"It's on the bottom of the chifforobe, Daddy." Winn thought of the half full bottle of whiskey in his valise. "Set it here on the bed and just hand me my clothes out of the dresser. Hope, maybe you better go let Mrs. Emerson know our plans."

"Oh my goodness, yes. She needs to know. I'll be right back to gather my clothes." She hurried away.

Frank reached for the bag and lifted it. In Winn's haste to replace it earlier, he failed to latch it completely and it flipped open. The bottle tumbled out onto the rug which prevented it from breaking. Frank calmly stooped to pick it up and tersely said, "I'm guessing Hope doesn't know about this?" He stepped toward the door and closed it.

Winn was a child again, caught red-handed stealing candy. "No, Hope doesn't know about it, a friend snuck it in for me. I had to have something to help me sleep; the medicine just eases it for a little while. If I take a swig with the medicine, I can get a few hours relief. She doesn't have to know, Daddy. Just put it in the inside pocket of the suitcase."

His father heaved a sigh. "You know what I went through to rid my body of this poison." He glared at his son and held the bottle like he was ready to smash it against the wall.

Winn let out a relieved breath when he lowered it to his side. Shaking his head, Frank said, "I understand how alcohol numbs the body, but it will eventually numb the senses. I'll go along with you because of your situation. But I'm warning you, Winston, go easy and taper off before it grabs your guts and yanks you inside out—it will, you know. Before realizing it, you will get to the point where you can't live without the foul stuff." He started to put it in the suitcase and then handed the bottle to his son. "You'll need a slug for the ride home."

Mrs. Emerson was in the kitchen taking cookies out of the oven. She looked up when Hope came in. "Will Mr. Prichard be staying for supper? I have plenty."

"That's so kind of you, Mrs. Emerson. No, he won't and actually we won't either." Seeing the surprised look on her face, Hope quickly explained Frank's offer and their immediate departure. "We do appreciate all you've done for us and I hope when Winn is able to go back to work, there'll be a room for us here."

"Of course you and Winn need to go home with his father, I most hardily agree." Drawing Hope to her for a hug, she said, "I'll continue to pray for the Lord's healing hand on Winn and for you in caring for him." Mrs. Emerson released her embrace. "Write when you'll be back and I'll let you know if I have a room."

"Thank you, Mrs. Emerson, I'll do that." They walked out of the kitchen together. "If I may, I'd like to leave a note for you to give Dr. Yates with the

Prichard's address where he may send our bill." She went to the table in the hall to use the notepad by the telephone. "Oh, and the Peabodys also, I need to write them a note but will send a letter when we get settled."

"I'll be glad to give a note to the doctor and the Peabodys."

Hope sat at the desk. "Guess I need to call Mr. Spencer and let him know where to reach us."

The landlady turned to leave. "I'm sure you have a lot to do. If you need my help with anything else, I'll be in the kitchen."

It didn't take Hope and Frank long to pack their few belongings. Winn's suits and other clothing filled most of their three suitcases. Hope stuffed the rest of her things in the paper and cloth sacks Mrs. Emerson provided.

The arduous ordeal of changing the bandage had to be done before leaving. Upon seeing his son's injury, Frank was aghast. The skin, now blue black, was swollen and sewn together like a horrendous red patchwork quilt gone badly awry. The gashes started from his foot to his thigh. *Dear Jesus. No wonder he's in such pain.* "I want to get you to my doctor as soon as possible, Winston. He's an exceptional physician."

Winn and Mrs. Emerson exchanged heartfelt wishes and good-byes. He was settled in the back seat of the car with ample padding for his leg. When the landlady handed Hope more towels and a pillow to place under and around it, Winn said, "For pity sake, the wheels could fall off and I wouldn't feel it."

Mrs. Emerson patted him on the shoulder. "Well, let's hope that won't happen or anything else." She handed Hope a small brown paper bag. "Dearie, here's some cookies for the trip." Before Hope could thank her, Mrs. Emerson gave her a hug and nodded to Frank. "Take care of these children; they've been very dear to me." Tears sprang into her eyes.

Frank was touched by her expression of love. "I fully intend to, Mrs. Emerson, and thank you."

Hope said, "Yes, thank you. You've been so special to us." She waved and stepped into the front seat of the car feeling like a chapter of her life was closing—so soon after the biggest change in her life of marrying Winn.

Winn was mistaken about the padding around the wound, every dip in the road felt like an enormous pothole. Sleep eluded him at the onset of the trip, there had been too much jostling about for him to rest. Vaguely observing tree tops in the passing scenery, he tuned out the cordial conversation between Frank and Hope in the front seat.

Riding to San Antonio, Winn felt like he did as a boy riding in the wagon with his daddy returning to Dallas, Georgia. After over a year with

Aunt Katy and Uncle John in Atlanta, he was summoned home to be Luther's overseer when Eddie was born. He was burdened with Luther's insolence and his mother's indifference. Now he was subjecting himself and his bride to Priscilla's dominance. *It's strange that after all these years I'm being taken back to Mother and Daddy's house. The difference now is that I'm in a car instead of a wagon, and I'm bringing my wife with me. I can only hope Mother has mellowed, but instinct tells me age has given her bitterness longer to simmer and boil over.*

In the haziness of the whiskey he took twice as much of the prescribed medication than directed. In Winn's clouded mind, sunlight hadn't had the grace to enter this day of pain and shocking turn of events. As dusk approached, the miserable hours deserved to be covered in darkness. Sleep finally overtook him.

About halfway to San Antonio, Frank stopped at a diner. Seeing Winn asleep, they decided to let him rest. After a sandwich and coffee, they resumed their trip.

Hope remembered the bag of cookies Mrs. Emerson gave her. "Would you like a cookie for dessert, Daddy Prichard?" After his refusal, she stuck her hand in the sack and was surprised to find an envelope. "Oh, she gave us a note." In the dim light of the moon she saw that it was the envelope she had given Mrs. Emerson at the first of the month. It contained the money for their rent with a note which read, *"May God bless and keep you."*

I expect to pass through life but once. If
therefore, there be any kindness
I can show, or any good thing I can do to
any fellow being, let me do it
now, and not defer or neglect it, as I shall not pass this way again.
—William Penn

THE RICHLAND RECORD

More Than a Newspaper—a Community Service
<u>A Weekly Publication Serving the Greater Richland Area</u>
Richland, Texas   Thursday, February 13, 1969
<u>Winston Randolph Prichard, Editor and Publisher</u>

News and Views of a Tactless Texan

Now that Hope and I are semi-retired, we enjoy revisiting places which hold memories for us. You notice I didn't say "happy memories" of which there are many, but our journey through this life has taken us on a few rough detours.

A recent weekend excursion took us to Liberty, east of Houston, where I worked a short time for the *Liberty Vindicator*. In 1928, jobs for linotype operators were scarce, and I was fortunate to be hired. I was courting Hope who lived in Hempstead. We exchanged letters almost every day, and on Saturdays I hopped on a Greyhound Bus for a visit with her. My early morning departure took me to Houston with a short layover before catching the bus destined for Hempstead. We visited and kindled our affection under the scrutiny of her protective Papa. In late afternoon, I caught the bus to retrace my path back to Liberty.

Liberty, established in 1831, was "The First City on the Trinity." It has the prestige of being the third oldest town in Texas and is the county seat of Liberty County. The township was a sleepy saw mill community until oil was discovered in the South Liberty field in January 1925. The discovery brought immense change and population growth. By the time I arrived, the weekly newspaper and printing plant was thriving which was a blessing for an out-of-work printer.

During our time there, I suffered a serious injury and was laid up for several months. For a couple of newlyweds, it was a most unwelcome occurrence. Early in our marriage, Hope was called upon to prove her strength and faith. Some valleys of darkness we walk through in life solidify a deeper love and admiration of the one God provides at our side.

Our recent walk down memory lane in Liberty took us by the boarding house where I lived and months later brought Hope as my bride. Motherly Mrs. Emerson, who owned the boarding house, passed away a few years ago. We have fond memories of her fine meals and Christian love toward us. Though we kept in touch for years after moving from Liberty, I don't know if she realized what her kindness meant to us during that difficult time of starting out.

The good Lord also provided helping angels in the form of friends, Dexter and Alice Peabody. Their concern and aide will be long remembered.

It makes one contemplate if we have made or if we are presently making a positive impact in the lives of others. Our simple acts of kindness could work wonders which may never be revealed to us. I truly believe those who go through life giving a helping hand deserve an extra jewel in their heavenly crown. Mrs. Emerson and the Peabodys should have lovely ones.

And that's -30- until next issue.

24

Eddie was watching for them and ran to the car, greeting his brother and new sister-in-law with a huge smile. As he helped Winn out of the car, Hope observed his gentleness. She had a good feeling about Eddie. *He's excited as a child waiting for his daddy to bring home a treat.*

With a ready hand, Eddie walked beside Winn as he hobbled on the crutches into the house. Winn made it to the sofa in the living room where his mother waited as if expecting dinner guests. Priscilla remained seated, offering no welcome greeting. Eddie returned to the car to help with the bags.

After catching his breath, Winn said, "Hello, Mother, looks like I've kept you up."

"It's not the first time." Her back ramrod straight, Priscilla spoke in the brittle tone Winn so well remembered.

"No, I suppose not." *Here we go, I haven't been here one minute and I already feel like a berated child. I have to let it roll off my back or we'll be in constant battle.* He moved his leg to a more comfortable position. "You're looking well, how've you been?"

"Winston Randolph, you have exhibited no interest in my well-being for quite some time. There is no need to feign concern about me simply because of your situation. Now explain how this accident of yours occurred."

It's really going to take all the patience I have and then some to get through this. He took a deep breath and submitted to her interrogation.

With Eddie's help, Frank and Hope gathered the things from the car. When Hope entered the senior Prichard's home, she noticed it was far above the means she was raised in. Not necessarily exuding wealth, but furnished in good taste with precise placement of accents, void of clutter. The first look at her mother-in-law reminded Hope of a wicked crone in Aesop's Fables. Priscilla Prichard was wearing a black dress with tiny white polka dots and a lace collar. Her gray hair was in a high bun, but the top and sides were fanned around her face so perfectly, it looked like a brimmed hat. She was dwarfed by the large wingback chair where she was seated, unmoving and unsmiling.

Hope's heart was racing with dread. *It's nearly midnight and she looks like she's dressed for church.* Despite the warmth of the evening, Hope shivered in the frigid presence of her mother-in-law.

Priscilla didn't stand when Frank introduced Hope, but she did extend a small hand. Hope scrambled to rid herself of the load she was holding. Taking her hand, she said, "It's nice to meet you, Mrs. Prichard." *Mercy, her face looks like it's pasted on.* Priscilla managed a frail semblance of a handshake. Hope actually had the impulse to bow. She looked at Winn, who had an "I told you so" expression.

Eddie brought a tray of coffee and cookies and set it on the spindle-legged table beside his mother. He offered the plate of cookies to Hope. "These are fresh from Burk's Bakery; I hope you like oatmeal."

Not wanting to refuse his kind gesture, Hope reached for a cookie but quickly withdrew her hand when Priscilla spoke with the biting tone of one reprimanding a dog. "Edward Thornton, they haven't even washed up yet." She looked at her husband. "Frank, show Winston to his quarters." She failed to include Hope in her command.

Embarrassment and disgust twisted around Frank's features. "Priscilla, let Winston and his wife, Hope, rest here for a few minutes." 'His wife, Hope' was emphasized. "I'm sure they would appreciate a cup of coffee, I know I would." He picked up a cookie. "Thank you, Edward, this is very thoughtful."

Hope didn't know whether to slink out to find a place to wash her hands or follow Frank's lead. She decided the latter and took two cookies, giving one to Winn as she sat beside him. "Yes, thank you, I love oatmeal cookies."

Eddie served the coffee as Winn continued to tell about the accident. "It was Hope's first time at the gulf. When we drove by a pier, she suggested we stop and get a closer look. Hope and I walked on it and near the end; I stepped on a rotten plank. My bare foot fell completely through. From there everything for me is a blur, although I heard Hope praying. It was a miracle there happened to be two men driving by who helped get me to a doctor. Our friends, the Peabody's, helped us considerably."

Hope stared at Priscilla. *Winn didn't exaggerate when he warned me about his mother, she seems so strange. Mama would be running about hugging and making us feel loved and welcome. What could she possibly be thinking behind those dark eyes?*

Eddie sat on the edge of his chair. "I wish I would've been there to help you, Winston."

Priscilla gave Edward an impatient glance and then looked intensely at Hope. "Couldn't you see the pier was old and probably rotten?"

Hope almost choked on her bite of cookie. Winn sprang forward and would have stood if possible. "Mother, don't start in with Hope. We both walked on the pier and didn't realize it was dangerous. I knew it wasn't in you to at least be civil for tonight. No welcome, no sympathy for what we've been through, not a word of thanks to Hope for taking care of me."

He was shaking with anger, frustration, and pain. All the anxiety of returning to his parents' home spilled out with unbridled abandon as he lashed out. Grabbing his crutches, he struggled to stand. "I'm going to the bedroom, come on Hope." Edward stood to help him. "Thanks, Eddie."

Frank was utterly speechless; the room was silent as Hope calmly gathered the bags contemplating what to say or do. Standing in front of Priscilla with arms full of all her worldly possessions, Hope was trembling with exhaustion and uncertainty. "I've been looking forward to meeting you, ma'am. I had no idea it would be under these circumstances. I appreciate what you and Daddy Prichard are doing for us." Priscilla's frown deepened when she heard "Daddy Prichard", but Hope persevered. "I will certainly do my part in household duties while we're here."

Frank picked up several suitcases. "Now, now, we won't talk of duties, we just want you to feel at home here, don't we, Priscilla?" He looked pointedly at his wife.

The woman's pursed mouth turned into a slit which with imagination could have been interpreted as a smile. "Of course. Good night."

Frank led Hope toward the back of the house pointing out the bathroom in the hall. "Hope, please overlook the scene tonight. Sometimes my wife can appear to be abrasive."

Appear to be abrasive? The woman is a prickly cactus plant.

They went through the kitchen to a laundry room before entering the large bedroom at the rear of the house. Eddie had placed the plate of cookies on a dresser. "Here are the cookies, just in case you get hungry in the middle of the night. Oh, and there's milk in the icebox."

Hope wearily let the sacks fall from her arms. "You're very kind Eddie, thank you." She studied him briefly. *He doesn't really seem as slow as I expected. If he wouldn't slump, he might be as tall as his daddy and Winn.*

Frank looked around to see if the room had been cleaned properly. A chenille spread and linens were meticulously turned down on the comfortable looking bed. "I see you found bedding. You did a fine job of sprucing up the room, Edward."

Eddie beamed with the compliment. "I was glad to do it." His eyes misted when he looked at his brother. "I've missed you, Winston."

Sitting on the bed, Winn was already unbuttoning his shirt, but nodded. "I've missed you too, Eddie."

Hope was relieved to see the brothers' sentimental exchange after the awkward experience with their mother.

Eddie turned to Hope. "If there's anything I can do, please let me know. I'm glad you're here."

"I appreciate that, Eddie." *What I'd like right now is a trip to the bathroom.* "Please excuse me." She glanced at the three of them as she turned to leave the room. Eddie hurried along with her.

Oh no, is he going to go with me? "I can find it, Eddie."

He squeezed past her and entered the bathroom. "Just let me turn on the light for you, Hope. The cord is in the middle of the room, it's hard to find in the dark." After a yank on the string, he quickly stepped into the hall.

Hope heard a shrill voice from the living room. "Edward Thornton."

Winn could hardly wait until Frank left the room so he could get to his bottle and take a swig. He then hurriedly found a hiding place for it before plopping down on the bed.

Hope looked around the large, tidy bathroom. There was a claw foot bathtub which she longed to climb into and wash away the ugliness of the woman in the large black chair. Unpleasantness of the abrasive encounter was still draped around her shoulders. *Should I ask Mrs. Prichard if I can bathe? Someone might need to use the bathroom. In the morning . . . I'll ask in the morning.*

On the way to the bedroom, she admired the beautiful pictures in the hall. She noticed an open door to a bedroom and surmised it to be Eddie's.

The kitchen floor was covered with linoleum in a small black and white diamond design. The spotless gas range was an Elite stove, made of white and black porcelain enamel like Mrs. Emerson's. Hope spied the ice box but didn't want to be caught snooping, so she hurried through the laundry room to the bedroom.

Lying across the bed on top of the turned down bedspread, Winn was already asleep. She stood in the middle of the floor surrounded by suitcases, various bags, and padding used for Winn's leg. This pitiful assortment was her only possessions in a house with unusual relatives and a husband injured and out of work. She allowed pent up tears to fall as her weary body melted in the middle of the floor. Drying her moist face, she stretched out across the padding and prayed. In a dreamlike state, she envisioned turbulent waters under the pier in Galveston as sleep washed over her.

Winn woke with the realization that Hope wasn't in the bed. "Sugar, what are you doing on the floor, did I kick you?"

"No, you looked so comfortable I didn't want to wake you." She stretched and stood to give her husband a kiss. "I slept fine." Amazingly she did have a deep and restoring sleep.

Hope grabbed fresh clothes and handed Winn his crutches. "I'd love to bathe, but don't think I should before asking if anyone wants to use the bathroom first."

"Hope, we're not going to sing *Hail to the Chief* every morning." He awkwardly hobbled on his crutches. "We'll use the bathroom without asking permission and if somebody is waiting, just let them wait—even Mother."

She followed with readiness to help if he faltered. In the bathroom, he balanced beside the basin and shaved while she took a quick bath.

Hope dressed and helped him with his trousers. "When you get rid of this thick bandage I can repair your pant leg where I opened it at the seam."

"You sure know how to make do in every situation, Hope. I'm sorry you have to deal with Mother. It's going to be a challenge, even for you."

"Life is chock full of challenges. Don't worry about me. I just want you to get back on both feet."

The aroma of bacon reminded Winn his stomach was empty. In the kitchen, Frank and Eddie were preparing breakfast. Winn sat at the table with a cup of coffee while Hope pitched in to help. She thought it strange that Priscilla wasn't making an appearance. "Is your mother under the weather, Eddie?"

"Oh no, Mother prefers dry toast and coffee in her room." Eddie took a plate of bacon, scrambled eggs, and toast to Winn.

The four of them ate at the kitchen table. Frank drained his cup of coffee. "As soon as you're finished eating, Winston, I'd like to get you to the doctor's office and have him examine that leg."

"What about work, Daddy?"

"I told them at the office I'd be out a couple of days on a family emergency. I can go in this afternoon, it's not like the *Light* is going to miss an issue without me."

Hope looked at Frank. "Is it all right if I go with you? I'd like to hear what the doctor has to say."

"Of course, Hope." *I can see she won't be like Priscilla with her lack of participation in my life or our sons'. I think she will make a real difference in Winston for the better. Now, hopefully, he will settle down.*

Frank took Priscilla's breakfast tray to her while Hope cleared the dishes. Winn noticed his brother was unusually quiet. "Hey, Eddie, I didn't have a chance to talk to you last night. My leg was getting the best of me."

Hope thought it was his mother who got the best of him, but bit her tongue and filled the dishpan with water.

Eddie looked down at the table; his shoulders were in a permanent droop. "I know, Winston, it's all right."

Winn playfully poked his arm. "Come on, what's the trouble? My leg's going to be all right. I'll be getting a job before you can say 'Jack Spratt ate no fat'."

Eddie gave a halfhearted smile. "I'll be happy when your leg heals. I've been praying for you. But I was sad last night."

Hope turned off the water and wiped her hands as she walked to the table. Winn said, "How come, Eddie?"

Eddie looked at Hope. His face was masked with gloom.

She was about to make an excuse to leave the room. *Maybe he wants to speak privately with Winn.*

Eddie's words were bundled in concern. "I heard Hope crying." There was a ready sob in his throat, but he quickly declared, "I wasn't eavesdropping." Glancing at his brother with a worried expression, he said, "I was going to knock to see if you needed anything and . . . and heard her, so I left."

Hope was both embarrassed and touched by this genteel, soft spoken man. She lightly touched his shoulder. "Eddie, you mustn't be concerned, I was very tired after the drive and relieved to be here." She hoped this would appease him. When she looked at Winn, sorrow was etched across his face.

I have made a pact with my tongue
not to speak when my heart is disturbed.
—St. Frances de Sales

25

Dr. Babcock carefully inspected the injury and removed more wood fragments that had worked their way up between the stitches.

Hope was anxious to see if the doctor would find any infection or mention amputation. She thought it best not to report what Dr. Yates in Liberty told them. Winn evidently felt the same; he merely related how the accident occurred.

Dr. Babcock applied ointment and wrapped the leg thickly with gauze. He encased it with splints. "The lacerations are deep as well as bruising to the muscle and ligaments. The splints will prevent movement or pulling on the stitches." While talking, he took Winn's temperature and blood pressure. "It's going to take some time for the calf and shin to heal. The more severe lacerations are in the lower leg. You need to take special care not to bend your knee until the stitches are removed which should be in at least another ten days. But that doesn't mean the tendons inside are healed enough to put any weight on that leg, Winston. I want you to rest and keep it elevated. I'll include you on my rounds of house calls."

The doctor called for his nurse to give Hope the new medication he was prescribing. "If all goes well, you may be able to go back to work in a few months."

"A few months? I thought you were going to say a few weeks, Doc."

"You're badly bruised, and the cuts are deep. Your skin will need time to fuse and heal over where flesh was torn away. If you rush the healing process, you may have complications and only prolong your confinement. Even now, you're lucky if amputation isn't necessary."

Winn impatiently reached for his crutches. "Okay, Doc, you're the boss. I think that ointment is helping a little already."

"It has a numbing agent in it that should last a few hours. It makes changing the bandage less painful." He turned to Hope. "Mrs. Prichard, I want you to look every morning and evening for any sign of red lines above the bandage. Call my office immediately if you do and I'll be by to see you in the morning."

Hope held the paper sack of pain medication and ointment. "Thank you, Dr. Babcock. We'll look forward to seeing you."

Frank shook the doctor's hand. "Thank you for seeing Winston right away."

After dropping Winn and Hope at the house, Frank went to work. The remainder of the morning, Hope arranged their few belongings in the large dresser with an adjustable mirror. This was the first house she had seen with a built-in closet, and their hanging clothes looked lost in the spacious area.

Around noon, Hope went to the kitchen to help prepare a meal. Eddie had already set the table with sliced ham, a fresh tomato and cucumber salad, thick slices of cheddar cheese, and bread. Winn hobbled to the table, and Priscilla made her entrance into the kitchen.

Priscilla actually leaned to give Winn a kiss that stopped short of his cheek. "It is good to have you home, Winston." Eddie pulled the chair out for her. She sat in a stiff practiced pose. "However, you should have been courteous enough to personally give me a report from the visit with the Doctor this morning. I expected as much."

Hope cringed at her tone. Winn reached under the table and patted Hope's leg. "Mother, I explained everything to Eddie and asked him to let you know since I was too exhausted to make my way to your room. You do understand don't you?"

The cup and saucer in Eddie's hand shook. "I did tell her, Winston, just like you said." He set the dishes on the table and hung his head as he spoke softly. "Mother, I told you all he said. I'm sorry I couldn't answer your questions."

Winn said, "I'm sure you did fine, Eddie."

Eddie smiled broadly at his brother and went about serving coffee.

Priscilla adjusted the salt and pepper shakers, her place setting, and silverware to her liking which was a centimeter from where Eddie had placed them. With a prim expression, she looked at Hope. "My husband tells me I was less than cordial upon your arrival. I was experiencing a great deal of anxiety about Winston." Looking at Winn, she pointedly repeated his words of moments before. "You do understand, don't you?"

Winn eyed her over his coffee cup. *She can sure slap people in the face with sincere insincerity. That's as close to an apology she's going to give.*

Hope said, "Certainly, Mrs. Prichard, it's quite understandable. I hope you slept well."

"It was a rather stress encumbered night, which left me with a headache." She inspected the table and seemed distressed. "Edward Thornton, where are the napkins?" He jumped to get four cloth napkins, but Priscilla didn't miss a beat. "It must have been hectic for you the past several days, Hilda."

All three heads jerked to give Priscilla a look of total disbelief. Winn said, "Mother, my wife's name is Hope, as you very well know."

With exaggerated theatrics, Priscilla's hand fluttered to her mouth as she looked at Hope. "Oh, I am sorry. This is all so new since Winn never mentioned a wife." Then with a smug air of conquest, she continued despite the distressed looks around the table. "Hope, I'm sure your personal time has been limited. Miss Abigail just down the street is an excellent beauty operator; she can give you a becoming hair style. I can make an appointment for you."

Winn looked at his plate and shook his head. His mother went on. "My husband tells me you worked at a newspaper office. A working woman cannot possibly achieve expectations of both a job and a wife. Since you are married now, surely you have no aspirations of continuing to work outside the home?"

Winn stared at his mother in amazement. *She did neither—never worked, yet seldom achieved expectations of Daddy or us. I knew she could be cruel, but I'm surprised how quickly she has begun to belittle Hope.*

Hope was puzzled as to a response. *Was that a statement or a question?* Her vision of a fairy tale continued. *This is like sitting before Cinderella's wicked stepmother.* A slow simmer began to take place in the pit of Hope's stomach. *Just keep my mouth shut, don't let my temper boil over like Papa says I do. I haven't even been here a day and I can already sympathize with Winn and Eddie and poor Daddy Prichard.*

As if she said nothing condescending to her new daughter-in-law, Priscilla turned her attention to Winn. "Now, Winston, perhaps you can tell me why you didn't see the need to inform us of your marriage."

He clenched his teeth while finding the ceiling extremely interesting.

After what seemed like minutes to Hope, she couldn't stand the silence and said, "It was just that we decided so quickly and all. He knew a trip to Hempstead for the wedding would be too difficult for you. He was so busy with work and . . ."

Winn shifted the position of his leg on the chair next to him. "Hope, I can answer for myself. Mother, I think you know very well why." His voice was without feeling. "I was going to tell you about it, just not for a while."

Priscilla daintily sliced her small piece of ham. "I see. I take it there was a ceremony of sorts in . . . where did you say . . . Hamstead? Is that where you live, Hope?"

Winn strived to keep his response calm. "Hempstead, Mother, that's where she lived; she lives with me now. Yes, there was a very nice wedding with a small gathering of her family in their home. The service was performed by the minister of her Pentecostal Church."

His mother's fork froze mid-way to her mouth. "Pentecostal?" She was about to make a remark, but saw the warning look on Winn's face and refrained. Clearing her throat, she gazed at Hope. "I suppose you wear no lip rouge or color on your cheeks because you attend a church that frowns on adornment, is that right?"

Hope's cheeks needed no rouge at that moment, this grilling was beyond anything she imagined. She could let barbs pass about herself personally and her appearance, but not her church. She saw that Winn was about to say something, but she beat him to it this time. "Mrs. Prichard, it's obvious you don't care for my looks or my denomination. Some don't agree with Paul's teaching in the New Testament about women keeping themselves free of adornment. But it's not my place to judge one way or the other and to my way of thinking, it's not yours either."

Priscilla slowly set her fork on her plate and opened her mouth to speak, but Hope was not finished. "I've been taught to look past outward appearances and give a body a chance." Her voice escalated with each word and again Winn thought of what Hollis told him about her when she is riled. Hope pushed away from the table and stood. "If I must stand up to some kind of scrutiny or comparison, I have to tell you I'm proud of where I came from and make no apologies for my upbringing or my beliefs."

Hope threw her napkin on the table. "If you're angry about not being invited to the wedding, I apologize. But obviously you are displeased with me for things I have no control over."

She twirled around to leave and turned back. "By the way, my church frowns on bobbed hair, but I don't think Jesus minds it. In fact, he might even think I don't need a beauty operator." She hurried to the bathroom, closed the door and stared at her flushed face in the mirror.

Priscilla was stone faced. Eddie had been open-mouthed throughout the entire encounter. When Hope left the room, he covered his mouth with his napkin, restraining laughter. Winn momentarily forgot his leg pain as he listened to his wife express most superbly all the things he had wanted to say.

Priscilla's words were biting. "Well, I must say, your Hope is overly sensitive, a sure sign of low self-esteem." There was a snicker across the table. "Edward Thornton, how dare you consider this situation humorous."

Winn wiped his mouth. "Mother, there's no reason to be critical of Hope. If you could possibly carry on a normal conversation without finding fault, you would see she's genuine and intelligent. She loves me and I love her, which should mean something to you."

"I was merely making a suggestion which I thought would be helpful. As a mother, I am naturally curious about the ceremony since I was not included." Priscilla patted the sides of her mouth with her napkin. "Lunch has become unpleasant, Winston. Your wife's temper has given me a loss of appetite." She gave Eddie an expectant look, and he hurried to pull out her chair. With head held high, her backbone was a steel rod as she walked toward her room.

On his mother's departure, Winn realized he was still clenching his teeth. He opened his mouth wide to relax his jaw. "Whew, it's going to be a rough month ahead." When he reached for the crutches, his brother held out a helping hand. "I'm okay Eddie, thanks anyway." *Eddie takes the brunt of Mother's verbal abuse. He's kind-hearted, so much like Daddy. His outward appearance ages, but his childlike qualities remain.* He patted Eddie on the shoulder. "All you're doing for Hope and me is appreciated."

The warm gesture was a soothing balm for a soul which sponged accolades. "I'm glad to do all I can, Winston."

Hope peered into the kitchen. *I guess she's gone back to her room, glad I didn't meet her in the hallway. Wonder if Winn is upset with the way I talked to her? He's right. This is going to really be difficult.* She stepped to the table and stacked the dishes.

Eddie said, "I can get this, Hope. You go help Winston get back in bed."

"Eddie, I'm sorry about making a fuss." She wasn't really sorry about the things she said to Priscilla, but she regretted losing her temper in the presence of Eddie who exhibited a sensitive spirit.

The man's features could turn from a smile to sadness instantly. "I'm sorry Mother said those things to you. She's really not mean."

Such a forgiving nature. "I know she's not mean. How could she be? She raised two wonderful sons."

Eddie's face transformed with a big self-conscious smile. At a loss for words, he nodded and went about his chore.

Winn was already in bed when she returned and closed the bedroom door. "There now, are you comfortable?"

He lifted his leg onto a stack of pillows and gave a little groan. "As comfortable as I'm going to get for a while, it appears." He pulled her arm to sit beside him. "Hope, I tried to brace you to be thick-skinned around Mother. She has always found fault with everyone and everything. Heck, if she went to Egypt, she'd complain about the shape of the Pyramids."

Winn's levity made her smile. "But, I don't understand her. She . . . she's so crabby. I never imagined a person could be so unpleasant." She rubbed the back of her neck. "She leaves hateful droppings all around—as awful as the droppings in Mama's henhouse if you know what I mean."

"That's one way to put it. I've learned to let her snide remarks and insinuations roll off my back. But I won't stand for her picking you apart, Sugar."

"But why? Why is she like that? She has a beautiful place to live and it's obvious Daddy Prichard cares a great deal for her. Eddie seems more like her servant than a son."

Winn rubbed her arm. "It must be hard for you to suddenly be placed in this situation. I've lived it and know her history. Mother was raised in a wealthy family who had servants. She wasn't interested in learning the simplest things about running a household."

"Or being kind. Just because she was rich isn't any excuse."

"You and I know that, but I'm trying to give you a little of her background. She's always acted like God made her superior." He laid his head back on the pillow and sighed. "My grandfather spoiled her, especially after the death of her older sister. After that, he gave his three children everything they could possibly want, but her brother and sister, Uncle Foster and Aunt Katy, are the sweetest, most giving people you could meet. I don't know why Mother's so different. Her mother was a kind Christian who tried to instill godly values in her children—it just didn't penetrate to Mother's heart."

Hope stood to straighten the room. "Your mother must've been born with a critical spirit. Do you think she knows the Lord at all?"

"Mother's critical all right, but I think she does believe. Years ago, when we left Georgia, she had a vision of Jesus."

This got Hope's attention; she moved to sit beside him again. "A vision?"

"Or a dream, but it was very real to her. Mother was worried about leaving behind the graves of all the loved ones who had died—her parents, sister, Robert, and the two babies. For some reason, she felt attached there as if she would be deserting them. It was night time, we were on the train and I had been sleeping. I woke to hear Mother tell Daddy she saw Jesus at the train station."

Hope took a quick breath of astonishment. "She was sure it was Jesus?"

"I never heard her speak more positively and the description was beautiful. She saw him dressed in flowing white at the train door and then she saw our deceased family members. They were happy and rushing toward Jesus who was waving them on board." Winn's voice was edged with emotion. "I've never told this to anyone for fear of ridicule, it's very personal." He wiped a hand across his face. "Anyway, Mother said Grandma was carrying one of my baby brothers, and her sister who had died was holding the other one. My grandfather was hurrying toward Jesus with his arm around Robert." There was a catch in his throat at the memory of his favorite brother.

Hope nodded with misty eyes. "God was showing her that believers are with Him and are always in our heart no matter where they're buried."

Winn studied his wife, seeing inner beauty shine clearly on her face. "You're a perceptive and understanding little gal."

"Well, that story gives me less understanding of her. The Lord loves her and consoled her at the time she needed assurance. If I had an experience like that, I'd be an angel the rest of my life." She stood and put her hands on her hips.

Her sudden change of mood amused him. "In my eyes you are an angel."

"No, I'm not an angel. I lose my temper." She stooped to pick up his neckties still stuffed in a paper sack. "I have to apologize to her."

Winn shook his head which was flashing warning signs in spades. "Oh no, face-offs always end in Mother's favor with her opponent a defeated boxer down for the count. No, Hope, you don't have to do that. Just forget about it."

"I can't. I don't like having anything go unsaid. Pretending everything is all right is like smoothing cake icing over a mud pie, it's still ugly underneath. I can't forget about it."

"You might be opening yourself up for more mudslinging than you can make pies out of, Hope."

What an absurd thing it is to pass over all the valuable parts of a man and fix our attention on his infirmities.
—Joseph Addison

26

Later, when Hope went to look for Priscilla, Winn was relieved to have an opportunity to indulge in his stash which was getting low. She found Eddie in the living room thoughtfully looking at a book and holding a pencil.

"Is your Mother in her room, Eddie?"

"Yes, she's resting." He held up his book. "Do you like crossword puzzles?"

She sat on the sofa next to his chair. "I don't know, I've never tried to do one." Her mind was on one track, and she didn't want to be derailed by a puzzle. "Do you suppose I could speak with her?"

Worry wound its way around Eddie's eyes. "Mother doesn't like to be disturbed from her afternoon nap."

"Oh no, I wouldn't want to interrupt her rest." *It's five o'clock, how long can her naps last?*

"Crosswords are very popular, there's one in the paper every day. I want to do more, so I got this book. Look, it's filled with puzzles."

Hope couldn't help but notice how enthusiasm lit up his eyes and she pretended to be interested. Winn hobbled into the room leaning heavily on his crutches. Hope said, "What are you doing out of bed?"

"I want to persuade you to let sleeping tigers lie."

Her posture held determination. "I told you, I'm not likely to do that."

He collapsed in the nearest chair. "Well, I won't let you face the tiger alone."

Eddie saw Priscilla standing in the doorway. "Did you have a good nap, Mother?"

"I did until I heard Hope's voice." She portrayed one of great suffering, yet somehow bravely bearing the burdens set upon her. Walking to her wingback chair, she patted her hair although it was perfectly in place. "What were you referring to about a tiger, Winston?"

He pointed to Eddie's puzzle book. "Just a clue in his crossword, Mother."

His answer surprised Hope. *He sure came up with that lie quickly.*

Winn changed the subject. "Since I didn't have a chance to tell you about my visit to Dr. Babcock this morning, I can answer your questions now. He did say the stitches could be removed in a week or so and I ought to be able to get back to work."

Hope leaned forward. "No, Winn, the doctor said the stitches might be removed in ten days. And he didn't say you could go back to work immediately after they're removed. You're badly bruised, and your muscles need time to heal."

He put his foot up on the coffee table. "Well, we'll see."

Priscilla was ramrod erect and frowned at his bandaged foot on the spotless table. "Edward Thornton, get a cloth to protect the table."

Edward jumped up. "Okay, Mother, I'll be right back."

Winn said, "For crying out loud, Mother, how much damage can gauze do?"

It was one of those infrequent times Priscilla preferred not to respond. After an uncomfortable moment of silence, Hope cleared her throat. "Mrs. Prichard, I wish to apologize for my outburst today."

Priscilla picked up a handsome accordion fan from the end table and flipped it open. Fanning her face, she looked expectantly at Hope waiting for her to grovel.

Sweat broke out on Winn's forehead. *I hate confrontations with her. She has never accepted fault. Guess that's why Daddy developed a passive attitude toward her.*

Edward returned. He gingerly lifted his brother's foot and placed a folded towel beneath it with the care of a mother laying her newborn in his crib. Returning to the chair, he picked up his book. After a few chilly moments of silence, Eddie said, "Winston, I need a nine-letter word for narcissistic."

His brother thought for a moment. "How about egotistic?"

Eddie grabbed his pencil. "Let me see if that fits."

Winn looked at his Mother. "Oh, it fits all right." Priscilla didn't miss his insinuation and slowly turned her head toward Winn with a face that took on the appearance of a fist.

With the intent of preventing any more unpleasantness, Hope said, "Mrs. Prichard, I was offended by your comments about my church and guess my temper got a little hot. Papa says I speak before I should sometimes and usually regret it." Seeing no change in Priscilla's expression, she went on. "Soo . . . that's what happened this morning. I'll try not to lose my temper again."

Priscilla stopped fanning. "I encourage you to keep your temper in check Hope, it is quite unseemly."

Hope's neck blotched with anger. *I fully understand what Winn meant when he told his daddy that his mother makes him crazy.*

Winn turned to his mother and grimaced as a pain shot through his leg. "Mother, Hope had every right to lose her temper, anyone would. You criticized her for not wearing a made-up face, you said her hair needed fixing, you even called her by the wrong name, and you insinuated her church didn't meet your standards."

Priscilla couldn't have been more shocked if he'd slapped her. "I said no such things."

Quietly, Edward said, "Yes, you did, Mother."

At that moment Frank entered the living room; their lively discussion had prevented them from hearing him arrive. Before seeing her husband, Priscilla said, "I have to defend myself from the three of you now?"

Frank went to his wife and gave her a kiss on the cheek. "Well, what's going on? All of you look like an editor without a front page story at press time." He gave a little laugh, but it didn't ease the palpable tension.

Winn spoke first. "Hello, Daddy. We were just having a little discussion about some words that were exchanged at noon. It's all over now. At least, I hope it is." He looked from Priscilla to Hope and back again.

Waving the fan, his mother turned her face away. Hope wanted to sprout wings and fly out of this suffocating cocoon of unpleasantness. "Hello, Daddy Prichard, come sit down. I think I'll get us all a drink of water. I know I can use something cool."

Edward stood. "I can chip some ice from the block the iceman brought this afternoon."

Hope smiled at him. "That's even better, I'll help you."

Frank studied the all-too-familiar frown on his wife's face. The once lovely features he had fallen in love with were now a memory difficult to recall. "I've only been gone for the afternoon and come home to a dispute, obviously more than a little discussion."

Priscilla was silent, perched on the fencepost of argument, a misunderstood and mistreated matriarch.

Winn's leg was throbbing. "Daddy, Mother was pretty pointed in some derogatory remarks toward Hope at lunch today. Hope was upset and had some retorts that . . . come to think of it, were pretty humorous."

Priscilla found her voice, and it was not pretty. "They certainly were not humorous, they were ignorant and childish."

In the kitchen, Eddie cut slices of pound cake. Hope carried the glasses of ice water on a tray. In the hall, she heard Priscilla's comments and stopped—too angry to enter the room.

Frank said, "Now Priscilla . . ."

"You weren't here Frank, you have no idea how she lashed out at me." Her head swiveled toward Winn. "Oh Winston, why didn't you try and make amends with Darlene? She was the one for you, not some backward girl from the sticks."

"Mother, you don't know what you're saying."

Hope didn't want to hear any more, and it was all she could do to balance the tray as she walked into the living room. "I think it will take more than the ice water to cool down the way I feel right now. Mrs. Prichard, I said I would try not to lose my temper, but your attitude toward me fuels it beyond my control." To her amazement, she set the tray on the coffee table, without spilling a drop. "I understand why Winn didn't invite you to our wedding; you would have spoiled it." Her brown eyes were unflinching as the woman looked stricken. Hope's voice was fluent with anger as the heavy artillery of her words was shot with accuracy. "You ignored my apology and have been rude to me from the get go, which I consider 'unseemly' to use your description of me."

Her eyes were tearful, but her face was set with frustration as she looked at Frank. "I'm sorry, Daddy Prichard, but I refuse to be belittled and compared to Winn's first wife. I may be from the sticks, but my mama is a loving person and taught me to be kind to others." The sobs yearned to burst forth, but she willed them back.

Her father-in-law went to her side and embraced her shaking shoulders. He felt like a man whose young pup had been attacked by his old hound. He had to save the pup, but cared too much for his faithful companion to whip. Winn had all he could take physically and emotionally. Fumbling with his crutches, he managed to stand. Frank released his hold on Hope; she walked beside Winn as they left the room.

Eddie met them in the hall. "You want a piece of cake?"

Winn managed to say, "No, thank you, Eddie. Maybe later."

His brother stood for a moment in the hall holding a plate of cake slices. Surmising the party that never got started was over, he silently returned to the kitchen.

No one can make you feel inferior without your consent.
—Eleanor Roosevelt

27

All was silent the remainder of the evening. Eddie perceived the need for Winn and Hope to be alone and made a supper tray for them to eat in their room.

The next morning, the last person Hope thought she would see in the kitchen was Priscilla. She was further shocked by Priscilla's cheery countenance.

"Good morning, Hope. I'm putting on a pot of pinto beans. They soaked all night, and I like to get them going early and simmer them low with a ham bone." She moved around like a little squirrel; scampering, stopping for a moment and looking about, before skittering across the kitchen again.

Eddie and Frank were seated at the table. Frank smiled. "Come join us, Hope."

Pausing at the doorway, Hope blinked with astonishment. "Good morning." Half expecting to step on a land mine, she gingerly entered the room. "I uh . . . was going to make a tray for Winn. He didn't sleep much last night and doesn't feel like coming to the table."

Edward rose from his chair and removed his dishes. "Come sit and have some coffee; I'll make a tray for him."

"All right, thank you." She was dying to know about Priscilla's drastic change of mood.

Frank could almost hear the questions rolling around in Hope's head. "Priscilla loves to cook every now and then. I always look forward to it." He walked to the stove and poured another cup of coffee. "I'm sorry to hear Winston had a restless night. I'll see him for a minute before I leave for work."

"Of course, I'll be right behind you." Hoping what he had to say concerned Priscilla, she grabbed two cups of coffee and hurriedly left the kitchen. Over her shoulder she said, "I'll be back for the tray, Eddie."

Looking expectantly at her father-in-law, Hope handed Winn a cup of coffee and sat hers on the bedside table.

Frank spoke softly. "Hope, my wife is a complicated individual. She changes moods like a chameleon changes colors, expecting others to adapt to her whims. After living with her for over forty years, I haven't figured if it's planned strategy or a subconscious thing. I'm sorry to say she has a tendency to test people or see how they handle being pushed."

Winn said, "She's been testing Hope ever since we got here. What's she up to now, the hurt, silent act?"

Hope looked toward the laundry room to make sure they weren't being overheard and then closed the door. "No, she's in there like nothing ever happened, cooking beans as pleasant as a bluebird."

"You're putting me on."

"No, Winston, she's right." Frank looked at Hope. "Most people shrink with Priscilla's disparaging words, but you stood up to her when you charged right in with that tray of water. I thought you might dump it on her." He chuckled. "Last night when I questioned her about what had taken place, she refused to tell me. And believe me, if she doesn't want to talk, she's a mummy. After a while when I was almost asleep, she said, 'that's a strong-willed girl'."

Hope stood akimbo. "That's it? That's all she said?"

Winn put his good foot on the floor leaving the injured one on the bed. "That was a lot coming from Mother. I think you may have passed her exam, Hope. She found out you're not easily intimidated and maybe she'll let up on you a little. But not completely if I know her."

Frank nodded. "Throughout our marriage, Priscilla's occasional good days give me a glimpse of the girl I fell in love with. Waiting for those infrequent times has enabled me to deal with the unreasonable woman she can be." His voice became husky with emotion. "Hope, you're family now, and I am speaking with complete honesty. You're exactly the wife Winston needs. I think my son and all of us are blessed to have you in this family."

Her admiration and love for her father-in-law was growing as strong as her dislike of her mother-in-law. She gave him a hug. "Thank you, Daddy Prichard. I can't tell you how much that means to me."

Winn nodded. "Me too, Daddy. I knew it would be tough dealing with Mother. But now maybe Hope understands a little more about her and that will make it easier for the degrading comments to fly out the window."

Frank reached for the door knob. "I need to get to work. Let me know what Dr. Babcock has to say." He opened the door, then turned back and said softly, "Try to block any interference from Mother until I get home, Winston."

"That's a tall order for a man in my condition." He tilted his head toward the injured leg and added, "It's a tall order for a man in the best of condition."

Hope was quiet. Winn knew her pretty well by now and waited for a revelation or a question. After a few moments it was the latter, a question he dreaded.

"Why did your mother like Darlene?"

He sighed and rubbed the thigh of his injured leg, it seemed to help defuse the level of aching. "She liked her because Darlene kowtowed to her. She played a game of her own to make Mother think she was obeying the rules of the game Mother plays with people."

"Well, that's confusing."

"You're right; I'll try to give you a better explanation. I brought Darlene here before we married and she bowed and scraped until Mother was convinced she could control her. Mother nagged me to marry her so she could have someone to do her bidding like she does with Eddie. Darlene all but kissed the hem of Mother's dress." He ran his fingers through his hair and shook his head. "Mother only saw her a few times and never realized the kind of devious person she is."

"But doesn't she know what Darlene did?"

"I don't know if Daddy told her, but even so, Mother has a way of not hearing what she doesn't want to accept. It's like there's a radio in her head that shuts down if information doesn't suit the way she wants to receive it." Sighing with resignation, he looked into his wife's fresh, honest face. "Darlene didn't have the backbone you have, Hope. She was dishonest, even with me. To answer your question simply, Mother thought she would be able to control Darlene, that's why she liked her."

"Winn, you must've had a hard time growing up with such a strange mother." She sat on the bed beside him holding her cup of coffee. "One day she's bad-tempered and helpless, the next day she acts like a different person, perky and going about the business of cooking."

He took a long drink of his coffee and set the cup on the bedside table. "I'd probably be an eccentric lunatic if it weren't for Edna Mae."

"I think you mentioned her before. She was the housekeeper, wasn't she?"

"Housekeeper, cook, and nursemaid to Mother and to each one of us boys. When I think back on it, I have to believe God sent her to us. She started working for my folks before I was born and was like a member of the family. Daddy said Mother continually plastered her to the wall with criticism and wouldn't even allow her to come through the front door."

"Was she a colored lady?"

"Not on your life. Mother wouldn't tolerate a colored person tending her house. Remember, she's prejudiced on every count. No, Edna Mae was white, but Mother considered her a servant who mustn't be seen entering her employer's home by the front entrance. But good ole Edna Mae put a smile on her face and came and went through the back door for . . . I guess almost twenty years."

"She must've been a remarkable woman to put up with your mother all that time."

He nodded. "Indeed. Daddy told me he asked her one time after she had been there a while how she tolerated Mother. She told him she asks God every morning for His love for Mother. Edna also said it isn't flesh and blood we fight against, but principalities of darkness, so we have to put on the armor of God and use His word as a sword. Daddy laughed about how Edna Mae picked up a big wooden spoon and swung it around like a swordsman. She had a way of making her point."

Hope's eyes lit up. "Oh, that's in Ephesians. It talks about the breastplate of righteousness and the shield of faith as protection against the fiery darts of the wicked. What a wise housekeeper you had."

"Edna Mae was a godly woman; she taught me many things that have stayed with me all my life. The times Mother was indifferent to something I wanted to show her or was excited about, it was Edna Mae who took interest and encouraged me. She helped me to understand we all have our peculiarities and faults. We must ask God to reveal how we can change and improve. She truly believed we can with His help."

Winn seemed more relaxed as he continued. "As I got older, I realized Mother concentrates on the faults of others so much she can't look at herself to even know she needs to change and the sky would fall if someone told her." Rubbing his leg, he went on. "After many years, Mother finally respected and loved Edna Mae, but guarded against revealing it."

Hope was thoughtful. "So there's a chance I can get along with your mother if I ask God to give me His love toward her. Wonder how many years it will take?" There was a light tapping and Hope opened the door for Eddie who was holding a tray with a bowl of steaming oatmeal and toast. "Oh, I was going to get that, Eddie."

"That's okay, Hope." He set the tray on the dresser. "How are you feeling, Winston?" He fluffed the pillows against the headboard for his brother to lean on.

"I'm fine as frog hair."

Eddie laughed, "I haven't heard that in a long time."

Hope said, "Is that some kind of joke between the two of you?"

Winn positioned himself against the pillows. "Grandpa used to say he was 'fine as frog hair' and then ask if I had ever seen hair on a frog. I'd shake my head, no. Then he'd say 'that's because it's so fine'." The brothers laughed as Eddie set the tray on Winn's lap.

Hope smiled at the two of them and sat at the foot of the bed. She was glad they were there in spite of their mother's odd behavior. "Eddie, Winn told me you have a paper route."

"I did, but Mother said she needs for me to stay near her, so I had to give it up."

Winn was enjoying the hot cereal. "Hope, you haven't eaten yet, have you?"

"No, I'll get something in a few minutes. That oatmeal smells good, did you cook it Eddie?"

"Yes, I did. I like to cook."

She was a little miffed that Priscilla made Eddie quit his paper route. "Perhaps you can get a part-time job while I'm here. That is, if you like to get out. I need to keep busy and will be happy to do whatever is needed, the cleaning or washing or cooking."

"Oh no, we send the laundry out and a cleaning lady comes in twice a week. Most of the groceries are delivered and Daddy often brings supper home from Fairfield's Café."

Winn nodded as he gulped his now tepid coffee. "I imagine Daddy arranges it all like clockwork, as usual."

"Yes, but Mother keeps him busy looking for new cleaning ladies after she runs them off. The one we have now has been here twice and may return tomorrow."

"Like Hope said, Eddie, you need to get out more even if you don't get a job."

"I like to make things in the shed out back. I attend church on Sunday and study my Bible every day."

Hope stood and reached for Winn's cup for a refill. "Sounds like you keep busy, that's admirable and I also admire how good you are to your mother, Eddie."

He sighed and looked at the floor. "I try, but trying to please her is a tedious pursuit. Sometimes when she holds up in her room, I think of her as a foreign country, walled and remote. I need her, so there is an alliance between us and I strive to abide by her proclamations."

Hope's respect expanded for this unpretentious, oddly intelligent man.

Winn had stopped eating and studied his brother while he spoke so earnestly. "That's profound philosophy you have, Eddie. But you're an important part of her world if you want to use that analogy. Remember what

John Donne wrote, 'no man is an island'? You and Daddy are allies, the only ships that approach her borders and supply her needs. She couldn't get along without you for a day."

Eddie seemed encouraged with his brother's words and nodded. A knock at the door caused Hope to jump. Behind the closed door they heard, "It's Dr. Babcock."

Hope opened the door and the room became smaller with his presence. "Doctor, we've been expecting you."

Feeling the closeness, Eddie said, "I need to see if Mother needs anything. It's good to see you, Doctor." He took Winn's tray and made his way through the laundry room passageway to the kitchen.

Hope watched as the doctor removed the bandage she had carefully applied last night. He was pleased with the leg's healing progress and with Winn's appearance.

Patience is the companion of wisdom.

—Augustine

28

As the weeks passed, Priscilla breezed in and out of her quarters like changing winds, an unpredictable forecast. Some days she presented herself as the chill of winter, the kind of cold that made her breath frosty as she spoke. When angry, she could rage like gales of a hurricane. Only when she was napping did tranquil breezes prevail through the household.

Listening to the *Grand Ole Opry* on the radio in the living room, Priscilla expressed her dislike of Minnie Pearl. She complained when the ice man dripped water on the kitchen floor, and reprimanded the grocery delivery boy's whistling as he came in the back door. Her tirades concerning the poor cleaning woman over trivial matters could develop into daylong diatribes.

Hope found ways to occupy her time. The Prichard's were well-read and she found a good selection of books on the living room shelves. She baked cakes and pies which the men immensely enjoyed. Although Priscilla cleaned her plate, she interjected complaints that the dessert needed more of this or less of that.

Autumn brought cooler days. While evergreens remained constant, some central Texas trees became bare of leaves without the grace to give warning by changing color. Some afternoons, Winn and Hope donned warm clothing to sit in Adirondack chairs in the yard. It was a relief when the splints were removed, and he could bend his leg. Hope attended church service with Frank and Eddie on Sunday mornings; she wasn't surprised when her mother-in-law didn't join them.

Edward became the means for Winn's liquor supply. Winn didn't want to hear input from his daddy about the evils of drink and saw no other way than to regretfully take advantage of his brother's willing nature as his undercover delivery boy.

Eddie did it without protest, but he disliked riding the bus to the seedy part of town to locate a backstreet dealer. He was concerned about his brother's drinking but rationalized that whiskey had its merits if it helped dull his pain. Most of all, he hated hiding anything from his parents and Hope and prayed he wouldn't be caught.

A few days before Thanksgiving, Winn sat in the living room with Frank after supper. "Daddy, I've been thinking about Hope and how long it's been since she's seen her folks. Would it be all right if I borrow the car for a few days while you're off work to take her to Hempstead for Thanksgiving?"

"That would be a thoughtful thing for you to do, Son. Do you feel up to it?"

"It's just walking or standing for any length of time that puts a strain on my leg. I can bend it fine now."

Frank set his book aside. "I'll be off by noon on Wednesday and won't go back to work until Monday. Of course you're welcome to take the car. Hope deserves a break, and I know she must miss her family."

Hope threw her arms around Winn's neck when he surprised her about the trip. "Oh, Winn, it will be the best Thanksgiving ever." Placing her hands on each side of his face, she kissed him. "I miss them so much. I hope Fayella and Buford will be there. Iris and Delbert always come, and I'll get to see their baby. I can't wait to see Betsy and Pearl. Thank you, Winn."

He laughed. "Well now, I think you like surprises."

"I do when it's one like this."

Fayella and Buford were there when Hope and Winn arrived on Thanksgiving Eve. It was a grand reunion.

On Thanksgiving Day, the Davidson's house was overflowing with family and joy, quite a contrast to the Prichard household. The table was filled with Octavia's home cooking when she called everyone into the kitchen. "Now y'all come on, gather round. Squeeze in where you can and let's thank the good Lord for His bounty."

Iris, holding their baby boy, stood beside Delbert. Buford put his arm around Fayella who had the appearance of a young girl. Winn managed to make his way to Hope who was standing by Mama. Pearl held her mother's skirt while Betsy snuggled between Winn and Hope.

Hollis leaned heavily on the doorway. Octavia stood on tiptoe to search him out. Assured he was close by, she began her prayer. "Sweet Jesus, thank You for this wonderful day. I'm mighty grateful for the table full of food, but most of all I'm grateful for our children all together with us."

Winn felt the true bond of family during those moments with Hope leaning against him; Betsy tucked close, and his mother-in-law speaking from her heart. He was always struck by her sincerity as she thanked God for each family member including her first grandbaby. He was humbled when she mentioned his name with pure love.

"I want to give my thanks for Your healing hand upon Winn so he could bring Hope here to be with us. I lift his family up to You, and may they be blessed with health and happiness. In the precious name of Jesus I pray. Amen."

When they returned to San Antonio, the weather was overcast, rainy, and cold. Sometimes Hope had a sixth sense about things. As she felt the chill of winter set in, a cold uneasiness flitted through her daily thoughts. Hope couldn't shake the feeling of foreboding, but she dismissed it as adjusting from the joyous visit with her family then returning to cope with her mother-in-law.

Every house where love abides and friendship is a guest, is
surely home, and home, sweet home, for there the heart can rest.
—Henry Van Dyke

THE RICHLAND RECORD

More Than a Newspaper—a Community Service
A Weekly Publication Serving the Greater Richland Area
Richland, Texas   Thursday, November 27, 1969
Winston Randolph Prichard, Editor and Publisher

News and Views of a Tactless Texan

Looking at the calendar, I realize this edition of the *Record* will arrive in your home the day after Thanksgiving. I sincerely hope you are still enjoying the savory leftovers at your table of God's provision for our country's annual celebration of thanks. More importantly, I hope you were and possibly are still surrounded by family, friends, and good neighbors.

America's first gathering by the Pilgrims to thank the Heavenly Father for a bountiful harvest is reported to be in 1621. George Washington proclaimed the first nationwide Thanksgiving Day celebration in America November 26, 1789, "as a day of public thanksgiving and prayer to be observed by acknowledging with grateful hearts the many and signal favors of Almighty God." Finally in 1941, President Franklin D. Roosevelt signed a resolution of Congress to officially observe the fourth Thursday in November as the traditional celebration of harvest.

My first memories of turkey and all the trimmings are in Georgia with Aunt Katy and Uncle John Webster. On that special day Aunt Katy was up early, humming as she prepared the Thanksgiving meal in her pristine blue and white kitchen. Uncle John hired a horse and carriage to travel across the cobblestone streets of Atlanta to pick up a destitute, invalid widow and her two children. He was a doctor and gave medical attention to the family without fee. Sharing the meal that day with the grateful little family made a lasting impression upon me of what Thanksgiving really means. Food sated their hunger, but it was evident that the Christian hand of friendship filled their hearts and uplifted their spirit.

Another memorable day of thanks for me was my first holiday with my wife, Hope and her family in Hempstead. Mama Davidson's cooking was known for miles around. There was always room for a crowd at her modest table, but nothing about her portions were modest. Before meals, she said the most heartfelt prayers I've ever heard. Before you took a bite of food, you knew you were in the presence of a woman who truly knew the One who provides for our every need.

Again, that's -30- until next week's column.

29

First Week of December 1928—

"There's a job over in Colt." Winn was sitting at the breakfast table reading a publication trade paper that Frank brought home.

Hope was at the counter rolling out dough for a pecan pie crust. "Where's Colt?"

Managing without his crutches, he stood and limped to stand near her. "It's in West Texas. I've been reading about it. Since a wildcatter struck oil a year or so ago, people have been flocking there in droves."

She picked up the dough and skillfully laid it in the pie pan, and then patted it in place. "I haven't heard you sound this excited since we saw the Al Jolson movie."

As she trimmed the dough and fluted the edges, Winn continued telling her about the town. "Colt is a boomtown now; we could be there at the beginning of something big. The newspaper is advertising for a linotype operator. I better call before someone else grabs it."

His urgency caught her off guard. "But Winn, are you sure you're strong enough to go back to work?"

"I'm strong enough to pace around this house like a caged animal. Ah, Hope, I can't loaf anymore, especially when we could be in a boomtown that's bulging with growth and opportunity."

A nervous feeling inched around the edges of her better judgment. "I thought we were going back to Liberty. Mr. Spencer said he could always use a good linotype man."

"I wouldn't be happy in Liberty knowing I might have a chance to start my own paper in a boomtown, Sugar. A gusher means lots of people and businesses and money—the things a newspaper needs. There's no telling how big Colt will grow, maybe large enough for two newspapers." He headed for the phone in the hallway. "I'll get a hold of the long distance operator."

Standing by the kitchen counter staring after him, an unwelcome heaviness draped around her shoulders. *Lord, guide him to make the right decision about this.*

Colt, Texas—

Hope was queasy as she stepped off the bus onto the dirt street by the Colt bus station. It had been a grueling trek starting on the San Antonio Southern Railway to Fort Worth, where they transferred to the Texas-New Mexico line as far as Odessa. The railway to Colt had yet to be laid; they made the last leg of the trip by bus. Each mile had been an endured misery for her. Suspecting she was pregnant before they left San Antonio, she was sure of it now. Winn was ecstatic with the news of becoming a father.

Hope was jostled by a man reeking of alcohol as they moved onto a crudely constructed boardwalk. The semblance of a bus depot was next to a sleazy-looking establishment. She stood with Winn while waiting for Mr. Gentry, the owner of the *Colt Messenger,* who was to meet them there.

In the street, a parade of trucks carrying lumber and equipment of every sort streamed along, angling right and left as the maze of vehicles provided an opening. There was no distinction of driving rules or indication of lanes. Pedestrians became moving targets as they darted between wagons, automobiles, trucks, and horse-drawn carts.

The bubble of enthusiasm was still afloat for Winn; to him the noise, cars, and people meant the possibility of advancement toward his dream. Wrapped in flying dust and gasoline fumes, only Hope's will kept her afoot. The determination to stand by Winn's side was still intact even after she found the bottle of liquor tucked in his valise before leaving San Antonio.

It happened when he was in the bathroom at his parent's house. She picked up the bag to pack; it didn't feel empty. In the inside pocket, she discovered the contents that had been hidden there. There was no denying it when she confronted him. Her disappointment and anger was almost insurmountable, but Winn convinced her it had been the elixir that made the last few months tolerable for him.

Waiting on the boardwalk, Hope's exhaustion was rising to a point impossible to rebuff when a car halted immediately in front of them. It brought a whirlwind of road dirt. She turned aside and then waved the thick air in front of her face.

A man jumped out and hurried around the vehicle. "You must be Winn Prichard." He extended a hand to Winn and pumped it up and down while looking at Hope. "And this must be Mrs. Prichard. You look like a breath of fresh air or I like to say an air of fresh breath."

She plastered a smile on her face hoping it would suffice expectations. *If I look like anything fresh, the dust has surely affected his eyesight.*

Winn gave him the pleasant face of self-assurance. "That's right, we're the Prichards. I take it you're Mr. Gentry."

"Right as rain, which we could use about now. But call me Howard." The man grabbed the scuffed suitcase sitting at Hope's feet and opened the trunk of his car. "Let's get to the cafe and have some chow. Is this all the luggage you have?"

"We shipped a few boxes which will probably be here tomorrow." Winn lifted his bag into the back of the new model Pontiac Landau. "Much obliged, Howard. Lunch sounds pretty good."

The man opened the front passenger door for Hope, but she stepped aside. "Oh, thank you, but I'll sit in the back. I'm sure you two have things to discuss." Wanting to delay the need to join in the conversation, she was more interested in viewing the circus being played out in the boisterous street.

"All right then, we always want to make the missus happy. That right, Winn?" He was a pudgy man with a ruddy but friendly face. Ginger-colored spots dotted his balding head.

Taking the opportunity to catch her breath, Hope settled in the back seat of the luxurious automobile. Watching the array sweeping pass the window, her comfort level was a minus ten. She was an alien amid humanity of every description marching to a drummer beating to the rhythm of greed. Hope turned her face away when they rode by scantily clad women standing in a doorway.

The café was crowded even though it was well after the noon hour. The men launched right into conversation about the overnight population explosion and expansion of the newspaper. Hope fought nausea with sips of cola and managed to nibble at the blue plate special. Feeling like a timid child who was bullied into taking an unreasonable dare, she might as well have been a nameless face in the crowd to the two men.

Hope stopped eating; her resolve to maintain the appearance of well-being was an effort. When she was able to get a word in, she said, "Mr. Gentry, I'm surprised to see places that look a bit suspicious of selling alcohol. Doesn't the Prohibition law apply here?"

"Well, Hope, I'm sorry to say that there are ways of getting around it, especially when there are under-the-table dealings with corrupt law officials. That's why the *Messenger* is so important. In my editorials I'm fighting to light the darkness that has spread throughout Colt with the invasion of racketeering."

Hope was appalled. "But, Mr. Gentry isn't that dangerous? I mean, from what I've already seen, it seems like the town is completely overrun with all manner of... of unruly behavior." Remembering accounts she had read about upright citizens being attacked when they strive to bring about decency, she was worried. "Won't there be opposition, even violence, toward the paper?"

Howard was not about to admit there had been threats, but dismissed her questions. "Oh, you mustn't concern yourself. It's not as bad as all that." He went on to extol the importance of the Colt newspaper capturing the nation's attention by continually sending news of the oil boom over the wire. "Just think of it, Winn, we're sitting on a keg of dynamite here, things are exploding all around us. People are coming in from everywhere and not just oil field workers. There are new businesses cropping up as we speak, and that means more advertising for the paper."

Mr. Gentry spoke the language Winn wanted to hear, and his enthusiasm was almost enough to make Hope forget her observations. The editor paid the cashier, and the threesome went on their way. Howard pointed out construction sites and proposed ventures in the settlement. "My wife says to apologize in advance for the poor lodgings available. People are moving in faster than construction can keep up with. The immediate need for building has brought carpenters, plumbers, electricians, and tradesmen from all over the country." He carefully guided his car onto a road which appeared to be carved out as recently as that morning. Hope surveyed a canvas city and wondered if their living quarters might be one of the tents.

Winn had never seen anything like this town which was burgeoning as steady as the car moved along. "I'm amazed, Howard, this looks like an army encampment."

"That it does and it sprung up overnight. I thought you might have to take temporary quarters in one of the settlements. But some shotgun houses were just completed. They went quickly. I was lucky to grab one for you to rent."

He turned onto a narrow dirt lane lined on each side with rectangular dwellings—all alike. Stopping the car, he pointed to one of the rough wood structures. "Here we are."

Midway along the block, workers shouted orders over construction noises of sawing and hammering. Howard and Winn got the suitcases out of the car and headed toward the cracker box of a house. Hope reluctantly followed and stepped inside the one large room, stark and smelling of fresh wood. There was a door in front and back and one window on each side with no plumbing.

Howard set Hope's bag on the plank floor. "Come look out the back." He motioned them to follow and opened the door. "They've only had time to put in one plumbing line straight across the back to the bathhouses you see there." He pointed to small square structures. "Each one is assigned to two houses, so you'll be sharing with the folks next door."

Hope thought it wasn't much better than sharing the outhouse back home with her family. Disappointment indented Winn's face. "Uh, I just assumed we could get a furnished place."

"No such animal 'round these parts, so I took the liberty of putting in an order for a couple of cots for you. They're supposed to be delivered this afternoon."

Hope gazed at Winn with the look of a lost sheep in the wilderness. He was speechless. Disillusionment washed over him as real as if he was standing in a downpour.

Seeing their disappointment, Howard said, "I know. Let's go to my house, I want to introduce you to my wife. We can gather some things to get you through the next few days."

Hope was never afforded much and she was willing to make do, but at this moment she wished in the worse way to be in Mrs. Emerson's comfortable boarding house back in Liberty.

> *Perseverance is not a long race;*
> *it is many short races one after another.*
> —Walter Elliot

30

The Gentry home was located in an older section of town, a distance from the din of confusion. Gertie Gentry was a woman of undetermined age. Her weathered skin gave evidence of many days in the sun while her spry movements could have challenged those of a youngster. As if personally responsible, she apologized profusely about the condition of their town.

"I'm so glad Howard brought you by." One look at Hope and it was apparent to Gertie that the young woman was at the point of complete exhaustion. "Have a seat; I'll be right back with coffee."

Ordinarily Hope would have offered to help, but she took the woman up on her invitation to sit. *Well, it's a relief to see some civility.*

Howard stepped to a desk and picked up a current copy of the *Colt Messenger*. "Here's this week's issue of the paper, Winn. It'll give you some reading material tonight."

Taking the paper, he said, "Speaking of that, I didn't notice an electrical line going to the house."

Gertie came into the room. "Oh no, Howard, they don't even have lights?"

Her husband looked sheepish. "Well, not yet, but I'm told the power company has expanded to just a few streets over. It shouldn't be too long."

Mrs. Gentry set the tray of coffee on the table. "That settles it; you two are not going to stay out there like pioneers with no utilities. You'll stay with us until that makeshift place Howard rented for you is livable."

Winn and Hope protested at the same time, but Hope drowned him out. "Oh no, Mrs. Gentry. I appreciate your kindness, but we'll be fine. I was raised with no conveniences."

Winn nodded. "It'll be like camping. But, I'd be obliged if you could take us to a store to pick up a few essentials on our way back, Howard."

After taking a few sips of her coffee, Gertie set about gathering things for the newcomers. By the time she finished, there were several paper sacks of linens, blankets, food staples, a kerosene lantern, and a tin coffeepot. Hope had seen some women cooking over campfires at the tent settlement and surmised that is what she would have to do as well.

When Howard picked Winn up for work the next morning, his persuasive fervor was still mountain high about the mushrooming town. Winn's thoughts were balanced on a teeter-totter. On the up side, he was hopeful for a future in Colt. Yet the unexpected conditions were revolting. He maintained a positive attitude and interjected appropriate responses in Howard's conversation. The car skirted around objects on rutted roads void of any vegetation in sight.

People emerged from hovels, tents, and vehicles. Howard pointed to a man creeping out of a rusted truck. "Look at that, would you? Like I said, it's lucky I was able to grab that little house for you and Hope."

Winn stared out the window at the piteous sights. He had been restless for new horizons, but his haste appeared to be another huge blunder. *What have I done? I never imagined it would be this primitive. And brown, not even a blade of grass anywhere. Poor Hope, I'm happy we're going to have a baby, but the timing is all wrong.*

Hope met the neighbor on the path to the bath-house. "Hello, guess you're the one we share facilities with. I'm Hope Prichard."

"Hi, Honey. Yep, I'm Dixie Cranston. Me and Donnie just got here yesterday. From what I've seen, we're lucky a friend got the house for us."

They chatted a few minutes until her husband came out of their house. "Hey, Dixie, hustle up your bustle, Babe."

Dixie said, "Hold your horses, Donnie. Come meet our neighbor, Hope. Her husband's name is Winn. They got here yesterday too." The short, thin man ambled toward them and pulled his homely face into a smile. Dixie pushed her long hair back from her face. "Donnie doesn't have to start work 'til tomorrow so he's going to take me to some stores. Lord knows we need a truckload of stuff."

Donnie gave Hope a brief handshake then put an arm around his wife. "Pleased to meet you. She's a talker this one is, but we better get a move on."

Hope stepped away from the couple. "Oh, don't let me detain you. It's very nice to meet you both." *What an unlikely pair, she's so nice looking and tall.*

Holding the nape of her neck, Donnie playfully pulled Dixie along. Laughing, she broke away and scampered toward the car. Before climbing in, she said, "Hey, Hope, why don't you and Winn come over tonight. We can talk about how we're going to survive this god-awful place."

Hope nodded and waved. She stood watching them drive away, her smile departed with them. Crossing her arms, she rubbed her hands up and down the sleeves of the thin sweater. *Hmm, god-awful. There's no such thing. It's either godly or awful. From what I've seen, this place is godless and pure-dee-awful.*

Reaching the bathhouse door, her eyes swept the property around her. *I guess it could be worse. At least I have joyful neighbors.*

Gertie had assured Hope she would be happy to take her shopping. But Hope saw no need to inconvenience Mrs. Gentry since it was only about a mile to town. *Shucks, I used to walk more than that to the cotton field from our camp on the Brazos.*

Hope set out mid-morning with her shopping list which included material for a maternity skirt and blouse which she planned to sew by hand. On her way, she took in the expanse of the sky. *It's so blue, no clouds, no trees, or tall buildings to obstruct the sky as far as the horizon in all directions. I was too tired to notice last night, but evenings must be beautiful with nothing to hinder the stars.*

Congestion in the street closed in around her. It was quite different witnessing unsavory characters and questionable business fronts from a passing car rather than face to face. Hope kept her distance from several bedraggled looking women sauntering the road. There was a rancid stench permeating from an alleyway. On a corner she avoided being sideswiped by a passing car and stumbled over an apparent drunkard lying on the dirt road.

The elevated price of merchandise at the mercantile was surprising; she only purchased a few items on her list. Hurriedly, Hope made decisions and on the walk back, shifted the parcels from arm to arm. Her pace quickened as waves of nausea began to undeniably swell. Her paper sacks slipped further down her torso, urgency to get out of the street was paramount. *Oh no, oh no. I've got to make it to the bathhouse.*

Reaching the back yard, she haphazardly tossed her packages toward the back door of their wooden box house. She fled toward the shared facility only to find the door latched, there was no alternative but to vomit on the ground alongside the building. Falling to her knees she wiped her mouth with the hem of her skirt. A sour remnant of aftertaste was as repugnant as the environment.

Winn's outlook had improved after a day of work at the linotype. He told Hope about the printing plant over a supper of canned pork and beans, bread, and jam.

"How does your leg feel, Winn?"

"Well, I'm not ready to run a race, but it's all right."

"I worry about it being too soon for a full day's work for you." Hope didn't tell him about the mishaps of her morning, but she did fill him in about meeting the neighbors and the invitation to visit.

Winn stacked his enamel plate and utensils in the wash pan. "That's great, Hope. It'll be nice to know our neighbors since we share a bathhouse with them."

She stood and placed her dishes on top of his. "It was so nice at Mrs. Emerson's to have the bathroom all to ourselves since there were no other boarders on our floor. You think knowing the people we share with will make it easier? I'm wondering if remaining anonymous would be better."

"No, no, Hope. What better way to know people that to share a bathroom? We can brush our teeth while they take a bath. Nice and cozy like."

Hope's eyes briefly widened with that shocked look Winn loved to induce with outrageous teasing. She put on a nonchalant expression. "Maybe you're right. Did I mention her husband is extremely handsome? Oh, and Dixie? Poor thing, I don't know how she snagged such a good-looking man."

Winn grabbed her around the waist and drew her close. "Okay, okay. Guess familiarity isn't a good idea."

The neighbors were nice enough, but Hope could find little in common with them, other than the primitive living conditions. Donnie offered to drive Winn to and from work since the newspaper plant was near the hardware store where he was employed as a sales clerk.

Preparing for bed, Winn said, "I'm glad we got acquainted with our neighbors and found out Dixie is home during the day. I feel better about you being stuck out here alone."

"It's a blessing that Donnie can take you to work." She failed at an attempt to stifle a yawn. "We've been here three days and I already have two friends, Gertie and Dixie."

Unbuttoning his shirt, he said, "You know, that idea I had may not be so bad after all."

Pulling her nightgown over her head, Hope murmured, "What idea?"

"The one about Donnie taking a bath while you brush your teeth. I mean, since you think he's so handsome."

She threw her pillow at him. He caught it and tossed it back to her, laughing.

On his day off, Winn accompanied Hope on her next shopping venture. They purchased a wickless oil burner, a small table and two chairs, along with a few other necessities which were delivered. Thankful the boxes of belongings arrived from San Antonio, Hope organized their small quarters. *Okay, Lord, I know we're to be content with whatever our circumstance, so help me to make do in Colt, Texas, like Apostle Paul in Philippi.*

"I think 'morning sickness' is inappropriately named," she said to Winn one evening. "I could aptly call it 'the all-day plague'."

Winn had carried their chairs outside where there was indeed a panorama of twinkling stars upon a dark velvet sky. He said, "All right, the heretofore mentioned malady shall now be known as "All Day Plague" as per Hope Prichard."

He made her laugh, but the heavenly canopy couldn't shut out various odors from campfires drifting their way. Her supper of Vienna sausage, cheese, crackers, and canned peaches was in danger of contracting the "All Day Plague."

In her loneliness, she found comfort in her worn Bible, and crocheting occupied some of her hours. With a good supply of thread and hooks, Hope worked on a baby sweater with matching cap and booties in cream-colored thread. She prayed for a healthy child who wouldn't be brought up in Colt, Texas.

While in San Antonio, Hope had kept up a correspondence with Mrs. Emerson and the Peabodys. With Winn's first paycheck in Colt, they sent the remainder of the money owed to Dexter for the doctor fee in Galveston. Frank had paid the hospital bill and doctor in Liberty and refused payment from Winn.

Letters from family reminded Hope that outside this vast sea of oil boom mania, there was a place of normalcy. Fayella's news was full of excitement about the house Buford was building on their land in East Texas. She also expressed happiness about Hope's expected blessing and her own desire for a child. Iris's notes were mostly about their son, Arlon. She reported he would have a little brother or sister much sooner than they planned, but was grateful just the same. It was difficult for Hope to come up with good things in her letters, but she did.

Living conditions were at poverty level and wages were below the national average. Produce and goods were sold for elevated prices and whisked off the shelf as soon as delivered, making extreme shortages. The frustrated attitude of people compensating in an overcrowded area fluctuated between impatience to downright meanness.

After work, Donnie parked the car in the narrow alley between their houses. Winn saw Hope at the outside faucet beside the bathhouse washing dishes. Throwing the enamel plates on a towel spread on the ground, her demeanor spoke of aggravation.

Getting out of the car, Winn said, "Thanks again, Donnie, for the ride." He approached Hope. "What are you in such a dither about?"

Hope tossed out the dirty dishwater and rinsed the pan before putting the clean dishes back in it. "Do you know how much a pound bag of sugar is back home?"

"No, can't say as I've bought much sugar." Walking with her, he took the dishpan and carried it into the house.

Flinging the rag over the back of a chair, she said, "At the IGA store in Hempstead it's eight cents, and do you know what that highway robber at Murphy's Market is charging?"

"I have no idea, but I'm sure you're going to tell me." He smiled at her indignation. Fresh coffee was in the pot on the warm coils of the oil burner. He poured a cup and reached for the sugar tin, but Hope grabbed it.

"Sixty cents." She poked him in the chest with her pointed finger and repeated, "Sixty cents for a bag of sugar—imagine that, and there were only two bags on the shelf this afternoon."

He held his coffee cup and looked at the sugar tin she clutched close to her chest. "That's quite a markup, but its supply and demand. We're a long way from Sugarland on the other side of Houston. It costs a lot for freight. You have to take that into consideration."

"What I'm taking into consideration is that it's gouging, pure and simple. And what you're going to have to take into consideration is there'll be less sugar in your coffee." She sat the sugar container on the table and crossed her arms in a huff.

Winn pulled out a chair and sat. Looking at her, he tentatively removed the tin lid and dipped one heaping teaspoon into his cup. When he reached for his usual second heaping spoonful, Hope pulled it toward her. He teased by stretching across the table for it; she picked it up and held it away from him. He got up and grabbed for it, laughing.

"Winn, you're going to dump it on the floor. If you do, you'll be cleaning up a good portion of very expensive sugar."

He pretended her grasp was too tough for him and held up his hands in mock surrender. She set the sugar safely on the table and their laughter was silenced by a tender kiss. Afterwards, Winn took a swallow of the coffee and winced. When he snatched a spoonful of sugar, Hope smirked.

With a guilty look, he said, "I'll work overtime for my two teaspoons of sugar."

Gertie was faithful to take Hope to town every week. Hope dreaded shopping, even accompanied by her friend. One morning, as they rode to the market, Gertie eyed Hope with concern. She was thin, and her usual sunny disposition was replaced by an aura of sadness. "You look worn out, Hope. Do you still have morning sickness?"

"Not as much, thank the Lord." She leaned an elbow on the window sill and cupped her hand over her forehead. "It's not that, Gertie. I just don't understand why most people are so rude. I smile and try to be pleasant, but have yet to be met with any act of courtesy." She quickly added, "Besides you and Howard of course and our next door neighbors. And it's depressing to see such lowlife everywhere." She flashed a wan smile. "Guess I'm just tired, that's all."

Gertie found a spot to pull her car over and turned off the engine. "Colt was a neighborly community before the oil strike, Hope. I've seen it turn into a sinful den of thieves. Sometimes I think surely God will send fire and brimstone and demolish it from the plains." She reached out and touched Hope's arm. "I certainly understand your frustration in dealing with the 'dog-eat-dog' atmosphere. But the main thing right now is the baby; you need to take care of yourself. Are you eating and getting enough sleep?"

Hope patted Gertie's hand which was resting on her arm. "You're so kind. Yes, my appetite is better. Sorry to worry you, Gertie. I'll try not to be such a grumpy Gus."

"It's comes with the territory, I mean being pregnant, not necessarily residing in Colt." Her car hummed as she started the engine and inched back onto the dirt road. "Howard and I talked last night about inviting you and Winn to the Christmas Eve service. We'll have dinner at our house and then go to church."

Hope's countenance brightened. "That would be wonderful. I wondered if the birth of Jesus would even be acknowledged out here."

After Christmas Eve dinner, Gertie pulled Hope aside and put a ten dollar bill in her hand. "Here's a little something to start a fund for the baby."

"Thank you, Gertie. You and Howard have been such a blessing to us. I don't know what we would've done without you." The unexpected generosity wrapped a warm bunting of happiness around her heart.

Gertie hugged Hope. "I remember what it feels like to be away from family and new to a community, but at least I had electricity and a car to get around in. I'm glad we've been of some help while you two are starting out."

Winn and Hope had agreed not to exchange gifts in order to save for their future. But Winn bought a present for Hope and asked Howard to hide it in his car. Late Christmas Eve, when Howard delivered the Prichards to their house, Winn covertly put it in the inside pocket of his coat.

Hope hung her wrap on the nail by the door while Winn lit the lantern on the table. When the room was illuminated, he held out the gift. "Merry Christmas, Hope."

Homesickness, pregnancy, and coping with dreadful living conditions had formed an emotional lump in her chest. Gertie's money for the baby touched her deeply and now a gift from Winn was the final prick that burst the bubble holding back her tears. "We said we weren't going to give gifts."

He led her to a chair by the table. "Sugar, don't cry."

Her sobs mounted. "I'm sorry to be so weepy lately." Holding a handkerchief to her nose, she blew hard and then sniffed. "I didn't get anything for you."

He perceived her reaction wasn't really about the gift. "Oh, Hope, you're wrong. You've given me so much more than I can ever give. You've given me your love and now you're carrying our baby." His arms encircled her trembling shoulders. "The gift isn't much, just a little something because you've been trying so hard and I love you."

The lantern light cast a shadow across his concerned face. Dabbing at the corners of her eyes, she said, "Okay, Winn Prichard, but I'm up to your tricks now. If we say there will be no gifts, then I guess I better have something ready."

"Aren't you getting something ready now?" He lovingly put his hand on her slightly swollen belly.

She smiled and tore open the wrapping paper to reveal a wooden box with the imprint of a needle and thread on top. With wide eyes, she lifted the lid of a small sewing kit. It was complete with a dozen colors of thread, various size needles, a thimble, and a pair of cutting shears.

He shrugged. "See, I told you it wasn't much."

Her hug told him differently.

It isn't what you have in your pocket that makes you thankful, but what you have in your heart.
—Author Unknown

31

In addition to running the linotype, Winn began putting in extra hours as pressman. With an abundance of new enterprises in Colt, there were demands for business cards, letterheads, and handbills as well as the weekly newspaper publication. Work took his mind off an occasional stab of leg pain and the circumstances in which he had placed Hope and their unborn baby. He figured the faster their funds grew, the quicker they could leave. As much as he hated to admit it, the rash decision of moving to a boomtown was a mistake.

At times, the wind across the plains of West Texas whipped around their modest dwelling so forcefully the couple feared the haphazard construction would give way. As winter winds whistled, they huddled with their cots close and blankets piled high. Hope had read about sand storms which plagued the Texas Panhandle, but experiencing one revealed that her imagination did not evoke the pure misery of it. A trip to the bathhouse was a dreadful undertaking with sand beating into her skin like a million tiny needles.

By March, Hope was truly weary from the everyday struggle reminiscent of the American frontier way of life. Physically strong, she was accustomed to hard work, but in her spirit, she knew their efforts were not on the right path to Winn's paper dream. That reality was the main culprit dragging her down. It was up to him to make decisions about his career, so Hope held her tongue and didn't complain. Instead, she prayed.

On the day of her birthday, the eleventh of March, she woke to see Winn smiling at her from his cot next to hers. "Happy Birthday, Hope."

"How long have you been lying there waiting to say that?" She rubbed her eyes and stretched, adjusting to wakefulness.

"Long enough to count your freckles."

"That long, huh?" She met his smile with one of her own. "Thank you for remembering my birthday, Winn."

He stood to take her hand and help her rise from the low cot. She said, "Oh, that made it easier. I think I'll hire you to stay here all day and help me get up from this cot and my chair."

Her effort at humor made his eyebrows come together in a frown. "I've been trying to find a better place to live, Hope. There's nothing. I'm sorry."

She slipped her arms around him and held him close. "I know you have, it's all right. This too shall pass. That's what Mama always said when something was difficult, and she was right. Eventually, it did pass. You have to just keep working toward your goal, and I pray that includes a place with indoor plumbing."

He rubbed her back and said, "You bet it will include a bathroom and proper kitchen, but I can't get that for your birthday."

"Hmm, scratching my back gives me chills." She held out her arm to show him the goose bumps. "A back rub is a good birthday gift."

"Well, that's not all—we're going out to eat tonight."

Looking at him with surprise, she said, "We are?"

"Yes we are; it's all arranged. Howard and Gertie are picking us up at six, and we're going to a café to celebrate your birthday."

"Oh, Winn, I can't fit into my wedding dress. I don't have anything to wear. Is it a fancy place?"

"Are you serious? A fancy place in Colt? No, but a little better than the greasy spoon we tried before. I've been planning this for you." He went to the table and picked up his money pouch. "Here, this is for you to buy something today, a dress or skirt, whatever you like." He began dressing for work. "Gertie is picking you up at ten, so skedaddle and get ready."

"I haven't seen maternity clothes in any store." Doubt and excitement were partners dancing around the prospect.

"Gertie knows where to take you, and she'll offer some help." A horn tooted. "There's Donnie. I need to go. I'll grab a bite at the diner next to the shop." He gave her a quick kiss on the cheek as he pulled suspenders over his shoulders. "Now, spend all of it. I know how frugal you are, so I put it aside for you to buy something that takes your fancy."

Later, when Gertie honked, Hope hurried to the car with a radiant smile. Gertie teased her. "Well, I think I'll drive all over town so you can shine your happy face upon all the dark corners of Colt."

Their mood was lighthearted as Gertie drove toward the older part of town. She stopped in front of a dress shop Hope would have never ventured in. Seeing the fine dresses in the window, Hope hesitated assuming their prices were beyond the seven dollars in her purse.

Gertie sensed her dilemma. "I thought we might look here first. They had an ad in yesterday's paper about a sale."

"Well, in that case, we certainly want to let them know we saw their advertisement."

Surprisingly, on the sale rack she found a dress with pleats flowing from intricate smocking across the bodice. Hope gently felt the soft navy blue material. "I really like the smocking and the round, white collar, but I shouldn't be so extravagant." She placed it back on the rack. *I have enough money for it, but I shouldn't spend that much for a dress.*

Winn had inquired of Gertie how much to give Hope for a dress so she was aware of the amount he had given her. Gertie retrieved it from the rack to examine closer. "Hope, I think you would be very practical in buying this. It's not really a maternity dress, but the pleats make it nice and roomy. You'll be able to wear it for several months and get more wear out of it after the baby is born."

Hope took the dress from Gertie. "You're right. It's a very sensible purchase." She smiled with her lips and her eyes.

The birthday dinner was in a café in the best section of town near the Gentry's residence. But even this eating establishment was not exempt from the boisterous, offensive element Hope hated. The table of four tried to ignore a party of rowdy patrons who came in during the midst of their meal. Hope had enjoyed quiet conversation with Howard and Gertie up until it became difficult to hear over the din across the room. *There's no getting away from loud people with filth spewing from their mouths.*

She was relieved when Howard announced they were going to their house. "Gertie baked a cake for you, Hope."

"I don't know when you had time to do that, Gertie, with running me all around."

They spent an hour visiting with the Gentrys before being driven home. When alone, Hope turned to Winn. "Thank you, Winn. This was almost as nice as last year when you came to Hempstead, and my family lassoed you to celebrate my birthday."

"That was only a year ago and so much has happened. There have been so many changes for you." He looked into her brown eyes, so loving and trusting. "You're only eighteen, Hope. I'm going to see to it that all your birthdays are nice. We have many, many more ahead."

There was no spring season to unlock flowers from the barren soil of West Texas. Frigid wind evaporated immediately into warm breezes in April. May brought little evidence of spring, and in June the air was so still it was an effort to find a wisp to breathe.

Enjoying the shade in back of their houses, Hope and Dixie took refuge from the afternoon heat. Hope sat in a chair avoiding the awkwardness of getting up from the blanket on the ground Dixie lounged on.

Holding up her hair, Dixie wiped moisture from the back of her neck. "You know, Hope, this part of the country only has two seasons—winter and August. In Houston there's flowers and shade trees. And you can ride over to Galveston for the gulf breeze and wade in the water at the beach."

Her comment conjured Hope's memory of their fateful trip to Galveston. She related Winn's accident, but left out the unpleasantness of recovery at his parents' home.

Dixie sat up and propped her elbows on her bent knees as she listened. "How terrible, he could've lost his leg."

"He almost did, and it was an answer to prayers that he didn't." Hope picked up a homemade paper fan from her lap and waved it leisurely near her face.

A forlorn look changed Dixie's countenance. "I wish God would answer some of my prayers."

Hope leaned forward toward the blanket. "He will, Dixie. If you've given your life to Him, He knows the perfect time and the best way for your prayers to be answered." *There are a few prayers of my own I'm waiting to be answered too, Lord—just a little reminder.*

Friday afternoon Hope was ironing. She used a towel for padding under a sheet on the table as her makeshift ironing board. The iron was heated on the oil stove asbestos ring.

She heard Winn whistling before he stepped into the house. Greeting him with a kiss, she said, "Hi, Winn. Why so chipper?"

"Sugar, I've paid all our bills and have a few dollars left over for our savings." He reached for the coffee tin.

She matched his jovial mood with a laugh as he dumped the money from the tin onto the "ironing board" to count it. "I figure we're a few bucks closer to our dream. Let's see how much we have now." Hope helped him as he straightened the wrinkled bills. He grabbed the iron and said, "Why don't we just press the wrinkles out?"

It struck Hope funny to see her husband standing by the table laughing while pressing money with the iron. "You iron out the wrinkles, and I'll count." They both had a good laugh as she counted eighty dollars.

A good laugh is sunshine in the house.
—William M. Thackeray

32

Hope felt more like facing each day when morning sickness had passed, although getting up from the army cot was becoming a bigger chore as the pregnancy progressed. She told Winn, "I'll trade nausea for awkwardness any time."

She had a list of things she thanked God for daily. Preparing meals on the small oil burner was certainly easier than cooking by campfire in the backyard like some had to do. The miraculous healing of Winn's leg was another reason for a thankful heart.

Looking at his leg, Winn said, "Wonder how long these scars will stay red."

"I don't know." Hope traced the zigzag puffiness along his calf. "It still looks pretty angry, but you're limping less and no longer need whiskey to tolerate the pain."

Ah, Sugar, if you only knew how hard it's been. He gave her a peck on the cheek and grabbed a towel. "I want to beat Donnie to the bathtub tonight."

He was harboring a ship's cargo of discontent, and his anchor of sobriety was in danger of dislodging. Winn had developed a pattern since young adulthood. For months he could resist the temptation of drinking. He could present a cheerful, happy-go-lucky front, but difficulties had a way of breaking down his resistance. To him, daily frustrations were like a glass splinter just under the skin, naked to the eye but an irritant that had to be addressed. He invariably addressed his stressful problems with alcohol.

Since the oil strike in 1926, the population of Colt almost doubled in two years. Upright citizens were attracted to Colt wanting to seize opportunities in legitimate investments, but the boomtown was also a magnet to lawlessness with bootlegging, prostitution, and gambling.

Donnie had been bragging about his winnings at poker, enticing Winn to join him in a game some night. Winn was not a gambler, but Donnie was flamboyant with more money than his sales clerk job paid. Flashing a wad of bills under Winn's nose, Donnie said, "I'm stashing it away, my Friend. Me and my old lady ain't long for this Stick Ville. A few more games like last night and we're heading back to Houston where we're going to have enough for a nice little nest."

Seeing Hope struggle with lack of the barest of conveniences day after day in a town where groceries were sold at a premium, Winn's wall of defense was cracking. The vision of his newspaper was becoming cloudy. Listening to Donnie on the way home from work one Friday after cashing his paycheck, Winn decided he had to do something. "You think I could get in on a couple of hands, Donnie?"

"Sure thing, Winn. Meet me at the car at midnight, and we'll head out to Wild Cat's. The guys meet in back. I'll vouch for you."

Usually a sound sleeper, Hope had become restless with the bulkiness of pregnancy. A faint sound momentarily nudged her out of slumber's domain. Repositioning herself on the narrow cot, she drifted back to sleep.

A few hours later, she needed to make a trip to the bathroom. The house was dark as pitch. She relied on memory to creep quietly so she wouldn't wake Winn. Outside she shivered with a chill of uneasiness as if she had stepped into the sharp bitterness of winter instead of a mid-June night. In ebon silhouette, the row of wooden houses was merely a continuation of the dirt they stood on, seemingly with no foundation for their existence.

On the path back to the house she paused, her eyes swept the sky. In her thin robe, she was cloaked beneath a blackened curtain pierced by pinpricks of a million stars. The vastness emphasized her weakness and dependency on almighty God. *Oh, Lord Jesus, keep us on Your path. Protect Winn and show him where to start his newspaper, if that is Your will for him.* With a hand on her growing womb, she acknowledged God's divine miracle of creation within. *Let this baby be healthy and strong. Give me strength in labor and wisdom to care for him . . . or her.*

Rubbing her arms, she felt that something was wrong and took notice about her. Donnie's car was not in its usual spot, but Hope was aware of his clandestine ventures, so it was of little concern to her.

Shaking off the uneasiness, she continued on the path. *It's so barren and though the town is overrun with people, it's a lonely place.* She knew the steps well and crept softly to her canvas bed that allowed little comfort. Closing her eyes to beckon sleep, she lay awake pondering the odd feeling of premonition. Her eyes flew open with the realization that the door was unlocked before her walk outside. *Maybe we forgot to latch it before we went to bed.* The thought consoled her enough for the return of slumber.

Saturday morning, as the sun emerged to light the humble collection of wooden houses, Hope roused. The cot next to hers was empty except for the rumpled sheet upon it. Accepting the fact that Winn was not there was slow in coming. *Wonder why he got up so early? Maybe he's out back.*

Raising the shade, she saw that Donnie's parking spot was still vacated. She made coffee, combed her hair, and selected one of the three blouses to wear with either the black skirt or brown one. *I hope Winn doesn't have to go in to work so he can go with me to the store for some material. These poor skirts can't see me through the next two months.*

The coffee was ready and before breaking the eggs in the skillet, she stood in the back doorway hoping to see Winn. Dixie came out of the bathhouse with a pained expression. "Hope, I'm worried. Donnie didn't come home last night. Do you think Winn knows where he goes for that god-awful poker game?"

A sinking feeling oozed from Hope's head to her feet. "Winn isn't here." She stretched her neck looking for any sign of him. "He didn't say anything about going to work today." She turned and walked to the table thinking perhaps he left a note she overlooked.

Dixie, still in her robe, followed Hope inside. "Maybe Winn's with Donnie."

"Maybe so," she said softly. *Well, that's no comfort.*

The two of them stood still for a moment lost in misery. Dixie said, "Well let's not worry; they're probably in a game somewhere. You know how those men can't stop when the stakes are high."

No, Hope didn't know; she didn't think Winn did either. "He's never done anything like this before."

"You'll get used to it, Honey." She looked at the burner. "That coffee smells good."

Hope was stunned. *I'll never get used to Winn disappearing in the night.* Her mind was whirling with fearful thoughts of her husband injured, unable to get help.

Dixie waited a moment for a response, but saw that Hope was shaken. "Sit down, Hope. I'll get you a cup of coffee."

Mostly in silence, the two women took sips from their cups. As people on the street began to stir with activities, first Hope and then Dixie searched the window for Donnie's car.

Dixie set her cup in the dishpan. "I need to get home. I know all kinds of thoughts are going through your head, Hon. Donnie's stayed out all night before and comes home with a pocket full of cash, so it's worth it, you'll see."

Hope gave a little nod. "I just hope they're all right."

Dixie patted Hope on the shoulder and left. Staring out the window, Hope thought nothing would make her happier than to see Winn walking toward the house. Mulling over Dixie's shallow words of consolation, she looked at the shelf where the tin can of money was kept. For an inexplicable reason, she picked it up and peered into it. Except for the lone ten dollars that Gertie gave her for the baby, it was empty.

Temptation is the fire that brings up the scum of the heart.
—Thomas Boston

33

People moved about and cars motored along the street like nothing was amiss, but in the Prichard house something was very amiss for Hope. A myriad of emotions were fueled by fear, anger, and worry. She was isolated, so far from anyone who could help. There was a phone in a little store about a half mile toward town, but who would she call?

She placed her hand on her belly when the baby kicked. *You're worried too aren't you, Little One. Don't be. I'm with you, and Jesus will never leave us or forsake us.* She continued to pray for Winn to come home and the wisdom to know what to do if he didn't.

Filled with confusion, she remembered he left a wife before and never looked back, but she had given him no cause to leave. Maybe the story about Darlene wasn't exactly as he told her. Doubts were agonizing in this isolated place. *I felt this loneliness last night before I knew Winn wasn't here.*

The baby's activity is what made her decide to eat something, for his sake. She browned a piece of buttered bread in the skillet and scrambled an egg. There was no ambition in her to wash the dishes. A collar on one of Winn's shirts needed turning and another had a missing button. She looked at the sewing kit he gave her and allowed a tear to slide down her cheek.

Looking out the window toward Dixie's house, her view of the street was limited; she stared at the empty parking space. Out the other window was no different. She paced until her energy was exhausted. She prayed until the words seemed like echoes bouncing off the bare wood walls—unheard.

Mid-morning she picked up the dishpan of dirty dishes, bar of Fels Naphtha soap, and a towel. "I need to do something. Moping never got anything done."

As she finished washing the skillet, she heard a car door slam from the street. Picking up the dishpan of clean dishes, she looked around the side of the house. Mr. Gentry's Landau was parked in front, and Winn was leaning toward the window talking to Howard. Dropping the dishpan, it landed in the dirt as she ran toward the road. As Winn turned from the car, Howard slowly drove away.

His clothes looked like they had been balled up and sat on. "Winn, are you all right?" She stopped before her arms went around him and stepped back. "You've been drinking."

"Let's go inside; we don't need to be a sideshow for gawking neighbors."

Forgetting the dishpan, she led him into the house. "Where have you been? What happened to your shirt?" His eye was swollen, and there was a bruise on his jaw. "And your face?"

"I threw up on my shirt and I was socked in the jaw." He added softly, "And a few other places." He limped toward the stove. "Any coffee?"

Hope was indignant. "You slip out in the middle of the night, take our savings, worry me half to death, finally come home and tell me you vomited on yourself, someone beat you up, and you calmly ask for coffee?" Her voice rose with each accusation, and her face was tight with anger. "Oh no, Winn Prichard. You sit down right now and tell me what happened. I deserve an explanation before I make coffee for you." There was no compassion in her tone. She yanked a chair out from the table, sat down and looked at him with livid expectation.

His shoulders slumped with this dreaded confrontation. His head, cheek, and groin ached and exhaustion encased his body so much that even his hard cot looked inviting. Ever since he married Hope, this was the last thing he ever wanted to happen.

Willing his body to move, he pulled out a chair and gingerly sat. Facing her was excruciatingly difficult. "Yes, Sugar, you do deserve an explanation." Putting an elbow on the table, he ran his hand through his tousled hair trying to come up with how to explain his actions. Apprehension of her reaction tossed the roaring riptide in his stomach.

Wearily he began. "We can't seem to get anywhere with the savings. Donnie's always egging me on with all his poker winnings. I thought if I went with him and won some money, it would be a quick way to get us out of this hell hole."

"You took our savings and gambled? I wouldn't want to use ill-gotten gains."

He breathed an exasperated sigh. "You don't have to worry about that—there are no gains."

"Where's the money, Winn? Did you lose all of it?" Nauseous realization set in.

"Sugar, I'm sorry. I thought I could double or even triple it to have enough to start over somewhere else."

She rested her head in her hands with elbows on the table. When she looked back at him her face was splotchy with anguished tears. "Double our money by tossing it down on a card table? I heard Buford say the only way to double money is to fold it half."

"He's right about that." Winn's remorse matched his physical ache. Fire was blazing up and down his injured leg.

Fury hung in the air around her so heavy, so real she wanted to grab it or grab anything and hurl it at him. "Our savings are lost and you drank the night away while leaving me here alone, not knowing if you were dead or alive. How could you, Winn?"

"I thought I'd be back in a few hours, I . . . I didn't know there would be bootleg liquor there."

"So the liquor made you sick?"

Looking up, he glanced at the coffee pot. Without a word, Hope stood to make fresh coffee.

"Thanks, Sugar." His voice was as weak as his body, but she required honesty. "We were in the back room of Wild Cat's."

Hope turned to face him with probing eyes. "Wild Cat's?"

His face flushed through the blue, black bruise. "Yeah, it's a . . . a place where poker players gather. Anyway, I drank quite a bit and won a few hands. I didn't realize how much I drank, but it was backing up on me. I had to get to the bathroom in the alley."

She stood with her arms crossed above the baby's bulge. Taking in this wretched story was a nightmare that she never imagined her husband would be telling.

He sat sideways in the chair to face her. "I walked out the back door and before my eyes adjusted to the dark, I was pushed from behind. When I turned around, somebody slugged me. I tried to fight, but my arms were held at my back while the other guy hit me until I vomited on him and myself."

"Oh, dear God." Hope's hand went to her mouth.

Winn's face spoke the shame he was feeling. "I don't know if I passed out or was knocked out. The next thing I knew, two policemen were dragging me to the paddy wagon. I was one of the first guests in the new Colter County jail with no money in my pocket. Our savings and this week's paycheck are gone."

She let it sink in for a moment; her knees felt weak. "How did Howard end up bringing you home?"

"After I slept for a few hours, the guard said I could call someone." Winn bowed his head and shook it slowly. "I hated to call him, but didn't know anyone else with a phone or anyone who could bail me out." Remorse was hot lava flowing through his body. "He's going to take it out of next week's paycheck. I thought I might get fired—he's pretty upset with me."

"So am I, Winn." She got a cup and filled it with strong coffee. Resisting the urge to toss it in his face, she slammed the mug down in front of him sloshing the liquid across the table. "What would it matter if you got fired, you want to get out of this town badly enough to gamble our savings?"

"We can't leave now. We're practically penniless." He wiped the table with his shirt tail and grabbed the sugar bowl.

"Practically? We are penniless." With a glance out the window she said, "What about Donnie?"

He took a sip and winced when the coffee burned his tongue. "He won the first hand and quit." His eyes couldn't meet hers. "He . . . ah . . . he went upstairs with one of the ladies. I didn't see him again."

She slapped her hands flat on the table and leaned directly in his face. "One of the ladies?" Her face was red with fury. "You were in a house of prostitution? You knew what went on there and stepped foot in that den of iniquity anyway? It's no wonder you were assaulted, that's what you deserved." Hope's lacerating words cut deep.

"Hope, please try to calm down." He stood and pulled out her chair. She allowed him to help her. He knelt and held her shaking shoulders. "You're right, Hope; it was what I deserved, but not what you deserve. Please forgive me."

Overwhelming torrents of exhaustion ebbed through her. She leaned heavily toward him, their heads touching. She whispered, "What are we going to do?" Thoughts of her husband in such a horrid place were tumbling—tumbling over in her mind. She began to cry. "The money, your hard-earned money. We could've bought train tickets and gone back to Liberty. Oh, Winn, Winn."

"Sugar, I'm going to work as hard as I can and make this up to you. I promise." He held her face in his hands. "Let's just get past this."

She straightened, moving away from him, unable to let go of the rage inside. "You were dishonest and sneaky. You put yourself among wicked people in an evil place and lost all our money." She was pushing words at him, raw and angry. "Besides the fact that you left me, pregnant with our baby, alone in the middle of the night with the door unlatched. That's a lot to get past."

The anger and frustration in her eyes sickened him. He dropped his arms. He had no words.

Hope felt utterly defeated by forces too strong to fight. All the yelling and harsh accusations couldn't bring their money back or change the fact that her husband was deceptive. Resigned, she said, "Go clean up. I'll fix something for you to eat."

> *Beloved, have you ever thought that someday*
> *you will not have anything*
> *to try you, or anyone to vex you again? There will be no opportunity*
> *in heaven to learn or to show the spirit of patience, forbearance, and*
> *longsuffering. If you are to practice these things, it must be now.*
> —A.B. Simpson

34

It was a quiet day, unpleasantly so. If hearts could speak, the words would be jumbled expressions of questions, sorrowful answers, hurt, and regret. Winn's facial bruise felt raw, but the punches he received on his torso and the kick in his groin were giving him the most physical discomfort.

Unlike Hope's compassionate nature, she didn't tend to her husband's superficial wounds. She told herself if they were more severe, she would look after them, but wanted the pain to pound into his senses the repercussions of his irresponsibility. It was an excruciatingly long day. The disappointment and ache she wore were heavy, even on her strong shoulders.

Winn kept a damp washrag on his face, but it did little for the swelling. He wrestled with the actions of the previous night replaying in his mind. No matter how much he willed the agonizing scenes to desist, they raced around his thoughts unmercifully. He heard Donnie's car pull in and was pretty sure Dixie would be angry as a cornered badger, but it wouldn't be the first time.

In the afternoon, he dozed off and on until he heard Hope's lackluster voice. "Winn, you feel like coming to the table for supper?"

Rising from the cot, he moved slowly, balancing his head on his neck. "Sure, it smells good."

Spooning the canned chicken noodle soup into bowls, Hope's countenance told of her disappointment and worry. An involuntary sigh came to her lips as she sat at the table and opened the tin of saltine crackers.

Winn said, "You want to pray, Hope?"

"I've been praying. Why don't you thank the Lord for our food tonight?"

He obediently bowed his head and offered a short prayer of thanksgiving. Stirring the hot soup, he tried to think of ways to assure Hope that he was truly contrite. "Hope, I could apologize a hundred times, but it wouldn't mean any more than this one time straight from my heart. Sugar, I'm sorry . . . sorry I made you worry, sorry for . . . everything."

Hope studied this man she had given her heart to, the pitiful expression he wore and the stubble of whiskers that had sprouted from his swollen jaw. "We both are feeling bad right now, Winn, for a lot of different reasons." She put her elbow on the table with a fist under her chin. "I'm so disappointed in you. You promised you would never lie to me. In the first place, I didn't know you drank." She hesitated and looked at him with eyes of hazy sadness. "No, in the *very* first place, you never told me you were married before."

Winn pushed his chair back and slowly stood, bringing his wounds to mind. He winced. "Are you going to bring that up every time something happens, Hope?"

"That's simple to answer—just quit making these horrible things happen."

"Humph. Simple for you. I can't go back and undo what's been done. I don't intentionally set out to hurt you." He stood by the side of the table, leaning on it. "I hadn't had a drink in quite a while before we married and didn't see any need to mention it. The accident with my leg and then this miserable place . . . I don't know . . . I just needed something to get me through."

"You know what I have to say about that. The only thing to help you in hard times is prayer and trust in the Lord." Her eyes revealed the disgust she had for his weakness in turning to alcohol. "More times than I want to bring up I've needed something to get me through, and it wasn't whiskey."

His head hung limply as Hope began to cry. Grievances again came down hard. All day her temperament had risen to extreme ire and fallen desperately close to despair. "I prayed for hours and wondered if my prayers could ever make it to Heaven from this horrible place. But He never forsakes us. I believe it was God who saved you from being killed. Oh, Winn, you could've been killed." Her body shook with sobs.

His body ached from the bruising endured, but his heart ached for hurting Hope. Rubbing his leg, he sat in his chair with downward eyes. "Deep down I know that, I do pray, but I guess I'm not as strong as you, Sugar. I wanted to get enough money to start over; I wanted the regret of bringing you here to go away if only for a little while." He dragged his eyes to look at her youthful face so soft to the touch; he noticed the roundness of her stomach kept her from sitting close to the table.

He stretched his arm across the table to touch hers. "I've been preoccupied with thinking about getting us out of this mess. Guess I haven't realized how the baby has grown. Are you feeling okay?"

"As far as the baby is concerned, yes."

He nodded. "That's good." His tone was solemn.

They sat in the quiet, partaking of the meager supper. The sun was setting, bringing dusk, obliging the darkness of their mood.

Finished, he shoved the bowl out of the way and crossed his arms on the table. He was calm and resolute. "This is what I want to do, Sugar. Part of next week's pay goes to Howard for bailing me out." He looked down at his arms, and then back at his wife. "The week after that, the wages will be for your ticket to Hempstead. I want you to stay there until the baby is born."

Hope's eyes widened with surprise, and he stopped her before she said anything. "I don't want our baby to be born here, and you need to be with Mama right now. In the meantime, maybe I'll find a job. The trade paper comes to the shop; they sometimes have ads for linotype operators." He had made the decision and was adamant. "My plan was to move before it was too hard for you. I wanted to have some cash to tide us over until we got settled somewhere. But obviously it hasn't worked out that way."

"But, Winn, we can go back to Liberty. Surely in two weeks we'll have enough for the both of us to go."

"No, I already called the *Vindicator*. Spencer said the paper is in a bind, he can't use an extra linotype operator. He was sorry, since he said there would be a job for me, but it can't be helped. I waited too long."

"I see." Perturbed, she clumsily stood and picked up the bowls and cracker tin. "When Pastor Wright married us, he said we are one. To me that means we make decisions together, and we talk about important things that concern the both of us—and our baby." She set the bowls in the dishpan and placed the cracker box beside the coffee can that once held eighty dollars. "You should've told me you talked to Mr. Spencer." Picking up the coffee tin, she said, "The money in this tin was our savings. You should've talked to me about what it would be used for."

"You're right, Sugar. Guess I was on my own for so long, just drifting when I had a hankering to, and spending my money where I wanted. A man of my age has a pretty hard time changing."

"It's just a matter of love and choice, Winn."

This was one of the things he loved about her; she cuts to the meat of the matter and doesn't mince words. He closed the distance between them and opened his arms which she readily stepped into and gently held his body next to hers. It was a healing caress, the kind that bonds with the knowledge of how much their love means to each of them regardless of their meager surroundings, their mistakes, and their hurts.

He breathed deeply of her essence and felt the baby bulging between them. "We are one, well actually plus one now. From now on I'll consider you in everything I do." He pulled back and looked deeply into her brown eyes. "I'll change, Hope."

"I need for you to let me in, let me into your life." She studied his bruised face, usually so clean-cut and handsome. In their pitiful situation, her adoration for him was overpowering. "You wouldn't have that swollen face if you would've consulted me about gambling our money." Hope couldn't stop the wan smile faintly touching her lips.

"Okay good, you're smiling now." Holding her at arm's length, he searched her eyes, and a hopeful expression burst through the sadness.

Hope said, "At this point, what else can I do?"

And be ye kind one to another, tenderhearted, forgiving one another, even as God for Christ's sake hath forgiven you.
—Ephesians 4:32 NASB

35

July 1929—

A first anniversary should be a monumental celebration, but for the Prichards, it was a solemn affair. The past year held both ecstasy and heartache—more than Hope thought possible. Her love for Winn was beyond understanding. It was almost supernatural, like the Lord put them together for a purpose and she must trust and hang on for the completion of God's plan.

They had pinched enough money for Hope's sojourn to Hempstead. Dread of their parting hovered over them both at the Colt bus depot. Her bus tickets already purchased, she also had train tickets from Odessa to Hempstead tucked safely in her purse along with a few dollars for food along the way. Compared to her heart, the suitcase by her feet was light.

Winn was trapped in a place he had come to hate; the love of his life carrying their baby was leaving. His paper dream was as elusive as a night vision disappearing with the dawn.

"Sugar, this is going to be a long day and night. I hope it's not too hard on you, especially since you have to wait so long in Fort Worth for the train to Hempstead."

"I'll be fine. You just be sure to keep your nose clean without me. No crazy ideas about gambling or bootleg whiskey, you hear?" Her voice was teasing, but her message was not.

"I promise. It's only work and home for the next month or so. As soon as you can get to a phone tomorrow, call the printing plant and leave a message to let me know you're okay."

She saw the bus making its way through the crowded street. "I want to see Miss Adkins at the news office. I'll probably use the phone there."

Several others also waiting for the bus gathered close by. With a protective arm around Hope, Winn held her place for boarding. "I guess you'll have some catching up to do with everyone." His face turned downcast. "I ah . . . I hope you won't put me in a bad light with your folks, Sugar." He knew Hope was not one to share her troubles, but guilt cast an ugly picture in his mind.

Their conversation was too personal for strangers to overhear. She pulled his head down and spoke in a whisper. "We're one, remember? What transpires between us is only for you and me to know."

Her forgiving and loving words were a soothing balm in his core. The moment had come; he would be without his anchor, his navigator. Visions of that horrible night he wound up in jail gripped him, and he hated himself all over again. Winn held her until the bus driver announced it was time to board. Guiding her up the steps, he found a place close to the front and placed her suitcase on the upper rack. The old valise was the one he had left in Hempstead the day they met. The latches didn't click shut completely; Winn had secured it with a belt.

Clutching her purse, small pillow, a wrap, and a paper sack with her crocheting, she settled in the seat. With a big assuring smile she said, "Don't worry, Winn. The Lord is with me." Anxiety was sculptured in his face. She laughed. "For goodness sake, you're not putting me on the *Titanic*. I'll still in be in Texas."

Accustomed to witnessing long good-byes, the bus driver tempered his impatience to get under way. He was a kindly gentleman who could understand a husband's concerns about letting his young, pregnant wife set out alone. Reassuring them, he said, "Don't you give a care now. The bus stop at the Odessa train station is the last one for me today, so I can help the missus and tote her suitcase to the train."

Hope smiled. "See, the good Lord is already taking care of me."

Winn shook the driver's hand. "Much obliged, sir. She's precious cargo."

"Yes sir, I can see that." Winn handed him a one dollar bill. The busman's eyes lit up, "Why, thank you." With a lingering look at Hope, Winn stepped off the bus. The driver swung his torso out the door and hollered, "All aboard to Odessa."

Standing below Hope's window, Winn held her hand until the bus edged out into the throng of vehicles and pedestrians. They both remembered when she held his hand in happier days as they bid good-bye at Butch's station.

Hope waved. He was a forlorn picture standing in the dirt street in front of that hovel of a depot. Their eyes were locked until the bus made a turn a block away. *Lord God, take away his desire to drink. Keep him safe, and let him find another job soon.*

> *The Lord will guard your going out and your*
> *coming in from this time forth and forever.*
> —Psalm 121:8 NASB

THE RICHLAND RECORD

More Than a Newspaper—a Community Service
<u>A Weekly Publication Serving the Greater Richland Area</u>
Richland, Texas   Thursday, May 14, 1970
<u>Winston Randolph Prichard, Editor and Publisher</u>

News and Views of a Tactless Texan

It is human nature to keep the good and dismiss the bad. But it doesn't hurt to occasionally examine some bumps in life's road and take inventory. Most of the time, hardships reveal our true character, make us stronger, and give us experience and wisdom for the future. Tough times, if we allow, shape us into the person God created us to be.

One such ordeal of extreme difficulty for Hope and me was our short time living in Colt, Texas. In 1927, oil was discovered there which changed the sleepy West Texas settlement into a riotous boomtown where life was similar to the wild frontier of America's Old West. I accepted a position as linotype operator at the newspaper hoping the burgeoning town could support another paper which I intended to establish.

Arriving there by bus in 1928, Hope and I were shocked by the chaotic circumstances which prevailed. Later, I read John Steinbeck's novel, *Grapes of Wrath,* about struggles during the Great Depression years. It vividly brought to mind the scenes in Colt of tent encampments and hardships of people who flocked there in droves. The dream of making fast money enticed folks from every corner of the country. I admit I was one of them, but living conditions at that time were not conducive for a young woman expecting a child. I learned that my bride was resourceful and able to "make do" in meager situations.

When I sit down to a meal, I am often reminded of prices in Colt during the boomtown days. Cost for the consumer was a matter of supply and demand, and the demand was greater than the supply. The masses expanded daily, and deliveries were slow in arriving to stock grocers' shelves. While a loaf of bread in other parts of the country sold for ten cents in 1928, the people of Colt had to pay five times that amount or more. Hope had been paying eight cents for a pound of sugar, and she was outraged at the price of sixty cents in the boomtown.

However, there are good, Christian people among the lawless. We were befriended by an honest couple who contributed to making our time there bearable. I'm glad to report that Colt survived its boomtown days and returned to the peaceful community it once was.

Hope and I are thankful for the lessons learned from painful events as well as the happy times of our life. No matter the error of our ways and situations we find ourselves in, we can learn and take away valuable lessons from every circumstance. Each new day ushers in the opportunity of beginning anew, dawn is a wonderful gift. We can make amends and determine to make improvements needed. The past can be a springboard to learn from, asking God for His forgiveness and thanking Him for the pleasures and progress. If I may impart a small bit of advice from our experiences, I would say take a good, prayerful look before a hasty leap toward a life-altering decision

Until the next edition, I'll close with the printers' symbol, -30-.

QUESTIONS TO CONSIDER

Discussion of books with friends, family, and clubs enrich and expand the enjoyment of reading. The following questions present possible events to come in Book Two of The Prichard Family Series which may also challenge us for personal insights.

- Should Hope give up praying for Winn since God gave him free will?
- Is Winn's paper dream a selfish aspiration? Should she convince him to give it up?
- What is keeping Winn from total surrender to the Lord? What causes him to turn to alcohol in stressful times?
- What can Hope do to remain strong in faith?
- Concerning the Prichard family—what could change Priscilla's haughty attitude? And what of Luther, the brother imprisoned?

When disappointment and issues of distress come up in your life, how do you handle them?

Is your personal faith and trust in Jesus strong enough to endure whatever lies ahead?

Do you have an ambition to attain? Are you convinced God placed that desire in your heart?

Is it possible for you to make a difference in someone's life? How?

The Prichard Family Series continues in Volume Two,
Pressing on With Hope.

CPSIA information can be obtained at www.ICGtesting.com
Printed in the USA
LVOW13s2042270614

392030LV00002B/5/P